The Fourth Ruby

Also by James R. Hannibal

The Lost Property Office
(SECTION 13, BOOK 1)

The Fourth Ruby

James R. Hannibal

Simon & Schuster Books for Young Readers
New York   London   Toronto   Sydney   New Delhi

SIMON & SCHUSTER BOOKS FOR YOUNG READERS
An imprint of Simon & Schuster Children's Publishing Division
1230 Avenue of the Americas, New York, New York 10020
This book is a work of fiction. Any references to historical events, real people,
or real places are used fictitiously. Other names, characters, places, and events are
products of the author's imagination, and any resemblance to actual events or places
or persons, living or dead, is entirely coincidental.
Text copyright © 2017 by James R. Hannibal
Jacket illustration copyright © 2017 by Petur Antonsson
All rights reserved, including the right of reproduction in whole or in part in any form.
SIMON & SCHUSTER BOOKS FOR YOUNG READERS
is a trademark of Simon & Schuster, Inc.
For information about special discounts for bulk purchases, please contact Simon &
Schuster Special Sales at 1-866-506-1949 or business@simonandschuster.com.
The Simon & Schuster Speakers Bureau can bring authors to your live event. For more
information or to book an event, contact the Simon & Schuster Speakers Bureau at
1-866-248-3049 or visit our website at www.simonspeakers.com.
Book design by Lizzy Bromley
The text for this book was set in Weiss Std.
Manufactured in the United States of America
0917 FFG
First Edition
2 4 6 8 10 9 7 5 3 1
Library of Congress Cataloging-in-Publication Data
Names: Hannibal, James R., author.
Title: The fourth ruby / James R. Hannibal.
Description: First Edition. | New York : Simon & Schuster Books for Young Readers,
[2017] | Series: Section 13 ; book 2 | Summary: Jack Buckles, a thirteenth-generation
tracker whose senses are on the fritz, and Gwen Kincaid, a clerk hoping to become an
apprentice quartermaster, are framed for stealing a legendary jewel—one of a set of rubies
thought to bring the owner loyalty, knowledge, and power—and they must locate the
remaining rubies before the thief does or risk his unleashing a reign of terror
worse than Genghis Khan's.
Identifiers: LCCN 2016053567|
ISBN 9781481467124 (hardcover) | ISBN 9781481467148 (eBook) |
Subjects: | CYAC: Stealing—Fiction. | Secret societies—Fiction. | Families—Fiction. |
Adventure and adventurers—Fiction. | Fantasy.
Classification: LCC PZ7.1.H3638 Fo 2017 | DDC [Fic]—dc23
LC record available at https://lccn.loc.gov/2016053567

To all those with a secret worth keeping:
may it remain forever unspoken and lead you to adventures untold

The Fourth Ruby

———· Chapter One ·———

NIGHT HAD FALLEN on London's Baker Street. The orange glow of the streetlamps reflected off pavement that seemed perpetually wet. A good number of pedestrians still walked the sidewalks, mostly heading home from the cafés. Teatime had barely passed, and in London, tea was more than just hot drinks.

A little south of Regent's Park and a little north of the Baker Street Tube station—near 221B—one particular pedestrian opened his palm and let an etched gold cube drop to the ground. He kept on walking. No one shouted after the man to tell him he had dropped something. No one noticed at all.

The cube clinked and clacked like a metal die, only not quite the same, thanks to tiny gems at each of the eight corners. It paused once, balancing on a single jewel for an unnatural space of time, then rolled on for another meter or so before coming to a complete stop. There it sat in the grime, glittering and anonymous, as a group of twenty-somethings strolled by. Their scarves and their laughing faces were reflected in a darkened shop window, amid lettering that read LOST PROPERTY OFFICE.

Once the laughing pedestrians were safely past, the cube shook and bobbled. Its sides split open, unfolding into eight spindly legs, each crowned with one of the tiny gems. The spider pushed itself up. It lifted a bulbous glass abdomen filled with sickly green syrup and then skittered across the pavement to climb a rainspout, utterly oblivious to the irony of its actions. Reaching the top unscathed, it raced across the roof, spiraled its way up a steaming vent pipe, and disappeared inside.

The creature descended for what seemed like ages, spiked feet clicking all the way. It took several branches, making lefts and rights into joining pipes, but always it continued downward, deep into a massive, secret underground tower known as the Keep.

Finally, the spider came within view of a blazing fire and

slowed. It crept, inch by inch, to the underside of a great mahogany hearth, training its tiny cameras on a pair of children seated in high-backed velvet chairs in an otherwise dark room. The boy, a teenager, sat staring into the blaze. The girl, younger, her tiny form dwarfed by the Victorian chair, gazed at him with an expression of concern. After a moment, the boy stood to inspect the hearth, and the spider scrambled back out of sight.

Then again, there might never have been a spider in the first place. Maybe the gold flashes the boy saw in his mind's eye had nothing to do with a metal cube or tiny gems clacking on pavement. Maybe the silvery spikes had not been the clickety-clicks of a clockwork spider skittering down a pipe. Maybe the glittering confetti he saw had not been pedestrian laughter at all. Maybe the boy had imagined the whole thing.

Jack Buckles, a tracker by birth, had been struggling with his unusually keen senses. A year before, he had defeated a grown man in a smoky bell tower using only sound and feel to guide his actions. But these days, even the noisy Quantum Electrodynamic Drones—better known as QEDs—that hummed around the Ministry of Trackers could sneak up on him. Jack's senses had been failing him for months.

Of course, on the off chance Jack's senses had been correct, if a clockwork spider had really crawled down into the Keep to look for him, then that would be very, very bad.

─── · Chapter Two · ───

JACK RETURNED TO HIS CHAIR, keeping his eyes on the fireplace. He could feel the weight of the inverted underground tower above him, with its black stone walls and unending levels filled with wood-paneled corridors. The Keep had become his prison. The Ministry of Trackers, the youngest of England's secretive Elder Ministries—behind the Ministry of Guilds, the Ministry of Secrets, and the Ministry of Dragons—had become home for his whole family, whether they liked it or not.

"You don't look so good," said Sadie, watching as he eased himself down in the chair again.

"I'm nervous. That's all."

Sadie pulled her ankles up into a cross-legged position

beneath her dress and leaned her elbows on her knees, auburn hair flopping forward. She stared at Jack as if she could see right through his skull and into his messed-up tracker brain. "No. That's not it."

Jack shot her a frown. "I've asked you not to do that."

His sister ignored the protest and shifted her eyes to an ornately carved mahogany door looming in the darkness behind his chair. "Is it time for you to go yet?"

"Yes." Jack did not stir.

Sadie seemed unperturbed by the contradiction between his answer and his actions. Her face remained as placid as ever. "Is the professor coming?" she asked, referring to Edward Tanner, the only remaining tracker of the eleventh generation. He wasn't known as *the professor* simply because he was Jack's teacher and mentor. Long retired from the usual ministry work, the elderly tracker now maintained tenure as a history professor up at Cambridge.

"He's molding young minds tonight."

"What about Gwen?"

Jack had known that question was coming. He sighed. "I don't think so."

"Because she's mad at you?"

"No."

"Because you're working with Ash now?"

"No." He gave a little shrug. "Maybe."

"Because Ash is a journeyman quartermaster, and Gwen is only a clerk?"

Jack said nothing.

"But you're only a clerk."

"Sadie." He gave her a *that's-enough* glare and the room fell silent for several seconds. It wouldn't last. It never did.

"Soooo, *why* can't she go with you?"

Jack rubbed his head. It hurt. Gwen hadn't shown up to see him off—twice in a row now. It wasn't his fault that he'd been assigned to a real quartermaster. And it wasn't his fault he couldn't study with her every day, or eat with her, or do whatever Gwen wanted to do whenever Gwen wanted to do it. His dad needed him. Couldn't she see that?

Jack slipped a hand into the pocket of his dad's leather jacket, the one he had taken as his own when he first found the armory and equipment locker in his dad's study. He wrapped his palm around a little red sphere with gold lattice-work, letting the silky pink coolness of the stone seep into his fingers. Feelings, sounds, smells—they all had color and texture to him, a side effect of his crisscrossed tracker senses.

He closed his eyes and released a long breath through

his nose. That same sphere had given him a brief connection to his dad the year before, on the night he had rescued him and confronted the Clockmaker at the top of Big Ben. On his return to the Keep, Jack had found a tiny scrap of packing paper folded up on the sphere's place in the armory, marked with a curvy Z. So he had named it the *zed*. After that night, no matter how hard he tried, he had never been able to reproduce the connection with his dad. He kept the zed with him at all times anyway. It calmed him, helped him think, helped him be the tracker everyone expected him to be. He couldn't say why. Maybe it gave him power. Maybe it gave him a little bit of his dad's tracker mojo. There were stranger artifacts with stranger abilities everywhere within the Keep.

The pain in Jack's head subsided, and he realized Sadie was standing over him. With the zed to settle him, he could see her without opening his eyes—by the blue-gray whisper of her breathing and the tan, sandpapery shuffle of her feet. He looked up anyway, because he wanted her to see the annoyance in his expression. "*What*, Sadie?"

"They're waiting for you." She glanced over at the big shadowed door. "All of them."

It was Sadie who finally opened the mahogany door,

leaning her little body back into the pull, with Jack standing reluctantly behind her. He winced as a thrumming white light assaulted his mixed-up senses, along with the bronze hum of the QEDs, and a black murmur of whispers. It was noise, all of it. But Jack could still make out some of the words.

Tracker.

Section Thirteen.

Freak.

Didn't they know he could hear them?

Jack left his sister in the little room and walked out onto a cobblestone lane. There were quaint cottage facades on either side. French, maybe. He couldn't tell yet. He crossed over to a broad semicircular platform set between two houses, and stepped up to a bronze rail to get a better look at what he was up against. Below him, level after level of arching bridges, steep stairways, and narrow streets were interwoven to form a village stacked upon itself. *English*, he thought, scanning the flats and storefronts that formed the circular periphery of every level. *Definitely English. What else?* Every home and store on the periphery was a mere facade—elaborate set dressings—but the eyes in the windows were real enough.

Section Thirteen.

Freak.

He shook his head, pushing back a creeping pain that shouldn't have been there—not after a year of training. Gray mist swirled in the light above him and in the darkness of the bottom level far below. The arena was so huge that it had its own weather system, gathering moisture in its upper and lower extremes. Sometimes, according to Gwen at least, it rained. Jack had never seen it. Then again, this was only his second time to enter the crucible. The bronze hum rolling across his brain intensified and two quad-style QEDs descended out of the clouds. Blue light glowed within round engine housings. Their cameras shifted to keep him in focus. Mrs. Hudson's voice, stern and cold, echoed from an unseen loudspeaker.

"Attention. The tracker has entered the arena. The Hunt is on."

Chapter Three

THE CLOCK WAS TICKING.

Jack and his quartermaster had thirty minutes to identify a stolen artifact, track it down within the arena maze, and steal it back again, out from under the wardens' big noses. This was the second round of the Hunt—the pinnacle of the Tracker Games. It all came back to ministry regulations, volume one, section six, rule nineteen: *Competition breeds excellence.*

Four groups comprised the agents of the ministry. Trackers like Jack were the firstborn sons of the four founding lines, the only agents to manifest the unique, hereditary tracker senses. Quartermasters were the Watsons to the trackers' Sherlocks, well trained in a host of skills and knowledge that came in handy in the field. Wardens guarded the artifacts, and sometimes the people, that the trackers and quartermasters recovered on behalf of the Crown. And clerks pushed paper, managed offices, and generally kept the entire house of cards from falling. All of them, from the lowest apprentice clerk all the way up to the Minister of Trackers, whose identity remained a closely guarded secret, came together each December for the Tracker Games.

This year's games were Jack's first.

There had been other events like warden wrestling, cane fencing, and the apprentice clerk deduction challenge, but the Hunt was the centerpiece—three rounds of what Gwen liked to call a one-sided game of capture the flag. Traditionally a tracker/quartermaster pair went up against a team of four wardens. The wardens stole an artifact and hid it somewhere within the multilevel labyrinth, and the tracker and his quartermaster had to get it back. Three rounds on three successive nights, best two out of three, and the Tracker Cup was the prize.

The wardens had claimed it every year for the last decade.

Thanks to Section Thirteen, no tracker had set foot in the arena for ten years, leaving the quartermasters to fend for themselves. The infamous regulation protected the ministry from the phenomenon of bad luck and the damage it might do when combined with the considerable abilities of a full-fledged tracker. Each of the four members of the thirteenth generation—Jack's generation—had been exiled to the corners of the earth. At that time, the twelfth generation had been exiled as well, to raise them. The twelves came back to the Keep for the occasional mission, but mostly they lived undercover, waiting for the day when they could return with the fourteens, to teach them the skills they had not been permitted to teach their own sons.

But Jack had thrown a wrench into the whole plan. He had stumbled—or rather he had been shoved—back into ministry affairs.

Nearly a year before, a French psychopath calling himself the Clockmaker had kidnapped Jack's father and threatened to burn London to the ground, forcing Jack to uncover his hidden past. After Jack had stopped the madman, the Ministry of Trackers had grudgingly opted to train him. He knew too much. His abilities had manifested early. Jack was dangerous, and sending him out into the wild unchecked was simply not an option. Now, against what many—including Jack—considered better judgment, *someone* had opted to throw him into the Hunt as well.

"Where've you been?" Ashley Pendleton pushed off from a stone facade not far from the mahogany door, leaning on a wolf's-head cane as he stepped down onto the cobblestones. There was nothing wrong with his legs. Canes were a sign of accomplishment among trackers and quartermasters, and at seventeen Ash was the eldest and most accomplished of the journeyman quartermasters. He gave Jack a conspirator's wink. "I was beginning to think the old girl had changed her mind."

"She can hear us, you know," said Jack, glancing up at the drones.

Ash scrunched his nose. "She doesn't mind."

"Maybe for you."

If Jack was the embarrassing son the Ministry of Trackers kept hidden in the dark, Ash was their poster child—tall and dashing, with a flawless black complexion and a winning smile. Girls swooned when he passed. Boys fell into step behind him. Only Ash with his undeniable charm could get away with referring to Mrs. Hudson—the ultimate clerk, the matron of the ministry—as *the old girl*. And only Ash could have convinced her to allow Jack to compete beside him.

The quartermaster wrapped an arm around Jack's shoulders and hurried him along the curving lane. "Don't look so worried. No one's ever been killed in the Hunt." He grinned, tipping up his newsboy cap with the tip of his cane. "Severely wounded, sure, but never killed. We've taken the first round, Jack. Trackers and quartermasters, together again. One more quick win and the cup will finally return to its proper place."

"Right. Quick." Jack let out a nervous chuckle. They had won the previous round, when the arena maze had been a wharf district straight out of Dickens, but there had been nothing quick about it. Ash had recovered the missing artifact at the last second. Jack had been next to useless. He didn't see this round going any better.

They passed beneath a wrought-iron arch into a small cemetery, the starting point for the night's maze. Something there would be missing—something unexpected. Ash paused at the edge of the gravestones and stooped down to Jack's height. "Listen, I know you're nervous. Years ago, there would have been four trackers to choose from, and the oldest or the best would have represented our team in the Hunt. But right now, you're all we've got."

"You call that a pep talk?"

"You didn't let me finish. I don't care that you're young,

or that you're a Section Thirteen. I never have. I believe in you, Jack. Now"—Ash swept the newsboy cap from his head and slapped him across the arm with it, gesturing toward the graves—"it's time to do your thing. Off you pop."

Jack returned the quartermaster's smile—half of it, anyway—and walked among the markers. It took conscious relaxation of his synapses to turn the chaos of his senses into order—the curse of a tracker. He *saw*, as Gwen called it, with all five senses at all times. Sounds became sights. Smell and taste became feel and sound. And the volume of it was overwhelming. Gwen had taught him to control the flood of data, or rather to master it by letting go of control. But lately that skill had eluded him more and more. He exhaled, concentrated on letting the noise in instead of shutting it out, and watched the data rise from the gravestones like spirits.

Whispers: still there, black wisps drifting across the cemetery.

Section Thirteen.

Freak.

He pushed them aside.

Scent of hawthorn: dark, antiseptic—the hedges around the garden.

Scent of grass: prickly and yellow-green—misshapen. That was something.

Bent and broken blades formed in Jack's vision, flickering as the static in his brain threatened to wash them away. "Footprints," he said, beckoning to Ash and pointing down at the trail. "A meter or more for every stride."

"Definitely a warden, then," said the quartermaster, and he had no trouble following the footprints the rest of the way. They led to a black marble obelisk that cast its shadow across a three-foot-long sarcophagus.

Ash held his cane over the casket, gauging its length. "Kind of short, wasn't he? Unless, of course, they chopped him up."

"Thanks for that mental image," said Jack, kneeling down beside him. "As if what I have to do next isn't bad enough." He cringed, leaving only one eye open—knowing that would not save him from seeing the casket's gruesome contents. And then he pushed the lid aside.

Empty.

So the artifact they had to recover had been inside the sarcophagus. Their next job was to determine what exactly that artifact might have been and where the wardens might have taken it. He pushed the lid the rest of the way off and saw block letters etched into the interior, faded but readable.

KING OF THE UNWANTED,

LORD OF THE LOST.

MAY HE REST IN PEACE

AND TROUBLE US NO MORE.

Jack sat back on his heels. "It doesn't even rhyme."

"Doesn't have to. I know what it means." Ash left him there and headed for the opposite gate. "It's Larry," he said without looking back. "The wardens have taken the clown."

——— · Chapter Four · ———

WELL INTO THE HUNT, Jack stood alone, waiting for what amounted to a spinning blade to come slicing across the arena. It was darker in the lower levels of the maze, away from the mock daylight at the top. The QEDs had installed a few streetlamps but not enough to banish the shadows. Ash had split their two-man team to search for the way down to the next level. They had less than five minutes left to find the clown.

The stolen artifact for the night's Hunt was a ventriloquist dummy that had been in the ministry for generations. Normally it sat high on a shelf in the warehouse of unclaimed items behind the Lost Property Office, the undisputed king of what the ministry called *the Graveyard*. Someone long ago had named the clown King Leer, because of its creepy, pock-faced smile. Everyone called it Larry for short.

A graveyard. Lord of the lost. In retrospect, the clues had been obvious, but Jack had missed them, and the rest of his night hadn't gone much better.

Following threads of red yarn from the clown's hair and too much Old Spice from one of the wardens, Jack and Ash had traced a path through the stacked labyrinth of streets and courtyards to their present level. Most of it had been Ash's doing. Jack felt like dead weight. He kept trying to sort out the data, but all he could see was noise.

Section Thirteen.

Freak.

Ash's titanium scout disc sailed across the arena, dipping way down into the mists gathering in the courtyard at the bottom. Jack tried to read its vector. He tried to hear the changing pitch of its whistle and predict its movement. He couldn't. The professor had warned him many times: a misjudged scout disc could take an agent's head off. At the last moment Jack ducked, letting it sink into the plaster wall behind him.

Ash had thrown the scout because he wanted Jack to pull a vision from it. He wanted Jack to *spark*, as the ministry called it, and translate the light captured by the titanium disc as it flew across the arena into images—maybe see a way down, or see where the wardens were lying in wait in hidden alcoves. But scout discs were no fun for an inexperienced tracker. Their sparks had a nauseating spin about them.

Jack steeled himself for what was coming and let his nerve endings sink into the cold metal as he jerked the disc from the wall, feeling the vibrations of the molecules. The low whistle of the disc's flight came through first, rising to a scream. The arena spun madly below. Jack couldn't stabilize it. He let go to keep from throwing up, and the scout clattered to the stones.

Section Thirteen.

Freak.

Jack sighed and shook his head.

Not wanting to disappoint Ash, he picked up the disc and tried again, this time slipping a hand into his jacket pocket and taking hold of the zed to calm his nerves. It worked. He managed to stabilize the spin. He saw the flight, and the data merged, moment upon moment until he had a full picture of the three bottom levels of the maze. A sentry stood like a statue in midstep, marching across a bridge at the center of the next level.

Subtle.

A flash of tweed appeared on the periphery. Jack shifted his focus and saw his least favorite of the wardens, half-concealed in an alley between two cottages, gargoyle face set in concentration.

Shaw.

The journeyman warden had never been fully convinced that Jack was not behind the entire Clockmaker episode. In the year since he and Jack had first run afoul of each other, Shaw had added several inches in height, though he remained as pudgy as ever. He was still considered small among the wardens, but big for a warden his age. Gwen often remarked that she shuddered to think what a full-grown Shaw would look like, or what he might be capable of.

The moment Jack released the zed, he felt dizzy. He had to lean against the painted door of a fake cottage to stay upright—probably a lingering effect of the spinning disc. After a quick breather, he headed for an alleyway directly above Shaw's position, hoping to catch the warden sneaking between levels, revealing the way downward. Jack staggered across the lane, pressed himself to the wall at the alley's edge, and peered around the corner.

No Shaw, only a tall cherrywood door at the very back. Jack crept up to it and eased the lever down. Unlocked.

There was no stairwell behind the door, no ladder or dumbwaiter leading down through the maze, and no Shaw, either. Jack had discovered an anteroom similar to the room where he had left Sadie. It wasn't part of the maze, and the door should have been locked, or covered by a facade.

Strange.

And stranger still, the room was occupied.

——— ·Chapter Five· ———

JACK HELD THE CHERRYWOOD DOOR open and stared into the room. "Professor?"

Edward Tanner, Jack's teacher and mentor, stared back at him, seated in his wheelchair with his usual threadbare blanket across his knees. He wasn't alone. A young man of Indian descent stood over him, wearing a worn black overcoat with far too many silver buckles and holding a gold cylinder and a glass vial of blue liquid in his open palm. He closed his fingers around the items and shot a fiery glare Jack's way.

Zzzap.

An orange lightning bolt flashed at the forefront of Jack's mind, more mental image than actual sound. When it was over, the professor and the young man had vanished.

Jack glanced down at his hand, easing it away from the door handle. Had he accidentally sparked? That had not happened to him for a while, but his skills *were* on the fritz. How else could he explain it? The professor was up at Cambridge.

Zzzap.

He heard the orange flash again, or saw it, this time at the very back of his mind. It had come from behind him. Jack ran to the stone wall outside the alley and looked out into the arena.

Nothing.

"What are you doing?" Ash appeared beside him, yanking him back from the edge. "I told you to keep out of sight." He took the disc out of Jack's hand and slipped it into the leather satchel at his side. "Did you see anything?"

"I . . . uh." Ash wouldn't care about the weird spark of the professor. Jack blinked, forcing his brain back to the Hunt. "A sentry. I saw a warden guarding the bridge at the middle."

Ash frowned. "Me too. You can't miss him." He started walking the other way, pulling Jack with him. "While you were staring at the obvious, I found a ramp to the next level, and I also figured out where they're keeping Larry." He slipped a pocket watch from his waistcoat and checked the time. "Three minutes. We've got to move if we want to win this."

Ash led Jack over a bridge and through a fake house to a tea shop, complete with a cacophony of smells that sent Jack's tracker brain reeling. He pressed a shoulder against a wall of tins and it rotated up, revealing a sloping stone hallway.

Jack struggled to keep up with the quartermaster's stride as the two jogged down the ramp. "How did you . . . figure out where the clown is?" he puffed.

"One word. Soil."

They reached the bottom, and Ash peered around the wall, out at the sentry. He sat back on his heels and twisted the wolf's head of his cane aside, tilting a telescope that was stored beneath it into place. He leaned it out past the corner and motioned for Jack to press his eye to the lens. "Take a close look at our sentry. He's got soil on his shoes. And he sure didn't get it from that bridge."

Jack focused on the sentry's wingtips. Sure enough, they were dotted with black soil.

Potting soil.

Jack had seen a flower shop in the spark from the scout disc, one level below the sentry's bridge. But he had also seen a flower cart down in the misty courtyard at the bottom. He shook his head. "There are two. We can't be sure which one."

Ash raised his eyebrows. "Can't we? The soil on the sentry's wingtips looks dry. No moisture. None on his pants, either. Sometimes the best clue is the one that you don't see, Jack. What do dry shoes and pants tell us?"

It took a few seconds, but the light finally dawned in Jack's brain. "The mist," he said. "If the sentry had been down in the courtyard with the flower cart, the soil on his shoes would be wet and clumped, and his tweed suit would be damp."

Ash touched his nose. "Now you're getting it. Our sentry's dry as a bone. So he hasn't been to the bottom level. That means he's been hanging out by the flower shop one level down. And I'll bet that's where we'll find Larry." He peeked out again, and Jack peeked with him. The sentry was guarding a ribbed drainpipe that ran from the street above, all the way down to the street below—the street with the flower shop.

Ash sat back again, furrowing his brow. He pinched the

collar of Jack's coat, rubbing the leather between his fingers. "I'm gonna need your jacket."

"What? Why?"

"Relax. You'll get it back . . . maybe." He checked his pocket watch and then held out a hand, snapping his fingers. "Quick, Jack. We're almost out of time."

Jack complied, and Ash took the coat, shoving the cane into Jack's hands in trade. He hauled Jack to his feet. "Now stay close."

Easier said than done.

The moment the sentry turned his back, Ash took off at a full sprint. Jack watched as he veered to one side, launched himself off the stone rail, and draped the leather jacket over the warden's basketball-size head. In one quick move, Ash dropped him to the pavers and tied the sleeves in a knot behind his neck.

Jack ran huffing up behind, giving the warden a wide berth.

"Quickly," said Ash, snatching his cane back and pulling Jack to the rail. He showed him the flower shop down below. Potting soil littered the pavers outside. Right next door was a doll shop, and in the window, Jack could see the creepy clown dummy that would earn them the Tracker Cup.

All they had to do was take it.

"Quick as you can, before the sentry recovers," whispered Ash, thrusting his chin at the iron drainpipe.

The quartermaster wanted him to spark, to draw images up the drainpipe like soda up a straw, and see if there were any other wardens waiting down there to ambush them. Jack glanced back at the sentry, who was tugging at the jacket covering his face. The zed was still in the left pocket, well out of Jack's reach.

"Hurry up." Ash pushed him rather roughly toward the drainpipe. "This is what you're here for, tracker."

"Right. Sure." Jack grabbed the pipe and tried to spark.

Static. Naturally. But what did it matter? Time was running out anyway.

"Nothing," he said. And then came the lie. "I mean. It's clear. I don't see anybody."

Ash needed no other prompting. He hopped over the rail and shimmied down the pipe.

Two wardens jumped out of the shadows and grabbed the young quartermaster the moment he touched down. Jack winced. He should have known better. Ash broke free, but the strap of his satchel snapped in the struggle and fell to the cobblestones at his feet.

Meanwhile, Jack heard footfalls behind him. The sentry was free, rushing his way. With no other choice, Jack hopped the rail and slid down the pipe, narrowly escaping the big teen's grasp. He landed and stumbled back, halfway between the two wardens and the doll shop. He had a clear shot at the clown.

The quartermaster kicked his satchel, and it flew between the wardens, landing a few feet away, so that a copper sphere rolled lazily out and settled between Jack's sneakers—an electrosphere. He swept it up and yanked out the ring and chain, spinning up the magnet inside.

Ash pumped his fist. "Yes! Take 'em down."

The electric charge building in the copper made Jack's palm tingle. He'd have to throw it soon, and he'd have to put it right between the two wardens if he wanted to take them both out of commission. He hauled back his arm for the throw and something—some*one*—caught his wrist.

Shaw stepped around to Jack's front. He wrapped his other paw around Jack's fist and gave him a tea-stained grin. "'ello, Thirteen. I've been waitin' for the chance to do this."

Jack heard Ash shouting. He heard thumps, pounds, and grunts. But all he could see was Shaw's gargoyle face, inches from his own.

The electrosphere fired its charge. Shaw clenched his teeth, absorbing the residual shock without letting his grin fade in the slightest. The rest of it coursed through Jack's body. The scant light that reached that deep into the vertical maze went out.

—·Chapter Six·—

JACK AWOKE amid a full-body convulsion that nearly shook him out of the wrought-iron chair he was sitting in. For a moment, he had no idea how he'd gotten there. Then it all came back.

The drainpipe.

The electrosphere.

Shaw's ugly grin.

Jack looked around and realized he was still on the second-to-last level of the arena maze, sitting in the orange glow of a streetlamp at a mock street café, next to a mock flower store and a mock doll shop. The creepy clown dummy that had leered at him from the window was gone. So were the whispers and the drones.

All was silent.

Ash came strolling toward him, Jack's leather jacket hanging from his hand. He laid the coat and his wolf's-head cane on the table between them and pulled out a chair, twirling it backward. "All clear. Was it, Jack?" he asked as he sat down.

Jack looked down at his hands. "It could have been."

"But it wasn't."

"It didn't matter. We had to do *something*." He shrugged. "But I couldn't spark."

Ash picked up his cane and ran his fingers over the bronze wolf's head. It was old, scratched and scarred. He had not been the first to carry it, not by far. "A lot of trackers have entered this arena before they could spark," he said, still examining the cane. "Most of them, actually. But none of them would have hidden that fact from their quartermasters. You *lied* to me, Jack. How could you?"

The quartermaster rolled his neck, and Jack could see that it pained him. His cheek was starting to swell. Jack got the feeling Ash had tried to save him from Shaw and taken a beating in the process. He wanted to say something—*thank you, I'm sorry*, anything—but he couldn't find his voice.

Ash looked away, down at the mist filling the bottom level.

QEDs were already dismantling the mock courtyard, picking up the stones and carrying them off. "I'm disappointed, Jack. I don't think I can trust you anymore." He stood, twirling the chair back into place. "I'm bringing Sullivan in for the third round. Maybe he and I can salvage this together. Two quartermasters, the way it's been done for the last ten years." He turned and walked away. "You're off the team."

——·Chapter Seven·——

THE FOUR TRACKER FAMILIES each had a small seventeenth-century manor situated around an underground cul-de-sac known as Tracker Lane, looking down on four gas lamps and a carved stone fountain that had recently been repaired. High above the houses, the upside-down roof of the inverted Keep tower jutted down through the cave ceiling, with its eight upside-down gargoyles snarling up at the stalactites.

Two of the four houses—House Fowler and House Shepherd—stood empty. The eleventh trackers of those houses were gone, and the twelves were off caring for the exiled thirteens. House Tanner remained occupied, but only part-time, since the professor spent most of his time at

Cambridge. Only House Buckles was full. They were prisoners, Jack included.

Jack especially.

He left the Great Stair—a broad wooden staircase that spiraled around the entire Keep—and hurried down the short lane to the cul-de-sac, not stopping to see if the professor was home. He didn't pause in the wood-paneled hearth room of House Buckles to say hello to Sadie, either. If she started interrogating him about the Hunt, he'd be stuck there all night. Jack did not even stop when his mother peeked out from the kitchen to offer him a post-Hunt snack.

"I made you a plate. Cold roast and beetroot."

"*Beetroot?* Really, Mom?" His mother had lived in America his whole life, hiding from the ministry. One year back in the Keep and she was as British as ever. He pressed on through the front hall. "I'm not hungry."

"You need to eat, Jack. You're skin and bones."

"I'm fine." He was already three flights up the stairs. She asked about the Hunt, but he pretended he didn't hear, slipped into his father's room, and closed the door.

A candle flickered on the nightstand, the one his mom always kept burning—the only light in the room. Jack didn't mind. The gaslights overhead would have shown him too much. He sat down by the four-poster bed and took his father's hand. There were tubes running into it. The doctors had put tubes everywhere—little ones running into his dad's arm, larger ones running up his nose and down under the covers, and a great big one stuffed into his throat. Jack sometimes wondered how his dad would react to the big one if he woke up.

Then he would chide himself for thinking *if*.

He opened his other hand and looked down at the zed resting in his palm. At the top of Big Ben, Jack had found his father, John Buckles the Twelfth, drugged and unconscious, kidnapped by a psychotic arsonist. And the moment he had pressed the zed between their two palms, his dad had spoken to him, offering encouragement. It was only later that Gwen had assured him his dad had never woken up. What Jack had seen and heard had been a sort of spark. The zed had acted like some kind of neural bridge.

It had never worked again.

Jack had tried. Over and over. He had pressed the little sphere into his father's hand every single night since the rescue. And he had tried to spark off its stone and gold, trying to see who else had used it. Either way, he saw only darkness. Once in a while, his nose bled too. He had gotten used to that part.

Each night, holding the zed in one hand and his father's limp fingers in the other, Jack prayed for him to wake up, but that prayer remained unanswered. Each night, a tiny part of him, a part that Jack despised, wondered if that was for the best.

The Ministry of Trackers had strict rules about the four tracker bloodlines. They had strict rules about everything, but the bloodline rules were especially so. The thirteenth generation was never to enter the Keep—or even learn of the ministry's existence. Jack had broken that rule, with a little help from Gwen. But that was only one of his two great offenses. The other was being born at all, and that was an offense he shared with his sister.

Section Eight of the ministry's regulations forbade members of tracker families from marrying, for fear of what the confluence of tracker bloodlines might produce. Jack's mother was born Mary Fowler, a daughter of the tracker Joseph Fowler the Eleventh. Not one to be left out of the family business, she had joined up and become a star quartermaster—partnering with the tracker John Buckles the Twelfth. Except their relationship had not been strictly professional.

When the ministry had sent John away to America, Mary snuck away and followed. She changed her name, pretending to be American, and they married in secret, crossing the

Buckles and Fowler bloodlines. Jack and Sadie were the result. The merger of tracker bloodlines terrified some in the ministry so much that the Buckles siblings were never allowed beyond the walls of the Keep without an escort. Jack was both a Section Eight and a Section Thirteen.

Freak.

His sudden appearance at the Keep the previous year had led to the outing of his parents' secret. But their punishment had been delayed pending a trial. As soon as Jack's dad woke up, the two would be judged and most assuredly locked away in a cell deep within the Keep. So, strangely enough, the same coma that separated Jack from his dad was the only thing keeping his family together. Jack was pretty sure his life was a textbook example of a catch-22.

"Will you come down and read with me before bed?" asked Sadie, peeking around the door.

She asked him that every night, and every night he gave her the same answer. Jack sighed and leaned back in his chair. "I need to be with Dad. Just in case. You know."

"Yeah. I know." Sadie pushed into the room, carrying a blanket and a pillow. She cast the one across his lap and tucked the other behind his head. As she straightened, she clutched a big gold pendant that hung from a chain around her neck, embossed with a dove flying upward into starlight. It was an heirloom, a gift from their mother, and it was far too big for her little frame.

Jack leaned his head back into the pillow. "Take that off, okay? You don't want it to choke you in your sleep."

She didn't argue. She unclasped the necklace as she walked out into the hall. "You're going to save him, Jack," she said, looking back through the door. "I know it."

He rolled his head over on the pillow to look at his father and the big scary tube going down his throat. "You always say that."

"Because it's true."

Chapter Eight

CLUTCHING A NOTEBOOK and a full thermos of breakfast tea, Jack trudged up a narrow stair, heading for Tanner's office. The steps and railing were chestnut, the picture frames oak and ash. With the exception of the arena, the vast inner workings of the Keep were made of wood and cloth, and the occasional bit of carbon fiber. No stone. No metal. No sense in a tracker getting a vision every time he leaned against a wall.

Jack left the stairwell on Sublevel Four, which was all mahogany, his least favorite of all the woods because it made everything so dark. Ash was only a few strides away, walking the other direction with Sullivan. Ash's swollen cheek was mottled with bruises. He wouldn't even look Jack's way.

Sullivan, on the other hand, gave Jack an *I'm-sorry-you're-stuck-being-you-today* shrug.

Jack hugged his thermos and notebook a little tighter and kept on walking.

"Ah, Jack." Edward Tanner rolled into view from an intersecting hallway, lifting a long, liver-spotted finger to tug his spectacles down his nose. "You're looking particularly ragged this morning."

Jack would have laughed if he had the energy.

The professor wheeled himself alongside his student. "Might that have anything to do with the Hunt?"

"You heard?"

"Who hasn't?"

"Great." Jack glanced down at the threadbare blanket across Tanner's knees, remembering the strange encounter the night before. "How was . . . Cambridge?"

"The usual." Tanner gave no sign that he knew what Jack was fishing for. Maybe it hadn't been a spark after all. "Lots of students. None as bright as you. I do wish I could have joined you, though—whatever the outcome." He slowed, touching Jack's arm. "There's no shame in it, boy. It wouldn't be a game if you couldn't lose once in a while."

Jack nodded, and the professor gave his wheels a push,

continuing on. "Every tracker's skills ebb and flow over the years. And remember, you started five years earlier than anyone else." He let out a little chuckle. "Come to think of it, the warden team defeated your grandfather and his quartermaster during *his* first Hunt. It took me weeks to nurse his ego back to health."

Thanks to his parents' violation of Section Eight, Jack had not one but two tracker grandfathers. He knew which one Tanner was referring to. Joseph Fowler the Eleventh had been the professor's best friend.

The old man grinned, shifting his gaze to the far end of the hall. "I was always dragging Joe out of one crisis or another." And then his smile faded. "Until the day I failed."

Again, Jack knew what he meant. The professor had lost the use of his legs in an attempt to save his friend on the day Joe the Eleventh died. Jack had never built up the gumption to ask him for the story, but the moment's pause felt like an invitation. "H-how?" he asked, stumbling over the delicate question. "How did it happen?"

The two entered a mahogany elevator—or what looked like an elevator—and turned around. The doors slid closed and the box shot sideways so that Jack had to steady himself against the railing.

The professor glanced up at him. "It was a terrible winter, boy. Terrible indeed. Bill Shepherd the Eleventh was hit by a train while searching for the Einstein-Rosen Bridge. Not two weeks later, the eleventh John Buckles tumbled off a cliff outside of Salzburg. So they say. But Joe . . . Joe was the first to fall, and I'm to blame."

"You?" Jack had never heard that part. "But you were the one who tried to save him."

"Yes. That's true. I tried to save him. I was also the one who dragged him off on that fool quest in the first place."

Centrifugal force pressed Jack into the rail as the side-a-vator entered a wide turn, working its way around the giant underground tower.

"You must understand, Jack. It was a time of transition." Tanner gripped his wheels to keep his chair from rolling backward into the rail. "The twelves and their quartermasters were coming into their own—field-ready, as they called it—and the ministry had little use for the old elevens. Old." He laughed. "Some of us hadn't yet breached fifty. We all had unsolved mysteries we'd gathered over the years, and so we dove into them. Unsanctioned missions—without the aid of quarter-masters. John and Bill each went off on their own. I roped Joe into joining me. I had caught the trail of the Timur Ruby."

The side-a-vator jerked to a stop, and the doors parted. Tanner rolled himself out into a long lecture room, passing between mahogany risers on either side.

"Timur?" asked Jack, following behind. He remembered the name from his history courses, of which he had plenty during the ministry school year. "As in Timur the Lame? Tamerlane?" Jack had found Tamerlane to be a terrifying figure. The fourteenth-century tyrant had built an empire stretching from Turkey to India, and in the process, he had slaughtered seventeen million people.

"Yes. Tamerlane. Well done, my boy." Tanner slowed to let him catch up. "It was said that his ruby was the source of his success, that it held the power to command men, so you can understand my interest. Over the years, I had traced its history to an East India Company ship that was lost with all hands in the mid-1800s. With your grandfather's help, I found it, run aground in an island cave at the edge of the Mariana Trench."

The professor halted his chair and turned to face his pupil. He raised his hands, cupped together. "There it was, boy, the famous jewel, resting in a silver bowl in the ruins of the captain's cabin. All we had to do was take it."

Jack leaned unconsciously forward. "And?"

"And your grandfather didn't hesitate." Tanner dropped his hands to his lap. "In his rush, Joe unbalanced the ship. It tipped into the sea, breaking apart, and before I knew it, a cannon had smashed through the cabin wall and pinned him down." With a sigh, the professor turned and rolled onward. "I dove in after him, kicking with all I had as half the ship slid down into the endless dark of the trench. The pressure was immense, threatening to rob me of consciousness. And then a piece of mast slammed into my back and it was all over. I woke up in a hospital weeks later without use of my legs. My friend, your grandfather, was gone."

Chapter Nine

JACK AND THE PROFESSOR stopped at the far end of the classroom, at a half circle of steps leading down to a set of double doors. "On to happier topics, eh?" Tanner slapped the arm of his chair. "Ready to rev this baby up?"

Jack mustered a smile. "I don't know why you waited this long."

The professor flipped up his armrest and pressed a red button, unleashing a hum like that of the QEDs, and the wheelchair rose up on a blue cushion of light. As Jack jumped ahead to open the doors, his mentor ghosted down the steps. "Can't tell you how often I've wished I could use my thrusters instead of those ramps in the Tube stations. But secrets must be kept."

They entered an octagonal study, its eight sides a mix of bookshelves, desks, and cabinets all built into the mahogany walls. Most areas of the Keep minimized sensory distractions, but the professor's office was full of them. Water trickled through the bamboo pipes of a desk fountain. A pair of clockwork zeppelins buzzed back and forth between the bookcases in a perpetual chase.

And there were spheres everywhere.

Polished spheres of every size and color sat on every shelf and desktop, some as big as bowling balls. They were samples of stone and metal, designed to teach young trackers how to spark. Over the course of the year, Jack had tried them all and seen the shadows and faces of Edward Tanners from generations past. Somewhere in the Keep there were other spheres, used by Jack's own ancestors, but Jack had never seen them. The Buckles office had been sealed, pending his father's post-coma trial.

Jack paused a few feet past the doors to lay a hand on his favorite sphere, a baseball-size orb sculpted from dragonite, so dark it was almost black, with deep rivers of iridescent red and blue. All the dragonite in London had been mined a thousand years before from a deep well fortress at the center of the city. Once a stronghold of the Ministry of Dragons, now it was the Archive of the Elder Ministries—the world's strangest library. Jack had no fear of sparking off the sphere. No tracker had ever sparked off dragonite. But whenever he touched it, he felt a golden wave of warmth pass up his arm.

"Your coat," said Tanner, snapping his fingers as his wheels settled to the rug. "We do have standards here, after all."

Jack let go of the sphere and relinquished his leather jacket. He wore a waistcoat and tie beneath, the uniform of all apprentice clerks at the ministry. He preferred the blue jeans and T-shirt he had worn in the arena, but Tanner wouldn't stand for it.

As the professor spun his chair around to hang up the coat, he knocked a paper from his desk. Jack saw a triangle with four circles—one at each corner and one at the center, with lines connecting them all. A scribble in Tanner's handwriting read *49 Divers*. Jack's mind jumped to the professor's story about the East India Company ship falling into the Mariana Trench. "Are you . . . still looking for the Timur Ruby?"

"It's become a bit of a hobby horse. You understand." The old man gave him a quick smile, tucking the paper into a drawer. "Now, I think we need to build your confidence after last night's . . . well . . . fiasco, not to put too fine a point on it. I have something new for you to try. Something quite advanced."

The professor slid a walnut box to the center of his desk. Inside, mounted on an onyx base, was a silver rod with golden baskets fused to either end. Each basket held a yellow gem the size of a golf ball.

Jack eyed the stones. Large, clear gems captured light and sound better than other minerals, making it easy for trackers to draw out the visions. Such gems were used for beginner spark training. He sighed. Tanner was patronizing him. "Professor, I know how to spark. Last night I just—"

"Do you?" The professor wheeled back, glancing up at him. "Do you know what sparking truly is?"

Jack shrugged. He thought he did. "The molecules vibrate against my nerve endings," he said, wiggling his fingers, "sending visions to my brain."

"Ehh." The professor bobbled his head back and forth. "That is a vastly simplified explanation." He gestured at the bamboo fountain on the corner of his desk. "By that logic, a spark flows through your nervous system like water through a pipe, moving in one direction, from point A to point B." Without warning, he caught Jack's wrist. "But this"—he flopped Jack's arm back and forth—"this is no mere pipe.

A tracker's arm is a cable, Jack. And how does data travel through a cable?"

Jack was beginning to catch on. "In both directions."

"Exactly. We're talking about two-way communication, boy. Interaction." Still holding Jack's wrist, the professor steered him toward a yellow gem. "It's time to reach beyond mere observation."

"Wait." Jack resisted the professor's pull, stalling. He eyed his jacket, but both it and the zed were well out of reach. "Um . . . why haven't you ever shown me this before?"

Tanner chuckled. "Because interacting with a spark is incredibly dangerous." With that, he pressed Jack's hand down onto the stone.

──── · Chapter Ten · ────

JACK STARED UP through a break in the fingers covering the gem—his fingers.

"Take a step, Jack."

He could see Tanner towering above, as if the professor were looking down at a figurine on his desk. But Jack couldn't answer, let alone move—just like any other spark.

"A leap of faith, my boy. That's what I'm asking of you. Take a single step out of that very comfortable spot you're in. Take the leap from observation to action." Giant Tanner's lips never moved, but Jack could hear him crisp and clear. He struggled to obey.

"No. No. Stop trying to move your muscles, child. You

don't have any. Separate consciousness from physicality and step out of there."

"Out of where?" The words were Jack's. He couldn't believe the sound of his own voice. He had never been able to speak during a vision.

"Well done! You're onto it. Now, let your mind wander."

Jack let go of the concept of legs and feet, of hamstrings and quadriceps, and urged his conscious self out into the room. In the next instant, he was standing at the center of the octagonal office. For a moment, he thought he'd lost the spark, but when he turned back toward the desk, he saw himself standing there, right next to the professor, fingers still resting on the jewel.

Freaky.

Tanner gave him no time to settle in. "Now, Jack, come and find me."

"I did. I'm right here, standing behind you."

"Not *that* me, you ninny. The other me."

Jack turned in a slow circle, feeling vertigo, like walking in virtual reality for the first time. The room shimmered as he turned. Everything had a micro-thin crystalline coating. There were two Jacks, him and the other him, but the office was short one professor. "I don't see any other yous."

"That's because I'm not in *your* gem, boy. Do you see the exit?"

"Yes."

"Then take it."

Jack headed for the double doors on wobbly legs.

"Wait!"

He stopped, throwing his arms out for balance. The office tilted and rolled like a ship on the waves.

"I almost forgot," said Tanner as the room finally settled. "Don't think about leaving. Think about going to another place instead. Do you understand the difference?"

"Um . . . yes?"

"That wasn't an answer. It was a question."

Jack frowned at himself and set his jaw, trying to look more confident than he felt. "Yes."

"Better. Go ahead."

With the next step, the door came rushing at him. There was a white flash, and once again, he found himself at the center of the office. "Um . . . Professor?"

"Don't talk to him-me. Talk to me-me."

Jack spun around. A man stood between him and the exit, wearing the same hound's-tooth coat and the same brown wingtips as the professor, but he was not bound to any wheelchair, quantum or otherwise. He stood tall, with light brown hair and a smooth complexion, free of liver spots and crow's feet—a younger version of Tanner.

Young Tanner laughed. "Don't look so shocked, boy. I wasn't always old, you know."

Jack blinked and swallowed. He could only manage one word. "How?"

Young Tanner patted Jack's arm. "Networking, my boy. Good for the career. Good for the soul." He pointed at the silver rod between the gems. "Silver is a superb conductor. It allows us to share the spark even though we're each touching a separate gem." He wandered over to a bookcase, clockwork zeppelins shimmering as they passed above him. "Mind you, we can only interact in here with items the gems themselves have seen. But over the generations those two beauties have seen every jot and tittle in this office." He pulled down a book and tossed it to Jack.

After a bit of fumbling, Jack settled the book in his hands. He could feel the compacted leather of its cover against his fingertips, even though he knew he wasn't actually standing there. All of this was in his mind. The real Jack—his physical self—was still at the desk, one hand on the jewel. On a whim, Jack held the book up to his nose, jerking his head back in surprise when he smelled the old ink and the musty pages. "So this—everything I'm experiencing—it's all . . ."

"Data." Young Tanner retrieved the book and slid it back onto the shelf. "These gems are silicates and carbon—the same building blocks used in the latest high-tech gadgets. Think of them as the world's oldest computers." He lifted a black-and-white photo—four men standing in front of a pyramid, wearing tweed suits and knee-high boots. "And trackers from the four families can access them. A few have even done it without physical contact."

Jack's amazed expression flattened into a skeptical frown. "You mean like tracker Wi-Fi."

"Is that so hard to believe?" The professor set the photo down. "Ever heard of a jewel curse? The most terrible crimes and notions of the worst rulers in history, trapped in crystalized carbon and rebroadcast for eternity, infecting all who wear the gem." He glanced down at Jack's arm. "Or perhaps a gem can trap something even more substantial. Like a conscious mind."

Jack followed the professor's gaze and saw his own sleeve was shimmering. His shoes were the same, becoming crystalline like the books and spheres and everything else in the office. His breathing quickened.

"You're losing your concentration, boy. I believe it's time to go."

"Right. Okay." Jack knew how to bail out of a spark. He pulled against the vision with his mind. Nothing happened.

"Oops," said Tanner. "Something wrong?"

If Jack didn't know better, he would have thought the professor was enjoying his growing panic. What would happen if he couldn't get out? Would his mind be trapped there forever? Would he become a ghost—the legendary curse of the Tanner jewels? That didn't sound good.

He pulled again. Still nothing.

"Your old skills won't help you, Jack. The moment you stepped out from the observation position, you severed your usual escape route."

The crystalline feel of the room grew stronger. A faceted sheet obscured every detail. "Why did you bring me in here if you knew I might be trapped?"

"In a word? Psychology. If I had warned you of the specific danger, you would have built a mental block. You might never have overcome it." Young Tanner placed a hand on each of Jack's shoulders. "But you jumped right in, didn't you? I am so proud."

Jack didn't feel like celebrating at that particular moment.

The faceted covering thickened. He could no longer make out the spheres or the zeppelins.

Tanner released him. "Remember when I told you to think about moving to another place, rather than leaving?"

Jack nodded, having lost the capability to speak. Another bad sign.

"Reverse that command. Think about leaving, Jack. Find an exit. A stairwell, a lift, a doorway—any exit will do."

The jeweled mahogany walls lost their color. Ripples of yellow flashed across every surface. Jack's heart raced, if he even had a heart anymore. His whole body had become crystalline.

The professor's calm expression turned dead serious. "I think I've pushed you enough for one day." He took Jack's hand and it became flesh again, and he leaned back and pulled.

Jack willed his foot to move, taking a step.

"Good. You've got it. Escape, Jack. Get to the door. Now!" The professor pulled once more, and Jack flew headlong through the doors.

In the blink of an eye, he was standing at the desk again. The crystalline shimmer evaporated. The office was real. He tore his hand away from the gem and patted his hips and waistcoat. *He* was real. "You saved me," he said to Tanner, now old and confined to his wheelchair once again. "You pulled me out of there."

"Nonsense. Not in my power."

"But you—"

The professor held up a hand. "I offered some forceful encouragement, as any good instructor must do on occasion. Only *you* have the power to pull your consciousness out of a spark, Jack. And you did." He thought to himself for a moment and then looked up at his student. "In fact, I think we should capitalize on your momentum."

"My . . . momentum?"

"Exactly." The professor tapped his chin with a long finger. "We have to keep moving forward with this line of training, really give you something to see."

Jack caught himself nodding. Despite the terror of the last few minutes, he did want to push into another spark. The freedom of movement had been intoxicating, like taking control of a dream.

The professor nodded with him, rubbing his hands together. "Yes. And I know just the place. Tonight. After tea. I have some errands to run, so I'll have to meet you there, but it shouldn't be a problem." He raised an eyebrow.

"Have I ever told you how to get to the Vault?"

Jack knew about the Keep's high-security storage levels, but he had never heard anyone refer to them as vaults. He narrowed his eyes. "Which vault?"

"*The* Vault, my boy. The one at the Ministry of Secrets—the nightly home of the Crown Jewels of the United Kingdom."

—— · Chapter Eleven · ——

THE MINISTRY OF TRACKERS had not been
content with imprisoning and training Jack. They also felt
it necessary to absorb him into the collective. According to
Mrs. Hudson, all trackers and quartermasters started out as
clerks, and Jack was no exception. When he wasn't training
with the professor or attending his academic courses, which
had been suspended for the holidays, he had a list of menial
tasks to accomplish.

Jack's clerk duties took him up and down the Keep, from
taking inventory in the low-security storage on Sublevel
Twenty-One to sorting unclaimed socks in the Lost Property Office at street level. And he never had to worry
about getting lost in between. Whenever he came to some

shadowed stair or secretive hallway where a Section Thirteen wasn't allowed, a QED appeared to shepherd him back to the right path.

Lunch would be a prawn sandwich and crisps, which Jack still called potato chips, eaten at his dad's bedside. And after that, it was back to work or school until teatime. His post-lunch duties had been suspended for a while so that he could train with Ash for the Hunt, making him feel at least a little like a real live tracker. But that was over now.

At the end of the day, Jack reported to the Matching Room beneath the Lost Property Office, where he and Gwen would be matching lost-item forms with found-item forms. It was a duty they had shared nearly every day before his doomed hiatus. Gwen's desire to become a quartermaster was no secret, and she had treated Jack's departure as a betrayal. She hadn't spoken to him since. Now that Ash had dropped him and he had to go crawling back, things were going to be all kinds of awkward.

QEDs buzzed about, carrying labeled plastic bags filled with the day's take of lost items, while three stories of movable filing cubbies shifted and rotated around one another, propelled by a single QED at the center, restocking the rainbow of forms. Gwen was already there, seated at a large oak desk on the sorting floor, separating white *Lost Property* forms and green *Enquiry* forms into two stacks.

Jack sat down next to her and began organizing the green forms by category. He kept quiet, hoping she would speak first.

She wouldn't. Not Gwen. Her honey-blond hair fell like a curtain between them. It smelled a bit like strawberries. He didn't mind.

After a long silence, covered only by the hum of the drones and the rather pointed *flap* of Gwen's papers, Jack couldn't take it anymore. "So . . . Ash—"

"Dumped you." Gwen pounced on the opening like a cat on a laser dot, throwing back her hair and scowling at him. "He tossed you like yesterday's kippers. I know." She slapped a white form down between them. "Purse."

"What?"

"Missing. Purse." Gwen rapidly tapped the form with her index finger. "Blue paisley. If you're back, then you're back to work, right?"

Jack sifted through his wallet-purse stack until he found a matching green enquiry form—filled out by the owner of the blue paisley purse. He placed it on top of Gwen's.

She slapped another form on top of that one. "Scarf. Yellow. Green stripes. Mrs. Hudson made me your guide,

Jack. We were supposed to be a team, you know?"

Jack nodded, unwilling to risk actual words, and placed the corresponding enquiry on the pile. During the night, long after Jack and Gwen were gone, the QEDs would match the pairs of forms to the actual purse, the actual yellow scarf, and all the rest of the lost items. And six to ten weeks later, each would make it back to its owner. It would take that long for no other reason than that was the *proper* time period for the return of lost items.

In the meantime, Gwen laid down another lost property form, one for a stocking cap. "But *you* wanted to run off with *Ash. You* wanted to be the hero of the games."

"None of that was my idea." Jack laid down a green enquiry from the stocking cap's owner. "I didn't ask to be on Ash's team. He asked me."

"Well, you *jolly*-well didn't say no, did you?"

Their individual stacks shrank. The combined stack between them grew. And every once in a while, they paused as one or the other filled in the blanks missed by the civilian—Gwen's term—who had filled out the form. Mrs. Hudson had made that necessity quite clear. Ministry regulations, volume three, section one, rule ninety-seven: *All forms, once initiated, must be completed.*

"I am glad to be back, though," said Jack, offering an olive branch after what must have been a half hour of silence.

"Really? *Are* you?"

Jack got the feeling there was no right answer. "Um . . . yes?"

Gwen knit her eyebrows together. "Huh. Because it seems to me that you ran off with a *real* quartermaster first chance you got." At the word *real*, she made quotation marks with her fingers. "And I was left down here, *slaving away* with *no one* to help." Gwen lifted the finished center stack above her head and two drones flew in with pincers ready, each taking half. Hands empty, she folded her arms across her chest. "No one at all."

The QEDs flew off to match the paired forms with the bagged items, and Jack looked down at the desk. On most days, at that point, it would be clean. But one form remained, an enquiry without a matching lost property form. He scanned the handwritten entries. "Missing wallet. A Russian archeologist named Lazarev. Says here he's a visiting professor at Cambridge."

Gwen nodded, still fuming. She snapped her fingers and waved a QED over. The drone took the form back to the moving cubbies, inserting it into the next day's cycle.

The desk was empty. Jack stood to go, but Gwen touched

his hand, and for a moment, he thought she might say something nice.

He was wrong.

"Aren't you forgetting something?" she asked as another QED flew in and laid a single paper on the desk. "We have to fill out the O-dash-ninety-six."

"Right." Jack slumped down in his chair again. "The O-dash-ninety-six. Sure."

Several months earlier, whatever undersecretary oversaw the QEDs had decided he or she should track the drones' customer service and instituted the O-96 QED Critique Form. Not to be out-formed, another undersecretary—the one in charge of regulations—had added a new subsection that dictated precisely how the O-96 should be filled out, lest someone inadvertently offend the drones and thereby reduce efficiency. Thus, any clerk who worked with QEDs had to fill out the O-96, but had to fill it out in exactly the same way every time.

"Response time?" asked Gwen, pen ready.

"Fast."

She checked a box on the first line and moved to the next. "Files and stacks?"

"Neat."

"Workload?"

"Average."

"Attitude?"

"Seriously?" asked Jack. "You people know they're just drones, right?"

Gwen's freckles flattened into a stern frown. *"Att-i-tude?"*

He sighed. "Friendly."

"Which is more than I can say for yours." She checked yet another box. "Drone condition?"

"Good."

"Yes." Gwen made the appropriate mark. "We're quite well polished today, aren't we?" She held the pen over the final box. "Total performance?"

Jack glanced at the drone. It inched closer, camera aperture expanding and contracting nervously. He rolled his eyes. "Good."

"I agree." Gwen checked the box and held out the form. The QED snatched it up and flew away.

———· Chapter Twelve ·———

JACK FOUND A FREESTANDING CLOCK on Oxford Street, right where Tanner had said it would be. The hands marked teatime, half past six in the evening. He took a left, passed through a gap between stores barely wide enough for a grown man's shoulders, and entered a pedestrian plaza lit with blue and green Christmas lights.

A few minutes earlier, Jack had walked right out the front door of the Lost Property Office. He. Jack Buckles. A Section Thirteen. *The* Section Thirteen.

No alarms had gone off. No QEDs had come flying in to stop him. Shaw had not come lumbering down the street with a net or an electrosphere. The professor must have made special arrangements. Jack had felt a twinge of guilt at the realization that the professor had gone to additional trouble, especially because Jack had traded his uniform for a T-shirt and blue jeans. But it was his first time out of the Keep in a while, and he didn't feel like walking around London in a waistcoat and wool britches.

Jack found a red telephone booth at the edge of the plaza, next to a man with no legs making chalk drawings. The artist nudged an upturned fedora with the back of his hand, jingling the few coins inside.

"Oh." Jack patted his jeans. He had not brought any change. After a moment's indecision, he removed a platinum card from his back pocket, one that simply read JOHN BUCKLES, and showed it to the artist, keeping it half-hidden in his palm. He glanced left and right to see if anyone on the plaza was watching. No one was.

The artist frowned, walked himself over to the red telephone booth with his fists, and gave the side of it a good pound.

The door opened.

Jack stepped inside, trying not to look as out of place as he felt—a wally, as Gwen would say—and the artist pounded the side again. The floor dropped away.

Jack dropped with it for a good three stories before jolting to a stop. He stepped out on unsteady legs onto a black granite floor and headed for a line of bronze turnstiles. He had not gone far before he noticed a familiar black-and-purple scarf on the other side. "Gwen?" His voice echoed across the station.

Everyone in the place cast a shocked scowl his way. A guard in a three-piece suit, wearing an armband that read MINISTRY EXPRESS, lowered his newspaper and glared. Jack had forgotten. The transportation service of the Elder Ministries demanded utter silence, a matter of avoiding cross talk between the secretive agencies.

Gwen's eyes grew wide for a fraction of a second before narrowing again in frustration. She tried to reverse course through a turnstile, but it locked, making a clamorous rattle, and the guard shifted his glare. She glared right back, waving a copper card similar to Jack's platinum version and rattling the turnstile again for good measure. The guard sniffed in displeasure, reached beneath the rim of his box, and pressed an unseen switch. The turnstile clicked.

Gwen pushed her way through and stormed over to Jack. "What do you think you're doing?" she whispered, shoving him back toward the phone-booth elevator with the tips of her fingers. She leaned left and right, trying to see around him. "And where is your escort? You know you can't leave the Keep by yourself."

Jack shrugged. "Apparently I can."

"Oh. You think this is funny?" Gwen checked over her shoulder.

The guard was watching them, one eye peering over his newspaper.

Jack lowered his voice. "It's fine. The professor—"

There was a pronounced *whoosh* as a cylindrical train pulled in to one of the platforms beyond the turnstiles, all gleaming bronze and steel beneath the purple glow of the huge maglev rings that formed its track. Gwen grabbed Jack's hand and pulled him along, whispering through clenched teeth. "It is *not* fine. And you're going to explain yourself as soon as we're on that train."

The station's four tracks were divided among two levels of open platforms. The bronze rings of the two upper tracks were suspended from the ceiling, so that the trains flew through them ten feet above Jack's head. The rings of the lower tracks rose up in arcs from beneath the floor, so that arriving trains surfaced like submarines bursting from the depths and dove down again once they were full. Jack and Gwen hurried toward one of those.

A trio of dragos—agents of the Ministry of Dragons—shuffled toward the next carriage over. All three were looking at Jack, their red scarves and the burn scars on their faces making their glares all the fiercer.

Gwen yanked him into their own car and pulled him down beside her onto a seat padded with sky-blue velvet. As soon as the door hissed closed, she folded her arms. "Spill it."

"What? I'm meeting the professor for some training."

"Don't 'what?' me, Jack. Section thirteen, rule nine: 'A Section Thirteen cannot leave the ministry without an approved and qualified escort.'" She opened a drawer beneath her seat, selected a pink glass bottle, and handed it to Jack. "Drink. You look dehydrated."

"I don't need an escort," he countered, accepting the drink. He took a swig and coughed. Burning, fizzy liquid bubbled out his nose. "That's . . . not water," he wheezed. "Tastes like . . . carbonated perfume."

Gwen recovered the bottle before he managed to drop it. "You do realize that you *are* English, don't you—despite your parents' little American charade? Eventually you're going to have to learn to like our food." She sat back and took a drink from the same bottle. "It's elderflower cordial. The Express has been stocking it for months. Where've you been?"

"Locked. Up."

Gwen touched her nose. "Exactly. Because you're a Section Thirteen, and a Section Thirteen *can't leave the Keep without an escort.*" She slapped the bench with each of those last few words.

The two of them leaned left as the train whipped to a stop. Tiles that read TOWER STATION came into view outside the portal window. "This is my stop," said Jack, standing up.

Gwen returned the bottle to its place and stood up beside him, kicking the drawer closed with her boot. "Then I guess it's mine, too."

Chapter Thirteen

THE ELEVATOR that brought them up from the station was concealed within a tiny cylindrical building marked LONDON HYDRAULIC POWER COMPANY. And that cylinder stood at the edge of the open plaza beside the medieval castle known to the world as the Tower of London. Jack pushed open the iron door, turned north, and kept on walking.

Gwen chased after him, slinging the tail of her scarf over her shoulder. "Where, exactly, are you meeting the professor?"

"Don't you have someplace else to be?" he asked, wheeling around.

"Of course I do. But I have to stay with you until I can hand you off to Professor Tanner."

Hand you off, as if Jack were a child passing between parents. "I. Don't. Need. Babysitting."

"Yes. You. Do." Gwen looked past him up the plaza, gauging his trajectory. "Are you . . . meeting Tanner at the Ministry of Secrets?"

"Maybe."

"How do you even know where the door is?"

Jack shoved his hands into the pockets of his leather jacket and frowned at her. Now she was just being obnoxious. He knew things. Maybe he hadn't *actually* known where the Ministry of Secrets was until the professor had told him that morning, but he sure wasn't going to tell her that. "Why shouldn't I know where it is?"

"Because it's the Ministry of *Secrets*, not the Ministry of Things-everybody-knows-and-we-all-discuss-over-tea, now, is it?"

"Then how do *you* know?"

"*I* know a lot of things." Gwen hooked his arm and pulled him north across the pavers, as if Jack hadn't already been heading in that direction. She snapped her fingers. "The Crown Jewels. *That's* why you're meeting him down in Spookville," she said, using the nickname for the Ministry of Secrets. Their agents were known as spooks. Agents of the Ministry of Guilds were known as toppers, thanks to their love of top hats, and the agents of the Ministry of Dragons were called dragos. In turn, the spooks, dragos, and toppers—who all considered the Ministry of Trackers to be a bunch of lowly commoners—referred to them as crumbs.

Jack said nothing, but Gwen was right. She excelled at deduction, which was often really annoying. The professor had promised him a few guided sparks on the famous gems in the Crown Jewels collection. During the touristy hours, the jewels were on display in the Tower, but there would be no privacy during that time. Ever. After teatime, though, the whole room descended on a slanted elevator, deep into the headquarters of the Ministry of Secrets, into the most secure vault in all of London.

They crossed Tower Hill Lane and entered a memorial that looked like a cross between a miniature Roman temple and an open mausoleum. Wide rectangular columns, plated with bronze, formed a long hall that supported a Parthenon-style roof.

Gwen came to a halt between the first two columns. "No one can get into the Ministry of Secrets without a spook escort, not even Tanner." She folded her arms, taking on an expression that Jack liked to call her Encyclopedia Kincaidia look. "Mo-Mos, book three, chapter eight, rule two: 'No person or animal shall enter a Ministry of Secrets facility unaccompanied by an agent.'"

"*Mo-Mos?*" Jack walked ahead of her into the hall, looking for a particular bronze panel.

"It's short for 'The Manuals of the Ministry of Secrets.'"

On the second column to the right, Jack found the panel the professor had told him about. Each one was embossed with the name of a lost merchant ship and the names of the crew that had perished with it. But this panel's names were uncannily anonymous.

SMITH, H. C.

SMITH, J.

SMITH, W. B.

The list of coincidental crewmen went on, every one of them a Smith—except for the captain, whose name was Johnson. "So you're saying you've read the top-secret spook manual."

"Manuals," Gwen corrected him. "Plural. And yes, I have."

"Then tell me how the Ministry of Secrets knows for sure who's an agent and who's not."

"Rule three: 'Agents of the Ministry of Secrets will have DNA access to all facilities that meet their clearance level.'"

"Humph. DNA access, huh?" Jack laid his palm flat on the many Smiths, raising an eyebrow at Gwen. The Smiths glowed for an instant, and then four of the huge granite tiles at their feet dissolved before their eyes, exposing a deep stairwell of glistening steps—white marble, flecked with silver.

"*That* can't be right."

Jack lowered a foot to the first step. "You don't have to come. You did say you had someplace else to be."

But Gwen only huffed and tromped past him, heading down the stairs.

He watched her go. "So I guess you don't, then."

Zzzap.

The smart remark had barely escaped Jack's lips when an orange lightning bolt flashed at the back of his mind, exactly like the one he had sensed during the Hunt.

Zzzap. It happened again.

Jack glanced around. Black taxis rolled by on Tower Lane. Pedestrians, huddled beneath their winter coats, hurried along the sidewalk. But he saw nothing that might have caused the strange flash. Gwen had reached the first landing. He rushed down the steps to catch up.

Chapter Fourteen

THE GLISTENING STEPS ended between two colossal figures—a white statue of a man with the head of a jackal and a black statue of a woman with the head of a bird. The two held aloft an ornamented block etched with hieroglyphs.

"To see yet remain unseen," said Gwen, scanning the block as she and Jack passed beneath it.

Jack glanced over at her, narrowing his eyes. "You can read that?"

She gave him a little smile, a single bounce of her freckles, the first freckle bounce he had seen in a long time.

They stepped down onto a midnight-blue marble floor. Set into the stone was a seal made from some dark silver alloy—tungsten, maybe. Two giant Vs lay one on top of the other within a circular boundary, and at their center was a lidless eye. Jack had the unshakable feeling that it could see them.

Hanging above the seal, a good twenty feet over their heads, was a copy of the mini-temple-mausoleum monument where he had found the Smiths, except the spooks' version included huge statues between the rectangular columns. Each faceless figure was dressed for a different era, in long capes, robes, or overcoats. Jack had the feeling they were all scowling down at him. Or rather, they were scowling up. The monument was upside down, and so was almost everything else. He nudged Gwen's arm and pointed. "Um . . . Gwen . . ."

Steps led up from all four sides of the temple. In the atrium above, men and women in striped suits and silk dresses walked inverted along bridges and balconies, defying gravity. Then it occurred to Jack that the floor at his feet had a bowl shape to it, terminating at the seal. It wasn't a floor at all. He and Gwen were standing on a shallow domed ceiling.

"Illusion," whispered Gwen. "Trickery. Stock in trade for the spooks. Mo-Mos, book one, chapter six, rule six: 'To remain unseen is not always to hide. More often it is to fool the eye.' The spooks call this the Mobius Tower. Supposed to be a nightmare for tracker senses." She snorted. "Doesn't look so bad." She reached deep into the pocket of her coat and withdrew a green bouncing ball. "I bet the whole thing's a hologram."

After a quick glance around to see that no one was watching, Gwen tossed the ball high in the air. It flew past the temple of faceless spooks, hit the inverted steps, and bounced down again. She gave Jack a scrunched-up smile and raised her hand to catch it. "See."

But the ball never reached her. It slowed and reversed course, returning to the steps and bouncing up them with diminishing gusto until it rolled across an adjoining bridge and bumped the foot of a spook with jet-black hair. He picked up the ball with a pale hand, shot a glare at the two teens, and slipped it into the pocket of his pin-striped suit.

Jack shook his head. "I have to get to the Vault. The professor said to take the south hallway from the seal, then down three levels, east, south, and east again." There were only two hallways leading away from the floor-slash-ceiling. Jack turned left, in the direction he knew to be south.

But Gwen grabbed his sleeve. "Wait." She looked up at the

inverted atrium and down at Jack again and then dragged him the other way.

"But we have to go south. That's—"

"Don't talk about it. You'll hurt your brain. Trust me."

Ice-blue lamps glowed in the marble hall that led to the next stair, reflecting off the tungsten trim. Jack and Gwen went down—the normal down—three levels and stopped at the adjoining hallway, where Gwen made a dance in the air with her fingers, as if doing complex geometry.

"Mrs. Hudson says the Mobius Tower is like an octopus beneath London, with tentacles reaching from the observatory at Greenwich to the headquarters of MI6, Her Majesty's Secret Intelligence Service. Remember every turn or we'll get hopelessly lost." She made one more gesture, nodded to herself, and pulled him to the right.

Their path ended at a small chamber, where a man and a woman sat on a bench against the left wall. His suit was black, with a silver scarf. Her dress was gray, with a tiny matching top hat resting amid tightly wound braids of black hair. They said nothing to the teens, but Jack noticed the woman's hand, covered in a black lace glove, moved within her partner's. Her fingers flicked and tapped in the spook touch code.

There were no exits. Strange artwork of the same tungsten alloy covered the opposite wall, and two lines of glyphs formed an archway at the center. The largest glyph was the ministry's eye seal.

"Dead end or doorway?" whispered Gwen.

Jack nodded at the glyphs. "You tell me."

She didn't answer.

Behind them, the spook woman's fingers were still flicking. She did not look happy. Jack clenched his teeth, trying to whisper without moving his lips. "You read the Egyptian inscription in the stairwell, didn't you?"

"That's not Egyptian. It's spook-script," countered Gwen, whispering through her teeth as well. "And I guessed, okay? All I did was recite the spook motto. *To see yet remain unseen.* With all those eyes, what else would it have said?"

Jack cast an embarrassed smile at the spooks.

The man looked disinterested, but the woman glowered back at him.

Gwen elbowed his arm. "Didn't your precious professor tell you what to do when you got here?"

The finger flicking stopped. The man stood up, exposing his true size for the first time. He was bigger than Shaw.

"Jack," hissed Gwen. "Anytime now."

Playing a hunch, Jack laid his hand against the seal. The arch and all its glyphs glowed blue for an instant, and then the marble dematerialized. It was a door. He glanced over his shoulder at the big spook. The man stopped, gave him a suspicious scowl, and returned to his bench. Gwen had been right about the rules. Jack's DNA was as good as a backstage pass.

He gave the two spooks a weak smile and a thumbs-up as Gwen yanked him across the threshold, into a room filled with glittering treasure.

"Whoa."

A sword on a velvet pillow was the first thing to catch Jack's eye. The whole of the blade was polished silver, and the hilt was pure gold, with guards formed into the heads of a lion and a unicorn. It was huge and epic—a sword for heroes. Beside it was another, with a hilt and scabbard covered in jewels. That one was a touch too gaudy for his tastes.

After the swords came a solid gold punch bowl big enough to bathe in, and matching jewel-encrusted goblets that could not possibly have been dishwasher safe. Jack saw gilded armor, sparkling tiaras, jeweled necklaces and bracelets—all protected by nothing more than the kind of rope chains you might find at a movie theater.

What he did not see was any sign of the professor.

Gwen had stopped deeper in, at the end of a long pedestal topped with seven crowns and one enormous scepter. She stood with her hands on her hips, frowning at him.

Jack gave her a little shrug. "The professor had some errands to run. Maybe he's delayed." He clasped his hands behind his back and walked past her, inspecting the crowns. He paused before the biggest—the one with the golden scepter lying on a pillow beside it.

By far, the largest stone in the vault was the massive diamond that topped the scepter, glittering in the spotlights like a captured galaxy. But Jack's eyes were soon drawn to the crown itself and the big ruby in its band. The flow of reds beneath the ruby's smooth surface merged the bright translucence of hard candy with the near black of thickening blood. He had a sudden, overwhelming desire to touch it.

Jack leaned across the rope. He would spark. Sure. That was why he had come in the first place, wasn't it? But he wouldn't step into the vision without the professor there to help him. He would just . . . look. His hand stretched out, almost of its own accord.

"What are you doing?" Gwen smacked him across the knuckles.

He pulled back, cradling his smarting hand. "I just . . . wanted to see. You know . . . spark."

"Well, don't. It's a bad idea. You don't know where that thing has been."

He started to turn away, then stopped. Why did he always let her push him around? Jack stepped up to the rope again. "I know what I'm doing, okay? You don't have to treat me like I'm brand-new anymore."

She opened her mouth as if to respond and then snapped it closed again.

Jack puffed up his chest and reached out again. He did take one extra precaution, though. He slipped his other hand into his pocket and wrapped his fingers around the coolness of the zed—to be safe, because the professor wasn't there to help him.

"Jack, don't—"

Gwen's voice went silent the moment his fingers made contact with the stone.

—— · Chapter Fifteen · ——

JACK HAD CERTAIN EXPECTATIONS going into the spark. The ruby was at the center of a crown. Kings and queens wore crowns in castle halls, or riding in carriages amid throngs of adoring subjects. He had figured the spark would drop him into some similar picturesque scenario.

He had figured wrong.

Jack fell right smack into the middle of a medieval battle.

His feet sank into stinking mud, weighed down by steel armor ornamented with gold—a king's armor. Bodies lay all around, some in armor like his, though much plainer, and others in rags tied on with leather straps. A knight with a plumed helmet and a purple cape swung an ax straight for his head. Jack raised a shield strapped to his left arm to deflect the blow.

Sort of.

Jack had no control over the shield, or his clinking, clanking armored body for that matter. Both belonged to whichever idiotic not-safe-in-my-castle monarch was wearing the ruby at the time. Jack was sparking the way he usually did, with no control over anything, not even his voice.

The knight swung again, shouting in French. Another soldier shouted back, and Jack caught the word *dyooc* at the end of the exchange. He mulled that one over as a broadsword in his right hand made an unsuccessful jab at purple-cape guy. He watched the sword bounce off the Frenchman's shield. *Duke*, maybe? Great. So a French duke was trying to kill him this time instead of a psychotic French clockmaker. Jack was moving up in the world, but why were they always French?

A cry from the right. The idiotic not-safe-in-my-castle monarch turned toward a short bearded man fighting his way through the melee, shouting at his English king in a thick Welsh accent. Jack couldn't understand a single word. When the vision turned back to the Frenchman, the ax was falling again. Jack's shield hung too low. On instinct, he jumped out of the way.

Mistake.

Big one.

Wet muck soaked Jack's sneakers. He felt the gray, seeping cold of it creeping up the legs of his blue jeans. *His* jeans. *His* sneakers. Jack had jumped out of the ruby's perspective and into the spark. And Tanner wasn't there to guide him out again. He tried to breathe, vaguely aware that each breath was more a case of firing synapses than expanding lungs. What had the professor taught him? Think about escape. Look for an exit. The battle raged around him. Men screaming, trying to kill one another. And then it hit him. What exit? Jack was *outside*.

The French duke's ax had hit its mark. Half the golden crown welded to the king's helmet had split off, including the ruby. The king lay in the mud beside it.

Unintelligible-bearded-Welsh guy cried out and dove at the duke with what Jack considered to be the world's smallest sword. The Frenchman knocked him away as if he had hardly noticed him. In truth, Jack had hardly noticed the Welsh guy either. He could not take his eyes off the ruby. He wanted nothing more than to rescue the beautiful red stone from the indignity of that revolting battlefield ooze.

The duke, it seemed, felt the same. The king moaned, struggling to get his knees underneath him and exposing his back, but the Frenchman failed to press his advantage. He dropped the ax and went for the ruby.

Something snapped inside Jack. He couldn't let the duke get the stone. "No!" he shouted, and he and the duke merged as one man. They lifted the ruby from the mud together, holding it up to the red sky.

Shink.

Jack looked down. The world's smallest sword protruded from his chest.

But it wasn't really Jack's chest. It was the duke's chest. Jack stepped to the side and watched the Frenchman fall. The duke awkwardly grasped at his back, unable to reach the hilt and remove the offending blade. Jack laughed out loud to see him struggling. He snapped his mouth shut in surprise. What he was seeing was horrible. Why would he laugh?

Unintelligible-bearded-Welsh guy pried the jewel from the duke's fingers and held it aloft, shouting, "For Henry!"

For once, Jack had understood him.

Oddly, Semi-intelligible-bearded-Welsh guy ignored the

actual King Henry, who was still on all fours in the muck, trying to regain his senses. Not that it mattered. The Welshman had barely gotten the words out before a black-smith's hammer slammed into the side of his head. A French foot soldier dressed in rags dropped him like a sack of pota-toes, right on top of the duke. The foot soldier snatched up the ruby and ran.

"Stop! Thief!" Jack gave chase. As he ran, everything and everyone around him took on a red, gemlike quality. A bad sign. But all he could think about was the ruby.

The foot soldier led him on a terrifying, muddy jaunt through the battle, ducking crystalline spears and dodging red swords, leaping over dying men with silicate cocoons forming over their bodies.

The two of them broke free of the melee at the edge of a red forest. The foot soldier ran into the trees, but Jack reeled to a stop. He had caught a flash of the familiar in his periph-eral vision. He looked, knowing he could not have seen what he thought. But he had. Not fifty feet away, leaning against the faceted mouth of a hillside cave, was his father.

Chapter Sixteen

"DAD!" JACK TRIED TO CALL OUT, but he choked on the word. He had lost his ability to speak again. He couldn't walk, either. Crystal blades of grass grew over his sneakers, fusing together.

Move, Jack, said a voice in his head. The figure ducked into the cave. *Now.*

With enormous effort, Jack broke free and ran after his dad, concentrating on escape like Tanner had taught him. The cave rushed toward him.

"And another thing," said Gwen. "I do *not* treat you like you're brand-new."

He was back.

Zzzap.

Before Jack could tell Gwen the spark was over, another orange lightning bolt flashed at the forefront of his brain. This time, he felt a punch in the gut along with it. He staggered back from the rope barrier and gaped at the pedestal, unable to speak. The largest crown had vanished. So had the scepter with the giant diamond, leaving nothing behind but a deep impression in a velvet pillow.

The Crown Jewels were gone.

Gwen grabbed him by the shoulders, shaking him. "What did you *do*, Jack?"

"I didn't do anything. I swear!"

Zzzap.

Another flash. Another miniature blast wave. Jack looked for the source and saw that the gold-and-silver sword he liked so much had vanished as well.

Gwen punched him in the arm. Hard. "Quit it!"

"I told you. It's *not me*."

"And yet, you and I are the only ones here. We're—" Gwen paused. She blinked. "You and I are the only ones here," she said again, a little softer. She took a step toward the empty display. "This is a heist, Jack. It's the *holy grail* of all heists, and we're going to take the fall for it."

Blue lights flashed in the chamber outside the vault.

"Oi! You, in there!"

"That didn't take long," said Gwen.

Jack rushed to the wall beside the entrance and peeked out. "The big guy's coming this way," he said, backing away again. He surveyed the wall. There were four tungsten glyphs to the right of the arch. One of them had to be the door control.

"What're you kids up to?"

"Just looking," called Gwen. "We don't need any assistance. Lovely collection. Really." She lowered her voice to a whisper. "Jack, hurry."

He mashed his thumb down on a symbol that looked like a man walking. No door materialized. Instead, the whole vault lurched into motion, rising like a giant elevator. The blue marble ceiling of the outer chamber came down to cover the opening.

"Come back here!" The big spook grabbed the rising threshold and hung on.

"Oh dear." Gwen rushed over and peeled his fingers away, one by one. "Sorry. Sorry. So sorry. We don't want these chopped off, do we?"

The spook dropped to the floor with a heavy *thump*, and the gap closed.

The two teens stared at each other. "Now what?" asked Jack, raising his palms.

Gwen didn't get the chance to answer. A digital voice started jabbering at them in a strange, stilted language.

"Spook speak," said Gwen, looking up at loudspeakers in the corners of the room. "Likely telling the whole place there's been a breach."

"They have a spoken language too?"

Gwen sighed and held up her fist. "Touch . . . Sign . . . Written . . . Spoken." She raised a finger with each word. "The spooks have all four. They have a knitting club and a football team too, if you're interested." She thrust a hand at the symbols. "*Would* you mind? If we let the vault go all the way up, there's going to be a small army waiting for us."

"Oh. Yeah." Jack examined the controls. The remaining glyphs were an eye, a disembodied foot, and a torch. He pressed the torch, because the eye looked like trouble and he had an aversion to touching feet of any kind.

The room slowed its ascent. Silver light breached the arch, growing to a full-blown exit.

"That'll work." Gwen grabbed Jack's wrist and dragged him through.

"What about the professor?"

"Seriously, Jack? That's your biggest concern right now?"

They raced through halls and stairwells, reversing the professor's directions, but only climbing two levels. Jack expected to emerge on the inverted blue dome and make a quick exit. Instead, they burst out onto a black marble balcony with a brass rail.

"Um . . ." Jack skidded to a stop.

Gwen slammed into the rail and stared upward, mouth hanging open. "Well, that's a horse of a different color."

The domed ceiling, the atrium, everything but the white temple of spies had changed from blue to black. And the tungsten trim was now brass, even the great eye seal.

"The Mobius Tower," muttered Gwen.

Jack peered down over the rail at the rest of the chamber. "Is this even the same room?" The bridges and balconies were all right side up, along with the temple of spies, which lay slightly above them, crowning its four broad staircases. Jack saw the man who had taken Gwen's rubber ball on the next balcony down. He pointed up at the two teens. "Thieves!"

"Here we go." Gwen pulled Jack back into the passage, and the two made a dash for the stairwell. Upon reaching the end, however, they found an intersecting hall of green marble, trimmed with copper.

"What—? How—?" Jack stuttered. "We just came from here, but it was blue."

Gwen took a right and kept running. "I told you we'd get lost if you took a wrong turn."

"So this is *my* fault?"

"Well, it's not mine."

They came to a promising stairwell of glistening white stone and took the steps two at a time, only to stumble out onto a matching white balcony. Gwen dropped her forehead into her palm. "You can't be serious."

They had crossed to the opposite side of the atrium, one level down from the last, despite having run the other way and climbed a set of stairs. Every bit of stone was now sparkling white marble, trimmed with platinum. And there were more spooks than before, a lot more, all pointing at the teens.

"I hate this place." Jack rested his hands on the rail, trying to catch his breath. The lights dimmed. The echoing spook speak went silent. Every person in the atrium disappeared except a pair standing on a bridge even with Jack's balcony.

Jack recognized the sinking feeling of a spark.

The young man he had seen with the professor spoke in hushed tones with a bald man wearing black robes. The older man offered the younger a square case, and the arm he extended from his robes was a prosthetic, made of a blue-green alloy. Gears turned within the ribbed structure, releasing tiny electric sparks.

Jack gasped.

The bald man looked his way, as if reacting to the noise. He had one clockwork eye, and the mechanical pupil focused, boring right through him.

"You coming, or what?" Gwen beckoned from a bridge connected to the balcony.

The lights brightened. The two men vanished and the angry spooks reappeared.

"We could jump from the temple," said Gwen, pointing up. "There must be a gravitational shift midway."

It was as good a plan as any.

A single spook blocked their path to the temple steps— pale, with black hair, gripping a green rubber ball in his fist. Gwen didn't even break stride. She whipped the scarf from her shoulders and lashed out at the man's ankles, yanking both of his feet out from under him. He landed flat on his back and the ball bounced across the bridge.

She snatched it up as she passed. "Serves you right!"

The rest of the spooks converged from below, climbing the white steps on all four sides. Jack and Gwen reached the top and she took his hand, looking up at the platinum seal more than twenty feet above. "Ready?"

Did he have a choice?

Gwen didn't wait for an answer. "One, two, three!"

They jumped as high as they could, reaching up together, and landed on the temple steps again.

Gwen scrunched up her face. "*That* was disappointing."

Zzzap.

Jack grunted with the impact of another micro-blast. The young man in the overcoat with all the unnecessary buckles appeared right in front of him, a black duffel bag slung over his shoulder. He had a strange tattoo on his neck, an *X* with three keys running through it from side to side.

"Thief," said Jack.

The young man grinned. He had a device in his right hand that looked like a stopwatch, made of dull metal so dark it was almost black. But before Jack could get a good look at it, the thief wrapped them both in a bear hug.

Zzzap.

Immense pain, like every atom in Jack's body had been turned inside out.

Solid ground. A blue marble floor. Another punch in the gut.

The thief released them and backed away.

Zzzap.

He was gone.

Jack and Gwen stood alone on the original blue dome at the center of the great eye seal. The thief had dropped them there and vanished. They didn't have time to look for him. They just bolted for the Egyptian statues and the stairwell to the street.

"If he can teleport like that," panted Jack, reaching the top first, "then why not go the extra twenty yards and take us outside?"

Gwen came up beside him, gasping for breath. "Why would he help us at all?"

The answer came to Jack an instant after he pressed his hand against a bronze eye in the granite above his head.

The blocks separating them from the memorial dematerialized.

They were free.

Zzzap.

And so was the thief.

— · Chapter Seventeen · —

GWEN AND JACK HOPPED aboard a passing double-decker bus and hurried to the tail end, sitting shoulder-to-shoulder, scrunched down below the top of the rear bench. Jack pressed against the upholstery and raised himself up just enough to tilt his head back and look behind them. He saw no spooks—upside down or otherwise.

"Tanner set you up," said Gwen, yanking him down again.

"You don't know that. Maybe they took him before he could get to us."

"Maybe *who* took him?"

Jack let out a frustrated sigh. No matter how he phrased it, the professor would look bad. He admitted to Gwen that he had seen Tanner with the thief the night before, but he quickly followed with a description of his spark in the Mobius Tower and the bald man's clockwork prosthetics. "I'm telling you, Tanner isn't behind this. What if *you know who* is back?"

The bus stopped, and a pale, thin man boarded—definitely spookish. He wore a long black coat, black gloves, and black trousers, and he took his time walking down the aisle, picking a seat only two rows ahead of the teens.

Jack gritted his teeth and lowered his voice. "What if the thief and the bald guy are working for the Clockmaker?"

"Don't be absurd. Lots of people in the Elder Ministries have clockwork prosthetics—dozens in the Ministry of Dragons alone." Gwen dug at the rubber floor with the toe of her boot. "And we have bigger problems than a French arsonist. That bald man you described is Ignatius Gall."

She said the name as if Jack ought to recognize it. He didn't. "Who is Ignatius Gall?"

"Only the number three man in the Ministry of Secrets." Gwen had raised her voice a little too much. They both flinched, but skinny-spookish guy kept facing forward, shoulders swaying with the motion of the bus. She dropped back to a whisper. "Gall is the UFTU, Jack. He's the Undersecretary for Things Unknown."

"The UF—?" Jack frowned. Sometimes he wondered if

Gwen was making it all up. "What kind of things?"

She pushed him. "*Unknown* things, you wally. He's powerful, Jack. And connected. Not someone we want to mess with." The bus slowed, and she grabbed the chrome handrail, pulling herself to her feet. "We're here. Let's go."

Once the big double-decker had driven off, Jack saw the London Eye peeking over a steep copper roof across the street. They had gotten off near the Thames, a long way from home. "I thought we were going to the Keep?"

"Can't. The spooks'll be all over Baker Street by now." Gwen hurried up to the next intersection and took a right.

Jack rushed after her. "Then where are we going?"

"We're going to find the one person who needs to know we're innocent before the spooks catch us." She took another right down a narrow lane and headed for the deep red awning of a restaurant. The gold calligraphy on each window read RULES.

"Evenin', Miss Gwen." The doorman tipped his short top hat.

"Good evening, Paddy." Gwen was all business. "Is she here?"

Paddy inclined his graying head toward the back of the restaurant. "As always, love. Usual spot."

Jack followed Gwen through the restaurant, taking it in:

Old paintings of ships and foxhunts.

Deep-red couches trimmed with copper-tinted rope.

Rich scent of beef.

Silvery scent of apples.

They found Mrs. Hudson at a table beneath a mural of Britannia, salt-and-pepper hair pulled back into a perfectly proportioned bun. She scowled at a piece of toast through a pair of handheld spectacles as if checking for the proper number of raisins.

Mrs. Hudson nodded, indicating the teens should sit down. "The Ministry of Secrets called. You two have been busy."

"Mrs. Hudson, we—" Gwen began.

But Mrs. Hudson cut her off. "Stole the Crown Jewels? Stashed them in a bus locker?"

"No. We—"

"Sold them already?" Mrs. Hudson scraped a bit of duck pâté across her toast. "Well, that *is* unfortunate."

Jack intervened before the ministry matron could jump to any more conclusions. "I was supposed to meet Professor Tanner in the Vault," he blurted out. "But the thief showed up first."

Mrs. Hudson set down her toast without taking a bite.

"Preposterous. The professor would never ask you to do such a thing. And the Ministry of Secrets would never allow it, not without an order from the Queen herself."

"But my DNA opened all the doors."

"*Your* DNA?" Mrs. Hudson raised her spectacles, scrutinizing his face, looking for the truth behind his eyes. "Interesting." Satisfied—or not, she gave no indication—she returned to her meal, slicing into a pale dome of pastry and frowning at the mess of gravy that spilled out.

Jack watched her stab a lump of kidney that had fallen out of the pastry. He blanched at the sight of it. "I'm telling you, the professor invited me. He—"

"Set you up? Played you for the fool?" Mrs. Hudson placed the lump of kidney between her teeth, chewed once, and swallowed.

"No. He must have—"

"Sold you out? F*rrr*amed you?" She added a pronounced trill to the *r*.

"He wouldn't do that!" Jack slammed his fist down on the table hard enough to make the dishes bounce.

Mrs. Hudson drew in a quick breath through her nose.

"I mean . . ." Jack tucked his hand away and looked down at his knees. "He'll tell you. Just ask him."

The caged fury on Mrs. Hudson's face subsided. "Edward Tanner left this morning on a research trip. As far as the ministry is concerned, *you*, Mr. Buckles, arranged this theft on your own." She raised an eyebrow at Gwen. "In fact, if Miss Kincaid cares to state that you dragged her into this against her will, she may come in from the proverbial cold. Right now. With no repercussions."

Gwen didn't even blink. "Jack didn't do this," she protested, giving him a nod. "I saw the thief. We both did. That's who the spooks should be looking for."

Mrs. Hudson folded her hands behind her plate. "The Ministry of Secrets reported only two intruders." She glanced from one teen to the other. "Do either of you have any proof of this third man?"

Jack and Gwen both opened their mouths to answer, then closed them again and looked down at their hands.

"I see. Well, I should *think* you would want to go out and find some."

Jack glanced from Gwen to Mrs. Hudson. "Say again?"

Mrs. Hudson picked up her utensils, narrowing her eyes at the mutilated pastry and its kidneys. "Joint regulations, volume three, section ten requires me to call the wardens and have you detained." She made a *tsk* sound with her tongue. "But the wardens are miles away. At the moment there's nothing between you and your freedom but an aging doorman."

Gwen raised an eyebrow. "So what you're saying is . . ."

Mrs. Hudson ignored her. She stabbed another piece of kidney and swallowed it whole. "*Should* you happen to find yourselves free and *on the lam*, I suggest you start by consulting *Gulliver*. Understand?"

Gwen let out a little squeak of a laugh and nodded.

Jack was completely lost.

"Good." Mrs. Hudson straightened, put down her utensils, and dabbed the corners of her mouth with a napkin. Then she screamed at the top of her lungs, "Paddy!"

Jack fell out of his chair.

Gwen dragged him to his feet. "Run!"

The doorman appeared in the aisle, hat in hand. "Yes, Mrs. Hudson?" He spun in a teetering twirl as Jack and Gwen ducked past him and shot out the door.

Chapter Eighteen

RIVULETS OF SWEAT ran down Jack's cheeks, icy cold in the December air. Gwen had not stopped running since they left the restaurant, and the last mile or so had been uphill. She slowed to a walk beside a cathedral. A huge white dome loomed overhead.

"Saint Paul's," panted Jack, catching up to her. "You're heading for the Archive. Why?"

She left the paved path at the churchyard, wandering off among the gravestones. "Didn't you hear Mrs. Hudson? She told us to consult Gulliver."

"Gulliver?" Jack rested his hands on his knees, breathing hard. "Is that . . . the name of the cat?"

Once his heart rate had dropped to a dull pound, he left

the path and followed her through the stone markers. Time had worn them down, leaving dents and divots filled with moss and lichen. "What is it with you people and cemeteries?" He stopped. "And what are you *doing*?"

Gwen had lain down on an empty slab, hands folded on her stomach like the effigies around her. The only thing missing was a flower.

"I know you're exhausted, Gwen, but . . ."

She rolled her head to the side and shot him an exasperated look. Then she balled up a fist and pounded twice. The slab tipped up on its axis, and Gwen slid down into the black beneath.

Jack ran to the grave, but the slab tilted back into position with a heavy *thump*, and before he could call after her, he heard boots on the path. Someone was coming. He ducked into the shadows behind the slab.

A few seconds later, the skinny guy from the bus strolled into view, looking left and right—searching. He fixated on the bushes on the opposite side of the path, and Jack took the opportunity to roll his body onto the slab. He pounded twice.

Nothing happened.

The spook froze, listening. He started to turn.

Jack pounded harder—three, four, five times. And just as he gave himself up for lost, the stone tipped up and dumped him into the dark. He sailed down a spiral slide, out of control, until his feet met solid ground and he crashed through a door, stumbling out into soft yellow light. There were books on every side, three stories of them, with wrapping balconies and wrought-iron staircases in the corners. Gwen stood right in front of him.

"The skinny guy," said Jack, finding his tongue. "From the—"

The clerk drew an urgent finger across her throat and pointed behind him. "*Look*, Jack. The *Archivist* is here in the Tracker Collection. Out of all the collections in the Archive, she's *here*, in *ours*."

Jack spun around, backing up next to Gwen, and saw a blond woman in a blue waistcoat and green skirt, sliding books one by one onto the shelves. The rotating bookcase that had spat him out clicked back into place beside her.

"Hello, Jack. How may I help you?"

He waved and immediately felt foolish for making a silent gesture at a blind person. "Um . . . hi." Jack had more pressing matters to deal with. He turned to Gwen once more. "That guy from the bus, Gwen. He—"

Gwen stomped her foot. She made her shut-up face and drew her finger across her throat again.

"There's no point in silencing him," said the Archivist, adjusting a pair of round glasses so dark they were almost black. "I already know about the Crown Jewels."

Gwen turned to stare at her. "You do?"

"Why do you think I chose to be here at this particular moment, as you subtly pointed out?" She slid the last of her books into place and headed for the long desk at the center of the collection. "Neither of you strikes me as a jewel thief. So, as I said before, how may I help you?"

That was good enough for Jack. He didn't have time to mull over issues of trust. "A spook saw me in the churchyard. He'll know we came to the Archive. This place'll be crawling with 'em in minutes."

Gwen smacked him across the arm. "Well, why didn't you say something?" she said, and strode off after the Archivist. "We came for a book. Fiction. Jonathan Swift."

Jack tried to follow, but he found that his legs were blocked. A big calico cat rubbed against his shins, leaving hundreds of white hairs on his jeans. "You again," he said in a flat tone.

The cat purred.

By the time Jack reached the desk, Gwen had poured herself a cup of tea from a silver service.

"What are you doing? I said we don't have much time."

"There's *always* time for tea." Gwen added a splash of milk and took a long sip. As she did, the cat hopped up onto the desk and began lapping away at the milk in the pitcher. Gwen stopped mid-sip, teacup hovering at her chin, and shifted her eyes to the Archivist. "Does he do that quite often?"

"More often than I'd like." The Archivist was thumbing through a ledger on the desk, running her fingers over the handwritten entries.

Gwen set down her teacup and pushed it away, scowling at the cat, but the calico ignored her. It finished its milk and curled up atop a broad leather-bound text, right next to Jack.

"Ah, here it is," said the Archivist. "A Swift book was added to the collection nine months ago." She frowned. "Strange, there's no name associated with the entry." She left the desk, nimbly sidestepping a leather chair on her way to a shelf across the room, and singled out a thin volume with a blue cover. She shook her head as she returned. "Shelved with the works of Theodorus of Samos, of all places. Who would do such a thing?"

The Archivist handed the book to Jack and walked away,

leaving him to read the silver lettering on the cover. "*Gulliver's Travels*. Oh," he said. "*That* Gulliver."

The cat dropped to the carpet with a *flump* and sauntered after the Archivist, who held open the door to the main Archive for it. A gondola with brass rails hovered at the threshold, burner rumbling. "I have something else that may help you," she said. "But it's down in the Ministry of Secrets Collection. I'll be back as quick as I can." She let the cat go through and followed, pulling the door closed behind her.

Gwen took the novel from Jack, and as soon as she opened it, she smiled. "I don't know what the Archivist was complaining about. The works of Theodorus of Samos were a perfect companion for this."

Jack frowned and gave her a shrug. He had never heard of Theodorus of Samos.

"Keys, Jack. Theodorus of Samos invented the modern concept of a key." She tilted the book, and he saw that the inside had been hollowed out. Resting in the pocket was a ministry access card much like his, titanium by the look of it, with an engraving that read PERCY KINCAID.

"Uncle Percy," he said as Gwen drew out the card. Her uncle, quartermaster to Jack's father, had been wounded by the Clockmaker, and Mrs. Hudson had released him for a long sabbatical to convalesce, sending him off to what she termed *the Colonies.* "Why would he leave his key card behind?"

Gwen slipped the card into her pocket. "More importantly, why would he hide it in a book in the Archive?"

"It's almost as if he and Mrs. Hudson knew something like this would—" Jack stopped as an undulating bronze hum drifted across his mind. In the quiet of the collection, he had no trouble processing the sound. "I hear something," he whispered. "Out in the main well."

"You mean the Archivist is back?"

Jack pressed a finger to his lips and started for the door. "If she is, then someone else is out there with her."

—— · Chapter Nineteen · ——

JACK CRACKED THE DOOR and peered out into the main Archive, a bottomless well of bookshelves, carved entirely of dragonite. He could see the deep purple fabric and gold netting of the Archivist's spherical balloon far below, lit from beneath by the gondola lanterns. Halfway up from there, a shaft of gray light stabbed into the well from the open doors of the Archive's Ministry Express station. Based on the hum, Jack had expected to see QEDs. Instead, he saw two men hovering there—literally hovering. Spikes of blue-white energy shot down from their heels.

"They're coming for us." Gwen had an eye pressed to the door beneath Jack's chin. "And with those ankle thrusters, they won't have to wait for the balloon."

"We need to get out of here." Jack started for the rotating bookcase.

But Gwen hooked his arm and pulled him back. "Not that way. You'll never lift that slab from beneath." She stared at the door for a long moment, then slid her hand down to his. "Do you trust me?"

"Not really. No."

"Right then. Just asking." She threw open the door and yanked him out into empty space.

The two spooks watched, stupefied, as the teens fell right between them, plunging down through the well.

Jack kicked his legs and clawed at the air. "What are we doing?"

"Steady on, Jack!" shouted Gwen, squeezing his hand. Her blond hair and purple scarf streamed above her. "It'll be over soon."

"That's what I'm afraid of!"

An instant later, they sank into the top of the hot-air balloon, and the force of the landing split them up. Jack tumbled over the side. He hooked the gold netting with two fingers, swung his legs inward, and found the gondola rail with his toes. He laughed, amazed at having survived.

And then his two-fingered grip failed.

As Jack reeled backward, grasping for the net, the Archivist leaped up to the gondola bench and caught his wrist. She pulled him in. "Are you quite all right, Jack?"

"He's fine. But *I* could use a little help, if you don't mind."

Jack leaned to look past the burner and saw Gwen's feet dangling above the rail. The calico stood on its hind legs beneath her, playfully batting at her boots. He rushed over to help.

"The spooks are coming down," said Gwen, once both feet had reached the bench. "They're already below the Ministry Express exit, and we won't get past them in this balloon. Is there another way out of here?"

The Archivist nodded. "Through the Ministry of Dragons Collection, assuming we can get there before they reach us."

"Oh. I think we can." Gwen crossed the gondola and took hold of the six tassels that controlled the balloon's air flaps, three in each hand. "Jack, you might want to grab the cat."

"I might want to what?"

She jerked the tassels down, filling the Archive with the hiss of escaping air. The ropes went slack, and the gondola dropped.

The calico, eyes as wide as Jack's, let out a confused "Brrr-rowl?" as it floated up from the bench. Jack pulled it to his chest, face-first, and wrapped his other arm over the rail to make sure he didn't float away himself. He glared at Gwen. "Wasn't one free fall enough for you?"

A second later, the Archivist stomped on the burner pedal. The balloon filled. Gravity returned. And the gondola bumped to a stop against an ancient door of black iron. Jack plopped down onto the bench, and the calico looked at him with what might have been gratitude. He held it up, smiling. "Don't worry. No matter what that mean Gwen does, I'll take care of you."

The cat sneezed in his face.

"Yeah," said Gwen. "You two were made for each other."

Jack had never been so deep in the well. The books on the shelves had given way to leather-bound papers and stacks of scrolls. Still, looking over the rail, he couldn't see the bottom.

"Quickly, children." The Archivist removed an iron key from her waistcoat and pulled open the gondola gate. She slipped the key into the lock. "They're coming."

"Wait," said Jack. "Wasn't there something you were getting for us?"

"Oh yes. I had quite forgotten." She produced a pocket-size text from her waistcoat. *The Great Balas Rubies* by Dr. Dimitri Lazarev. You might be interested to know that

Professor Tanner has spent a great deal of time with this. It appears to be his current favorite."

Before Jack could ask how the Archivist knew Tanner was involved, Gwen had taken the book. "Lazarev," she said, sliding the text into her pocket. "Why does that sound so familiar?"

"Haven't a clue. Now. You really must go." The Archivist turned the key and yanked open the door, flooding the gondola with a burst of stale, musty air. "Take the lift at the far end. Don't stop for any reason. Understand?"

Jack nodded, unnerved by her tone. How bad could a library be?

"No reason whatsoever, Jack." The Archivist repeated her warning as she ushered him through. "This collection is nothing like the others."

Chapter Twenty

THE DOOR CLANGED SHUT behind them and a dozen different tones thrummed against Jack's brain, interfering with his senses. "Can't see a thing," he muttered. "She could have at least given us a lantern."

He heard a tiny click. A wide beam cut through the dark. Gwen shined the light on her own face and pumped her eyebrows. "Voilà." She had produced a big steel flashlight—what she would call a torch—making Jack wonder how deep the pockets of that coat actually went.

"What happened to your penlight?"

"Self-defense." Gwen swung the oversize tool up and down like a hatchet, then handed it to Jack. "London isn't as safe as it used to be."

"London was never safe for me." He shined the light ahead, illuminating a line of script carved into the dragonite where the passage turned. The words were Latin, which was part of Jack's Ministry of Trackers schooling. But he knew Gwen would still translate them for him, whether he needed her to or not.

"'*Aperta . . . flamma . . . Prohibetur*,'" she read, true to form. "'No open flame.'"

They looked at each other for a long heartbeat, and then they walked on.

The passage curved left and right at random, with the occasional set of steps, always leading up. All the while, the pulsating tones in Jack's head continued, getting stronger.

"Can you hear that?"

"Hear what?"

"Nothing."

Lantern sconces jutted out from the walls, filled with cloudy liquid. "Must be a flooded conduit," Gwen suggested, nodding up at them. There were doors as well, on either side of the tunnel, made of dragonite instead of wood or iron. Whenever the teens drew near one, the thrumming in Jack's head intensified. After several minutes, words formed amid the tones.

The flame. Fire. The flame.

Something slammed against a door on Gwen's side of the tunnel, shaking dust from its hinges. She squealed and pressed into Jack. "I don't like this place."

"Yeah. Me neither."

Some of the doors were short, others twice as tall as Jack. Hurrying around the next bend, the two saw one that reached the full height of the passage, the size of a small hangar. At that moment, a sharp *creak* echoed through the tunnel.

Jack spun and fixed his beam on the bend. "The spooks are in the passage." He heard the *clang* of a door closing and the light *shink* of a bolt shifting into place. He glanced at Gwen. "But why would they lock the door?"

"Let's not find out." Gwen tugged at his sleeve. "We have a good lead, let's keep it."

Jack didn't move. Something had changed. A white glow steadily grew in the passage, emanating from the sconces. They weren't flooded after all.

Gwen saw it too. "Bioluminescence. Water lights."

"No open flame," said Jack, nodding. And then the thrumming in his head shifted into high gear.

The flame. Yes. The fire. Fire. Flame. The flame. Yes.

New sounds joined the chaos. A hundred hinges creaked at once. Jack squeezed his eyes shut.

"Um . . . Jack?" Gwen gripped his arm.

"It's all the noise," he said. "I'll be okay."

But when he opened his eyes, he found that Gwen wasn't looking at him. Her gaze was locked on the bend in the passage. A snout—long, gray, and rubbery—poked around the corner. It snorted, sending up a puff of mist. Then the whole creature ambled into view, taller than Jack, walking on a single knobby knuckle at the base of each leathery wing.

"It's a dragon," whispered Gwen, pulling Jack back a step.

"Yeah. That much I got."

Another one appeared behind it, with green metallic scales, crawling along the floor in serpentine bursts. And then another, hovering on buzzing wings. Every time the teens stepped backward, new dragons appeared. There were dozens. The spooks hadn't followed Jack and Gwen into the collection. They had released the dragons and locked the door.

This was an assassination.

The dragons varied in color, from the darkest blue to light green, to the sickly pink of the small one hovering above the rest. All the eyes, however, were the same coal black. Whenever Jack looked into them, the dragon under his gaze would look away. The creatures bowed and bobbed like courtiers before a king. But always, they inched closer. The gray one that had appeared first let out a chortling groan and lowered its head.

"Look, Jack. It's okay. He's friendly." Gwen stretched out her hand to pet its snout.

Jack was not getting that vibe at all. "Careful, Gwen. I don't think you should—"

The dragon bared its yellowed teeth and snapped. Gwen jerked her hand away.

"—do that."

The dragon's chortle became a growl, and the others joined in, still inching forward. But as Jack raised the flashlight in defense, they all stopped. The gray dragon cocked its head to one side. It yelped, and the whole pack scrambled, slithered, and waddled out of sight.

"What now?" asked Jack.

The chamber filled with a deep, metallic grind. Slow, pounding impacts shook the dragonite floor. The teens turned around, cringing. The hangar-size door was open.

The flame. Yes. The fire. The flame . . .

Now.

Jack doubled over, grabbing his head and letting out a pained cry. One voice. It had been only one voice amid the tones the whole time. *That* voice.

A huge snow-white head ducked into view, capped with scimitar horns covered near to the tips in leathery skin. The tips themselves were translucent, as if they were made of quartz. White vapors fell from its jaws like drool and pooled on the floor in great wispy clouds.

The dragon stared Jack down with those same coal-black eyes. *The flame. The fire. Yes. The flame. Now.*

Jack gritted his teeth and glared up at the creature. "Get out of my head!"

Instantly, the dragon shifted its gaze to the floor and the thrumming tones dropped to nothing. The words grew soft. *The flame. Please, the flame.*

The pain subsided. Jack breathed in and out. Had his command made the dragon back off?

Not entirely.

The creature came fully out of its cage, cutting a swath through its own vapor, digging its quartz talons into the dragonite walls and keeping its wings close to its body. Jack could feel the desire to spread them aching in his own subconscious.

The dragon reared up on its hind legs, balanced there for a long moment, and then dropped onto its wing knuckles with the reverberating *boom* of a falling tree. The motion put its head little more than a foot from Jack's.

The flame. Yes. The fire. Please, the flame.

Jack backed away, and the dragon's eyes followed, trained on his right hand. Gwen's flashlight. He had forgotten to switch it off. "It thinks the flashlight has real fire."

"What are you talking about?" Gwen backed away with him. "Jack, what's happening?"

The dragon stopped and fixed her with its black gaze, as if contemplating the words she had just spoken. Then it looked Jack straight in the eye.

Jack. Now the dragon knew his name.

The thrumming came back hard and fast.

The flame, Jack. The fire, Jack. Yes, Jack. The flame . . .

Now, Jack.

Jack stood his ground, fighting back the blinding pain. He shut off the flashlight and shook it at the creature. "No! See? No flame. Get back in your cage."

Gwen looked from boy to creature and back. "Bad idea. Don't antagonize it."

But Jack's gamble worked. The dragon reared up, taking on an utterly dejected expression. Jack marched up to it, close enough that if the creature came down again it would crush him. "Cage."

The flame, Jack. Please, Jack. The flame.

He pointed with the flashlight. "I said, 'Cage.' Now!"

Finally, the dragon twisted its giant frame and toppled over, letting its wings slam down inside its cave. As it lumbered away into the shadows, the voice became a whimper. *The flame.*

Gwen pulled Jack into a run. "Let's go, before the others come back."

The elevator the Archivist had told them about waited ahead, not far past the big door—an old iron frame with wood-plank walls and a rope pulley at the back.

Gwen got there first.

Jack was only a few steps behind when he noticed the dragon's tail lying across his path, concealed by the fog of drool-vapors still carpeting the passage. He tried to jump over, but the tail whipped up, tangling his legs and sending him headlong onto the dragonite. Blue sparks shot out from beneath the flashlight in his hand, igniting the vapors. A trail of fire snaked its way into the dragon's cave.

Jack heard a great *foomp*, like the catching of a furnace. The whimpering voice in his head became a victorious roar.

The flame!

—— · Chapter Twenty-One · ——

"DON'T WAIT FOR ME. Go. Go!" shouted Jack as he scrambled to his feet.

Gwen needed no urging. She hauled down on the rope, lifting the oversize dumbwaiter off the floor.

As he ran, Jack caught a glimpse of the dragon emerging from its cage. The eyes were no longer black. They glowed orange, throbbing like embers. It opened its jaws. Yellow fire grew in its throat.

Jack made a desperate leap and hit the base of the elevator at his belt line, elbows slamming down on the wooden floor slats. Gwen pulled him the rest of the way as a stream of fire lit up the shaft below.

The flame, Jack!

"Shut! Up!"

"I didn't say anything," said Gwen, returning to the pulley.

Jack grabbed the rope and pulled with her. "I wasn't talking to you."

The dragon poked its head into the shaft and twisted its neck to look up at them, throat glowing.

"I was talking to *him*. Look out!" Jack pushed Gwen to the edge of the box and hopped back to the opposite side, pressing his body against the ironwork as the dragon let loose another blast. Tongues of fire licked at them through the slats. When the stream subsided, the planks continued to burn. "Really?" said Jack, setting to work at the pulley again. "A wooden dumbwaiter in a dungeon full of dragons?"

Gwen reached out with a boot and stomped through the burning planks. The pieces fell, smacking the dragon in the face. It groaned and ducked away, but not for long.

The pulley hit its upper stop, and the teens jumped out onto black slate stairs. An instant later, flames filled the elevator. The rope burned through. The iron frame crashed down through the shaft, and the dragon let out a long, angry howl.

"That should hold him," said Gwen. "At least for a while."

A sheer wall of slate blocked their path at the top of the steps, but a big iron lever stuck out from the wall beside it.

Gwen pushed it down. Gears ground. Chains clinked. A section of the stone slid up, and the two stepped out onto an aging wooden dock.

"So . . . we're still not outside." Jack frowned as the door dropped into place behind them.

"No, but this will work," said Gwen. "I know where we are."

They had reached an underground pool, where brown stone columns rose up from the water to support a high arched ceiling. A single gas lamp burned on the central column, lighting a bronze sign that read THE BARBICAN.

Jack pressed his ear against the slate door. The dragons had started a ruckus below—a riotous blend of shrieks, screeches, and honks that might easily have been mistaken for street noises. "The dragos have their work cut out—"

Gwen pinched his other ear, cutting off his remark and twisting him away from the wall.

"Ow!" he cried, swatting her hand away.

"Exactly how did you do that?"

"How did I do what?"

"You *know* what. You and that dragon had a . . . a *moment*."

Whatever had happened with that voice in his head, Jack wasn't ready to discuss it with Gwen. "I don't know what you're talking about."

She looked at him sideways, walked over to a skiff tied up at the dock, and began tugging at the knot. "All right. You don't have to tell me. Maybe you'd rather wait until you and Ash patch things up so you can talk to *him*."

"Gwen—"

"And what about the fire, hmm? How did you manage to light off a whole squadron of dragons?"

"You saw what happened. The flashlight hit the floor and caused a spark that lit the vapors."

Gwen stood up from her half-loosened knot and shook her head. "Impossible. That floor was dragonite. And nothing sparks off dragonite, not even metal." Before Jack could protest, she raised her hands. "I'm not talking about tracker sparks, Jack. I'm talking flint-and-steel-banging-rocks-together sparks. It can't be done with dragonite. That's probably why the dragos house their little menagerie at the Archive. Dragons are as much mineral as animal, so they can make their own sparks by scraping their talons across normal stone."

At that moment, Jack could not have cared less about the science of dragonite, or how he managed to make a spark with unsparkable stone. The spooks were after them. The thief was out there somewhere, getting away with the Crown

Jewels. He and Gwen needed to keep moving. "You said you knew where we were." He thrust his chin at the sign across the water. "What's the Barbican?"

"Right. The Barbican," said Gwen in a flat tone, giving him a look that told him they'd be coming back to the dragon topic later. She knelt down to finish untying the boat. "Eighteen centuries ago, this dock was part of a Roman fort that straddled a channel running between the Walbrook and the River Fleet." She gestured at iron portcullises on either side of the pool, with bronze plaques that read THIS WAY TO THE WALBROOK and THIS WAY TO THE RIVER FLEET. "These days, all three waterways run underground, part of the Ministry Express transportation network." She tossed the rope down into the skiff and stepped in after it, glancing over her shoulder. "You coming?"

Jack hesitated. The skiff looked like it had seen better days. The wood had turned gray. The bronze plating on the gunwales was scratched and worn. "Coming where?"

"As it happens, the best place in all of England to find a burglar lies on the shores of an underground river, Jack. Hop in. We're going to the Thieves' Guild."

Chapter Twenty-Two

GWEN TOOK THE BOW, and Jack sat in the stern, paddling with the boat's single oar toward the portcullis marked FLEET. There was a digital reader on a post a few feet from the gate, and Jack reached out to press his ministry card against it.

"Nope. Gimme." Gwen snatched the platinum card away, paired it with her copper version, and tossed them both over the side. "How do you think the spooks knew we were on that bus, hmm? We swiped those to pay the fare." She drew out her uncle Percy's titanium card and pressed it against the reader. A red LED turned green and a spindle of chain beneath the surface clinked into motion, lifting the portcullis dripping from the water. "Everyone is looking for Jack Buckles and Gwen Kincaid. *No one* is looking for Uncle Percy."

She hung a lantern from the bow and lit it with a match that was tucked inside its glass door. As the orange glow expanded, a brickwork tunnel opened before them. Gwen took Jack's oar away and laid it down across the benches. "Take a break. The current will carry us to the Fleet, easy peasy."

"Right. Easy peasy." Jack got nervous whenever Gwen used that phrase. It meant she was worried about something and compensating for it. "And the Thieves' Guild is on the River Fleet?"

"Sort of." She gave no sign that she had heard the concern in the question. "This channel pours into the River Fleet, and the Thieves' Guild lies on another tributary, farther south." She sat cross-legged on her bench and opened the book the Archivist had given them, flipping through the first few pages. After a moment, she said, "Huh. That's weird."

Jack watched a yellow spiderish creature drop from the bricks and plop into the water to escape the light of their lantern. "Yeah. It is."

"Not the tunnel crab, you wally." Gwen slapped his arm with the book. "*This*. Tanner's book. It's all about balas rubies—which is kind of like saying faux rubies or fool's gold—they're not exactly the most expensive jewels in the world."

"So?"

"So the thief took the Imperial State Crown and the Sovereign's Scepter, including the First and Second Stars of Africa—the two largest clear-cut diamonds in the world. If Tanner was behind this, why would he fixate on the crown ruby? The diamonds are far more valuable."

"Because the professor isn't behind this, Gwen. He's a victim, like us." Jack thrust a frustrated hand at her book. "Whatever he was or wasn't reading before the heist doesn't matter. You're chasing rabbits."

The boat drifted close to the brick wall, and Gwen pushed off, sending it back to center. "Let's assume that I'm not, just for a minute. Okay?"

She wasn't going to let it go. Jack hunched down on his bench. "Fine."

"Good." She held the book up for him, open to a picture of the very same ruby Jack had sparked on before the heist. "This is the Black Prince's Ruby, arguably the least valuable of the big jewels in the crown, not to mention cursed."

"Cursed?" For a moment, Jack forgot his defense of the professor. "What do you mean 'cursed'?"

Gwen lowered the book, gaze lingering for another second. "I told you not to touch it."

"Gwen . . ."

She held up a finger to quiet him and then read a few paragraphs, summing up as she went. "The Black Prince's Ruby is thought to inspire loyalty for its wearer, and was named for Prince Edward, who always carried a black shield into battle. Prince Edward died of dysentery"—Gwen glanced up—"ew." She looked down at the pages again. "—not long after receiving the stone from the Castilian Don Pedro the Cruel as payment for protecting him from his brother."

Gwen scanned another page. "Apparently, that didn't go well. Once Edward had left with the stone, Don Pedro was betrayed by his formerly loyal ambassador and got stabbed in the face anyway. Coincidentally, Don Pedro himself had gotten the ruby a few years earlier by slaughtering an ambassadorial entourage at a dinner party, murdering Abu Sa'id, an eastern usurper to the Moorish throne."

She read a few more lines to herself and then rested the book in her lap. "Nearly every person to wear that ruby was betrayed, murdered, or died from a horrible disease. It was cut from the heads of not one but two kings of England on the field of battle."

Cut from the king's head. "Henry," Jack muttered, remembering the Welshman's cry.

"Yes. Henry the Fifth, to be more precise. He lost the ruby at Agincourt and was spared only because the Duke of Alencon paused to pick it up and got himself skewered in the process."

"By a Welshman."

"Correct." Gwen cocked her head. "How do you know that?"

He shrugged.

"You were there, weren't you?"

"Yeah, okay? That's what I saw in my spark. It was horrifying." Jack told her everything he had seen in the battle, leaving out the part about his father because that was a Pandora's box he didn't feel like opening just then. "I'd say the men showed more loyalty to the stone than to Henry," he said as he finished. "A French foot soldier ran off with it, so how did it get back to England?"

Gwen turned the page and scanned a few more lines. "Here it is. Your foot soldier brought it to the royal tent after the battle, expecting to get paid, and spent the rest of his life in a British dungeon." She tapped the page. "Cursed, Jack."

What had the professor said? *The most terrible crimes and*

notions of the worst rulers in history, trapped in crystallized carbon . . . infecting all who wear the gem. Jack shuddered, remembering his own hideous laugh at seeing a man killed. Had the curse in the stone infected him as well?

Gwen kept reading, musing out loud. "But why would the professor study such a dangerous artifact if it was already locked away?"

Jack never got the chance to answer. The shadows beyond the lantern light stole his attention. They looked too black, like an empty void. "Um . . . Gwen? What did you mean when you said this stream *pours* into the River Fleet?"

"Just something I read. Why?"

The void reached the lantern's glow and Jack finally understood. Both passage and stream ended in a waterfall. He tapped Gwen's shoulder and pointed, unable to get the words out.

She looked up from her book. "Oh" was all she had time to say.

——·Chapter Twenty-Three·——

JACK GRIPPED THE BENCH, Gwen clutched the book to her chest, and both of them cried "Aaaah!" as the boat pitched over the falls.

They dropped all of six feet.

The bow hit first, dousing the lamp, and the stern slapped down behind, sending a shower of smelly water over Jack. Once Gwen had the lantern glowing again, she looked up at him and gave a little start. She fished out a plastic bag of wipes and pointed at Jack's dripping face, making a circular motion with her finger. "You've . . . um . . . got a little something . . ."

Jack snatched the wipes away. The new passage was wider than the last, with faster water and an odor that filled his tracker brain with green fog. Big, spoked control wheels stuck out from the bricks, paired with giant faucets that dumped brown water into the flow. He scrubbed his face and looked down at the result. The wipes were the same color.

Jack threw up a little in his mouth.

Doorways and stairwells drifted past, along with smaller waterways that fed into the main line or branched off at sharp angles. Any one of them could have been the tributary that would take them to the Thieves' Guild. "How far?" he asked, scrubbing the front of his jacket with a new wipe in each hand.

Gwen was looking out at the passage ahead. "I didn't know you could interact with your sparks." She glanced back over her shoulder. "That's huge, Jack. You could have told me. In the sorting room, I mean. Or on the train."

Jack appraised the two wipes, now completely brown. He threw them down into the boat. "No. I really don't think I could have."

Gwen spun around to face him. "What's that supposed to mean?"

"It means that between the ear-bashing you gave me in the sorting room and going all Mrs. Hudson on me for leaving the Keep, I never had the chance."

"Well . . ." Gwen's retort stalled at her lips. She pressed them together again. "Is there anything else you haven't told me?"

The boat had picked up speed. The stairwells and branches leading away were sailing by, but Gwen looked unconcerned. Jack glanced down at his wet sneakers. "I'm losing my abilities."

That seemed to catch her off guard. "But you just learned a whole new way to spark."

"Only with the professor's help. And in the Vault I . . ." Jack caught himself. He didn't want to tell her about the zed. What if it was some kind of artifact? What if she made him give it up? "Well, I almost didn't make it out, okay? I can't control my sparks, Gwen, and it's getting harder and harder to see data. The headaches are coming back. Everything is noise again."

Her expression softened. She touched his hand. "Like I said, you could have told me."

He looked down at his knees and shrugged.

Gwen cleared her throat. "Well, you *do* look pretty awful and not only because you look like a drenched sewer rat." She took his chin and turned his face side to side. "You have bags under your eyes. You're not taking care of yourself, Jack. You never eat. You spend all your time at your dad's bedside."

He pulled away from her. "Really? You want to start this again. My dad is in a *coma*, Gwen. The doctors are useless.

The ministry wants to lock him away. Mom has her hands full taking care of Sadie. If I don't worry about Dad, who will?"

She had shrunk down into her scarf, and Jack realized he had been yelling. He let out a breath. "So where is this branch we're looking for?"

She glanced up at him for a moment and then turned to the front again.

"Gwen, I'm sorry I yelled, okay?" Then Jack realized she wasn't pouting. She was watching the walls ahead. They were solid brick, with the occasional batch of pipes and control wheels. No more branches. He slapped the bench beside him. "You're lost, aren't you? We missed the turn." A misty, gray rushing noise rose in the base of Jack's mind. Somewhere ahead, the Fleet would dump into the Thames. What would that look like? Another waterfall?

"I am not lost. The Thieves' Guild passage is . . . hidden. That's all. The entrance is found by way of a secret mark."

"And if we don't find it?"

"This tunnel shrinks to become a filter, a sort of pipe filled with steel teeth that breaks up debris before the Fleet shoots out into the Thames."

"So we'll be . . ."

"Ground to pulp. Yes."

143

Jack dropped his head into his hand. "So there's that."

The tunnel shrank, as predicted, and the gray rushing noise grew into a frothing white roar. Jack took up the oar and jabbed at a steel control wheel sticking out from the wall, attempting to trap the paddle and halt their race toward certain death.

He missed.

He growled and fixed his sights on another wheel, hanging down from a mass of pipes on the ceiling. But then he noticed something odd. That wheel was missing some of its spokes. It cast an X-shaped shadow across the pipes behind. As he watched, the pipes and their fittings aligned to form the rough image of three keys laid across the X. Jack gasped. He knew that symbol.

As quickly as they had all aligned, the pieces drifted apart. But the X marked a rusty iron rod sticking down from the bricks. Jack smacked it with his oar. The rod shifted like a lever.

A heavy *chunk* sounded from the bricks. A section of wall swung out to block their path, and the bow smashed into it, sending up sparks from the bronze gunwale and turning the boat. They went flying down a slope of rushing water and splashed down into a slow-moving current. As everything settled, both teens looked up and saw a big copper X set into bricks above them, with three keys laid across it made of gold, silver, and iron.

Gwen dropped her gaze from the X to Jack. "How did you—?"

"The man who stole the Crown Jewels had the same symbol tattooed on his neck."

"That's the mark we were looking for," she said. "The mark of the Thieves' Guild."

Chapter Twenty-Four

JACK ROWED THEM OUT of the little passage into an underground lake the size of several football fields. A hundred voices echoed across the water. Ramshackle structures dotted with yellow lanterns rose like bleachers from every shore. And theirs wasn't the only boat on the water. A barge passed within arm's reach, piled with lumpy sacks that might have contained anything from potatoes to dead bodies. The pilot, a brawny fellow in a threadbare suit, stared Jack down.

Jack lifted his chin. "Hey."

Brawny-threadbare-suit guy shifted his gaze to the line of tunnels behind them, pushed down on his punting pole, and coasted on.

Gwen slapped Jack's arm. "'Hey'?" She thrust her chin at a

line of docks. "Steer us over there. And check with me before you speak again."

Once the boat was tied up, the two worked their way along the crowded waterfront. Burly crewmen brushed past them, loaded down with sacks and crates. Hucksters hocked their wares off the barrel. As Jack and Gwen squeezed by, a huge bruiser caught Jack's arm, bald head covered in silver tattoos. "What's yer hurry, boy? Buy a pretty bobble for the pretty girl, eh?"

Gwen pulled Jack away. "Not interested."

But as soon as he turned to follow her, Jack bumped into a miniature stage. An angry marionette in black tails and a top hat pointed at him with a flopping finger and yelled, "Watch where yer going!" while a second marionette—a little boy—picked its pocket. The bystanders laughed. Jack turned beet red.

"*Stairs. Now.*" Gwen tugged his lapel to get him moving again.

They dodged a girl juggling butcher knives, ducked under a giant painting that Jack could swear he had seen in photos of the Louvre, and climbed a set of stairs to the relative safety of a cobblestone street. From that elevated position, Jack could see the variety of boats at the docks.

There were skiffs and barges, a few steam-powered craft, and even a Chinese junk at the far end. A girl not much older than Jack broke from the crowd and passed between two beefy thugs that guarded the junk's gangplank, without so much as a glance at either of them. She had a streak of red down one side of her jet-black hair.

"That'll be the guild master's barge," said Gwen, following his gaze. "We'll start there."

"*That's* your plan?" Jack had to swallow his shock as a giggling threesome in grungy petticoats strolled by. As soon as they had passed, he leaned close to Gwen, lowering his voice. "You plan to waltz into the lair of the master thief and ask him to rat out his star player? You think Fagin is just gonna hand over the Artful Dodger?"

"Honor among thieves, Jack. The Crown Jewels are off-limits for the guild. Always have been. Our thief broke the rules. The master won't tell us anything. Naturally. But our visit will set off a mad hunt for his Artful Dodger. All we have to do is keep out of sight and follow."

The cobblestone lane brought them past the center of the docks, and a plume of fire caught Jack's eye. A teen in a blue cloak stood above the crowd on a flashy gold drum, shooting fireballs from both hands. Two collided above his head, exploding into a flaming triangle, and the crowd erupted into applause. From Jack's angle, however, he could see a contraption hidden within the boy's frilled sleeve. Jack watched a wad of material shoot out of it, igniting as it passed over the boy's palm.

"The Thieves' Guild and the Magicians' Guild are tight," said Gwen, stopping to watch the show. "Along with the Tinkers' Guild. All three have . . . overlapping interests."

She was right about the magicians. There were others. A young woman sawed herself in half, and a Persian man in silk pants made his tattoos leap from one bicep to the other. At the edge of the crowd, an Asian boy in a worn tux held his hands over a barrel and formed a glistening, long-stemmed rose out of ice. But the stem was too delicate. It snapped, and the half-finished bloom fell to the dock and shattered. His sparse group of onlookers turned away. In desperation, the boy shot fierce streams of white over their heads, making it snow. Most only brushed the flakes from their shoulders and walked on.

Again, Jack saw up the magician's sleeve. And again, he saw a contraption, silver this time. But as the boy made more snow clouds, nothing emerged from the shooter, as if it was only there for show. Confused, Jack looked to the boy's face and found that the young magician had fixed him with a hostile glare, boring into him with ice-blue eyes.

A hand touched Jack's elbow. "Don't look, Jack. He doesn't want you to see."

"But why would he—?" Jack stopped mid-question and looked down at his side. "Sadie?"

His sister smiled up at him, dressed in her favorite green skirt and sparkly lavender Keds.

She wasn't alone.

Ash stood in the middle of the lane, a few feet in front of them. He lifted his wolf's-head cane and tipped up his newsboy cap. "Hello, Jack."

Jack backed away, pulling Gwen and Sadie with him, but then he heard heavy footfalls behind. He wheeled around and saw Shaw stepping out from an alleyway.

The big warden blocked the road and punched a meaty fist into an equally meaty paw. "Going somewhere, Thirteen?"

Chapter Twenty-Five

JACK STRUGGLED to catch up with what was happening. How had his sister wound up in London's underworld, escorted by Ash and Shaw?

"I didn't want to believe it," said Ash, tapping his cane on the cobblestones. "But here you are, in the Thieves' Guild with the rest of the criminals." The tapping stopped. "Jack, what happened to you?"

Jack ignored him. "Sadie, what are you doing here?"

His little sister shrugged. "Helping."

"She's a natural, she is." Shaw thrust his chin at the little girl. "Led us right to ya the moment we arrived down 'ere. Per'aps she's got wot tracker brains you 'aven't."

"I heard Mom say you'd be hungry." Sadie held up a

bulging leather satchel. "Look, I packed you some dinner."

"Oh, Sadie, what have you done?" Jack lifted the satchel's strap over his head and checked the contents. All he could see were gobs of paper-wrapped toffees. Leave it to a nine-year-old to pack dinner. "Penny chews?"

"Your favorite." Sadie winked and shot another glance at the bag.

Jack scrunched up his brow. His sister almost never winked.

"Chew your candy on the way back to the Keep," said Ash, taking a step closer. Shaw did the same, closing the net.

A three-story shanty stood at the edge of the lane, opposite the docks. Jack grabbed Gwen and Sadie and backed against the door. He jiggled the handle. Locked. "I didn't do this, Ash. You have to believe me."

"Tell you what. Come back with us and sit tight while the ministry investigates. The truth will out, Jack. Always does. I think we learned that together."

Gwen had wrapped an arm around Jack, as if cowering away from Shaw. Then he felt her slip a hand into the satchel and grope around. "Stall them," she whispered.

The satchel.

Sadie's wink.

Of course.

Jack gave Gwen a tiny nod and then coughed. "Uh . . . wow, Ash. Shaw? Really? I can't believe you're working with this ginormous lummox."

"I said 'stall them,'" hissed Gwen. "I didn't tell you to insult the big one's intelligence."

Ash leaned on his cane and raised an eyebrow. "I had to let my last partner go. After that, my options were limited."

"Tha's right," added Shaw, advancing another step. "And them limited options was me."

Gwen sighed. "Never mind."

Crack!

A blue cloud filled the lane, and Jack felt himself yanked through the doorway. Cheers erupted from the magic show spectators on the dock below. Gwen, it seemed, had shoved a handful of puffers—pea-size tracker smoke bombs—into the space between the door and its frame, blowing it wide open.

The three raced up a staircase and out across a plank walkway that bridged the alley behind the shanty. Ash came running around the corner and jumped, swiping at Jack's heel with his cane. "You can't hide, Jack. Not from me."

Another door: unlocked.

A left, a right, and another left down a hallway with bloodred carpet and peeling wallpaper.

A crash behind them.

Jack looked back and saw Shaw's gargoyle scowl. "Faster, Gwen!"

They ran up dozens of steps and across more rickety walkways, climbing higher and higher through the shantytown, until they burst into a room filled with ruffians playing cards. Every grisly, snarling face turned to stare at them.

Gwen would not be stopped. "Excuse us, please. Coming through."

There were bumps and jostles, a few squished toes. The crowd filled in behind them, and Jack heard Shaw growl, "Let us through."

Another voice, deeper and far more menacing, growled right back at the warden, "Wot's yer problem, mate? You threat'nin' that young miss and 'er friends?"

The rest was lost in a barrage of angry shouts.

The teens and Sadie pushed through a heavy door and emerged on the uppermost street of the cavern, where the houses were built of stone and sturdy timber up against the rock wall. Jack pulled up short and put his hands behind his head, breathing hard. Not far away, a set of steps led up to a tunnel entrance. "We have to get out of here," he said, turning toward the stairs.

Gwen jumped in front of him. "Wait. We can't leave yet. We haven't learned anything."

"Yeah? Well, we sure can't stay. The Hunt is Ash's specialty. How long do you think we'll last down here if we hang around?"

Instead of answering, Gwen produced a spring-loaded knife and flipped out the blade with a pronounced *shink*.

"Uh . . . Gwen?"

Without explanation, she turned him around and scraped the knife down the back of his leather coat.

"Hey, what're you—?"

"Relax. I didn't hurt it." She spun him back around and showed him the blade, now covered in powdery blue residue from the puffers that had gone off behind him. She swiped a pinkie through it and rubbed a little on the stones at their feet. "If it's a hunt Ashley wants, then it's a hunt he'll get."

Jack craned his neck to look over his shoulder, turning backward in a circle. "Is that stuff only on my back, or is it all over my—?"

"Quit messing around. Those ruffians won't hold Ash for long." Gwen jogged up the stairs, stopping twice to rub the blue powder on the steps and on the mouth of the tunnel at the top. Then all three of them retreated down a plank walkway on the low side of the street and hid behind a set of linens hanging from laundry wires.

Seconds later, Ash and Shaw walked by. The young quartermaster crouched at the base of the steps and inspected the residue Gwen had left for him. He looked up at the tunnel and clenched his fist. "They're out already. Come on, Shaw."

The warden lagged behind. "You sure 'bout that?" He turned as he spoke, looking straight at the linens.

Jack held his breath.

"Yes, I *am* sure." Ash was halfway up the steps. "Look here. More residue from those puffers. One of them must've stepped in it. Quickly, man. We're losing them."

The warden took one more long look at the linens, grumbled to himself, and lumbered up the steps after Ash.

Once he was sure they were gone, Jack crept out from behind his sheet. Across the walkway, mounted on a tin shanty, was a brass plaque. He read the name out loud. "Divers Run."

"A diver is an old term for a pickpocket," said Gwen, ducking out from behind another sheet with Sadie. "It's a play on words, as in 'divers run from the bobbies.'"

"It's more than that." Jack turned to look down the walkway, which descended by ramps and steps all the way to the docks. "It's our thief's address."

— · Chapter Twenty-Six · —

WITH ASH AND SHAW out of the picture, Jack had time to think, and he remembered the satchel. He lifted the flap and dug through the penny chews. Aside from the puffers, Sadie had brought him a four-barrel dart gun, two electrospheres, and a copter-scout—a wind-up sphere whose top half could spread out to become helicopter blades. "You packed this?" he asked, handing her a toffee. He tossed a vanilla chew to Gwen and chose a strawberry one for himself—his favorite.

"Mom was busy," said Sadie. "Tracker Lane was absolutely crawling with spooks and wardens. She says she misses you, but she knows you have to do this."

Jack knelt down in front of his sister, helping her unwrap

her candy. "I'm sorry I was so slow to clue in to your plan."

"That's okay. Gwen got it. That's why you two are so good together." Sadie popped the toffee into her mouth. "She completes you."

A hint of red crept into Gwen's cheeks.

Jack stared at his sister for a long second, half-chewed strawberry toffee hanging from his teeth. "You have to go."

"What? Why?"

"Jack—" Gwen protested.

He held up his hand. "This is too dangerous. She needs to get back to the Keep."

"All right. And what's your plan? Send her up the steps? Ash and Shaw are long gone. She'd be all alone, stranded in the middle of London."

Jack stood, looking up and down the wooden walkway for some kind of help. Nothing materialized.

Sadie squeezed his arm. "You need me." She looked as serious as any nine-year-old could.

Right. Like he needed to babysit a little girl while he was chasing a thief, clearing his name, and trying to save his mentor. At the moment, however, Jack had no other choice. "Fine. You can come." He turned and started down the walkway.

"Yay!" cried the nine-year-old, catching his hand. "So . . . where are we going?"

"Forty-nine Divers." Jack scanned the shacks on either side as he walked. "I saw it on a paper in the professor's office. That can't be a coincidence."

The addresses were hard to find, each formed by a number of wind chimes or potted plants, or encrypted as symbols carved into a shingle. Gwen identified a 53 written in ancient Babylonian. "Thieves," she grumbled. "They make everything so complicated."

They found the number 49 painted on a rusty rail car, tucked in among the wood-and-tin shacks—an old bedroom car, with its burgundy-and-beige paint job half eaten away. Jack scratched his head, gazing down the walkway to the underground lake far below. "But how did they . . . ?"

"This has to be the place," said Gwen, pushing on the door.

"Gwen, it's a thief's hideout, I doubt it'll be—"

The door squeaked open.

"—unlocked."

She scrunched up her nose. "Locks aren't much use around here, for obvious reasons."

Jack went in first, drawing the dart gun. If the thief was in

there, he wanted to be prepared. A night lamp on a desk at
the far end cast a dim red glow over the space. Beside it sat
a complete human skull, mouth gaping open in a scream.
Jack swallowed. If their thief was going for super creepy, he
had hit a home run.

Gwen hit a switch and a string of yellow lights flickered on overhead. No one was home. Jack motioned Sadie
inside. "Shut the door." Then, considering how easily they'd
gotten in, he added, "And lock it."

There was a small kitchen on one end and a bed on the
other, with the desk in the middle. "He's kind of messy,"
said Gwen, lifting a red sheet from the floor to check
beneath the bed. When she came up again, she was holding
a leather case.

"That's the one I saw Gall hand the thief," said Jack, stepping over to have a look.

Gwen laid the case on the bed and popped it open.
"Look. Custom pockets." There were two rows of square
cutouts in the black foam liner and two matching rows of
round cutouts below them, with one extra at the bottom.
"Empty," she said. "Whatever Gall gave the thief, he took
it with him."

Based on the car's interior decor, the thief was obsessed with two things—death and the color red. Neither gave Jack a warm, cozy feeling. Ghostly, hooded forms were painted on the walls, flying in and out of graveyards, ragged cloaks trailing behind. And a single giant wraith glowered down from the ceiling, with nothing but a hint of bone and two flaming eyes beneath the hood of its bloodred cloak. Who on earth could fall asleep staring up at that?

Gwen rifled through the desk drawers. "Nothing of use over here, either." She tossed a stack of flyers down next to the skull. "Just ads for small-time metal bands and the standard desk-drawer stuff—pens and paper clips and the like."

That was enough for Jack. He would be happy to get out of there. "This guy is gone," he said, guiding Sadie toward the door. "We should get out of here and go for the guild master, like you said." But as he reached for the door, he noticed a shadow pass across the window blinds. He flicked off the lights. "Someone's coming."

All three retreated to the desk and huddled down.

The lever jiggled. The door rattled against its frame. Something scraped against the lock.

Jack set his aim and tightened his finger around the trigger of the dart gun. He wouldn't have much time to shoot, and he wasn't about to let Creepy-death-obsessed-teleporting guy anywhere near his sister.

The bolt clicked back and the door swung open with a bone-chilling squeak.

Jack fired.

Chapter Twenty-Seven

"OI! WATCH IT!"

Jack's dart had embedded itself in the steel doorframe an inch above the head of a black-haired girl in a dark jacket and red jeans. She was squatting down, leaning across the threshold, and she had been picking the lock by the look of things. The girl bolted upright and flicked on the lights, glaring at Jack and his gun. "Put tha' thing away, 'fore ya hurt someone, ya get me?"

Jack stuffed the gun into his satchel. He leaned against the desk to steady himself as he stood. He had intended to disable a deadly thief. Instead, he had almost killed a girl his own age.

Gwen was not shaken in the slightest. "Who are you, and what are you doing here?"

"I should ask you the same, yeah? This is *my* place, innit?"

"No. It *isn't* your place." Gwen's enunciation had become exceedingly sharp and proper. She nodded at the lock picks. "Try again."

Before the girl could come up with another lie, Jack interjected. He recognized the red streak in her hair. "She was on the docks. At the guild master's boat. I'm pretty sure she works for him." He gave her an apologetic head tilt, as if outing her true purpose there somehow added insult to the injury of nearly killing her.

The girl studied him for a moment, then turned and started working the dart free from the door. "Yeah, awright. The thief who lives here broke the rules o' the guild, an' I'm lookin' into it for the master." The dart came free with a jerk, and she spun, flinging it at Jack. It sank into the desktop between his thumb and forefinger. She winked. "Name's Raven. Turnabout's fair play, innit . . . ?" She let the question hang, waiting for Jack to fill in his name.

Minutes before, he had been shocked by the sudden appearance of Gwen's pocketknife, but this girl took dangerous to a whole new level. He peeled his hand away from the dart and gave her a half wave. "Um . . . Jack."

Gwen rolled her eyes. "And this is Sadie. And I'm Gwen,

not that it's any of your business. We've already searched the place. There's nothing here. Move on."

"You'll pardon me if I don' take your word for it, yeah?"

Raven strolled around the car, eyeing the open case as she passed.

When she got to the desk, Jack shuffled out of her way. "Um . . . what can you tell us about the guy who lives here?"

She opened a drawer, frowned at its contents, and closed it again. "We call him the Phantom, 'cause he gets in an' out o' the tightest spots. No trace. No witnesses."

"*We* were witnesses," countered Gwen.

Raven paid her no notice. "No one down here'll cross the Phantom, 'cause *zap.*" She snapped her fingers in Jack's face, making him jump, and then traced a fingernail across his neck. "He can slit your throat, an' then vanish into thin air. Some say he was born doin' it—that he's . . . unnatural."

Jack swallowed at the thought. But he shook his head. "He . . . uses a device. Some kind of stopwatch."

"Which he probably stole," added Gwen. "Because he's a thief. Like you."

Raven ignored the gibe. She slapped her hands down on the desk, looking around. "What 'bout his slick, yeah? Didja find that?"

Gwen regarded the question with pronounced skepticism. "His what?"

"His *slick*. A hiding place. It'll be somethin' quick, activated by a lever, or a pedal or somethin'."

Jack would have done a face palm if Raven hadn't been standing so close to him. Of course a thief would have a secret stash. He let his gaze drift over the room, settling on the desk.

Drawer handles: too obvious.

Lamp: red but otherwise unremarkable.

The screaming skull: way too scary to look at for long, *which would be perfect.*

Looking closer, he saw scratches at the corner of the jaw. "The skull," he said, nodding to Gwen. "I think you can close its mouth." He had no intention of touching it himself. Jack didn't know if he could spark off bone, and he never wanted to find out.

Gwen pursed her lips at him and pressed the head down. The bleached-white teeth clacked together. A V-shaped compartment flipped out from the side of the desk.

"Oo, this one's handy, yeah?" Raven playfully flicked Jack's ear. "I can see why you keep him 'round." She jockeyed herself in front of the secret drawer before Gwen could get there. And after a moment's inspection, she grinned. "What have we got here?" She withdrew a leather pouch from the compartment and dropped it on the desktop. It toppled over and gold, silver, and platinum cubes tumbled out.

An etched gold cube with green jewels at each corner rolled to a stop right in front of Jack. He picked it up, remembering his vision before the Hunt. "What . . . is this?"

Gwen took the cube and turned it over, showing him a pair of giants stamped into the opposite side—the symbol of the Ministry of Guilds. "Guild coin." She dropped the cube into the pouch and scooped up the others, dropping them in as well. "The favored currency of the more anonymous guilds. Cubes of precious metals are as good as cash practically anywhere." She pulled the drawstrings, cinching the pouch closed, and put it aside. "Leave it alone. We're not interested in the Phantom's dirty money."

"Maybe *you* ain't." Raven swept the pouch off the desktop and in an instant, it was gone. Jack never saw where she put it. "There's more, yeah?" she said, reaching into the compartment again. "Check it out." She produced a rolled document, removed the rubber band, and unfurled it on the desktop. "Blueprints."

The other two leaned in while Sadie bounced on her

tiptoes behind, trying to get a look. The drawings depicted a walled compound and several buildings.

Jack could see no labels of any kind. "Blueprints of what?"

"Don't know," said Gwen, shaking her head. "We'll have to go back to the Archive to find out."

"Amateurs." Raven leaned across the desk, brushing against Jack, and slid the lamp over so that its red light shined down on the paper. Glowing lines and symbols appeared in the blank spaces beside the buildings.

"Neat," exclaimed Sadie, wedging herself between Jack and Gwen. "Invisible ink."

Raven tousled the little girl's hair. "Stock in trade for a good thief, innit?"

"The Kremlin," said Gwen, pointing to a glowing notation in the upper left corner. She chewed her lip. "As in Moscow."

Jack knew that look. She had figured something out. "What? What've you got?"

She drew out the professor's book and laid it down on the plans. "The Phantom stole the British crown out from under our noses," she said as she flipped through the pages. "And now we find blueprints in his place detailing the location of *this*." She stopped at a glossy picture of a diamond-studded crown, topped with a huge egg-shaped ruby. The caption beneath read RUSSIAN IMPERIAL CROWN, KREMLIN ARMORY, MOSCOW.

Jack placed his hand on the book, holding the pages open for her. "There's going to be another heist."

"Exactly." Gwen slid the blueprints over, bringing another of the Phantom's handwritten notations under the lamp. The glowing scrawl read MIDNIGHT, 11 DEC. "And it's going down tomorrow night."

Chapter Twenty-Eight

JACK DIDN'T LIKE the implications of Gwen's deduction. Like the big stone in the British crown, the largest jewel in the Russian crown happened to be another ruby from the professor's favorite book. "Professor Tanner's not behind this," he said, eyes following the book as Gwen put it away.

"I didn't say he was."

"You didn't have to say it."

She pursed her lips at him. "Either way, the Phantom will be in Moscow tomorrow night. And if we want to clear our names—"

"And save the professor."

Gwen rolled her eyes. "*And* save the professor . . . *if* he needs saving . . . we've got to follow."

While Jack and Gwen argued, Raven rolled up the blueprints and shoved them inside her coat. She started for the door.

"Oh, no you don't," said Gwen, blocking her path. "We need those plans."

"Well, I need them more, yeah?"

Gwen clenched her fists, freckles scrunching up in anger, but Jack touched her shoulder. "Raven did know about the slick. And the invisible ink. She might be useful."

"You *could* team up," offered Sadie, fishing in Jack's satchel for another toffee.

The two older girls stared at each other for a few more seconds, until Gwen let out a dissatisfied huff. "Fine. We'll bring her."

"More likely, I'll bring you." Raven pushed her way between Jack and Gwen. She smirked as she reached the door, holding up a little red sphere. "Oi, what's this, then?"

Jack patted his empty pocket. She had taken the zed. "Wait. Don't—"

Gwen gave him a *told-you-so* frown and snatched the sphere out of Raven's hand, slapping it backward into his chest.

She lowered her voice to a growl. "If we're going to work together, you keep your filthy hands out of his pockets."

There was a moment of awkward silence. Jack blushed.

Raven's grin spread a little wider and she lifted her other hand, brandishing Uncle Percy's titanium key card.

Gwen snatched that away too. "And mine." She stepped around the thief and yanked open the door. "Now, let's crack on, shall we?"

"Crack away," said Raven, crossing her arms. "One thing first, yeah? How exactly are you plannin' on gettin' to Moscow, eh?"

Raven had the solution, which absolutely infuriated Gwen. The thief led them around the rim of the cavern to a shop built into the rear wall. A chaotic assortment of junk stuck out from the timber facade, along with a sign that read TIN-KERS' GUILD TRANSPORTATION AUTHORITY. "The TGTA," said Raven, yanking down on a gold braided tassel beside the door. "Fastest bus in town . . . if ya got the stomach for it."

The rope she pulled released a steel ball that spiraled down a track into a metal cylinder. There was a flash within and a puff of white smoke, and a top spun out the other side, traveling down a ramp into a miniature elevator.

"What does that do?" asked Sadie, eyes fixed on the contraption.

The miniature elevator dropped, and the top spun out, tumbled down another ramp, and fell over a ledge. It landed on a seesaw, which sent a brass pointing finger swinging out to press a button. A buzzer sounded inside the shop.

Raven glanced down at the little girl. "Rings the bell, yeah? What else?"

A voice called from inside. "Come in!"

The thief pushed open the door.

"You mean it was unlocked this whole time?" asked Jack, following her through.

But Gwen caught him by the belt loop before he crossed the threshold. "Listen," she whispered. "This is a tinker's place. No matter what you see in there, do *not* use the words 'overcomplicated' or 'unnecessary.' Or we'll end up right back out here on the street. Understand?"

He nodded, and she pushed him over the threshold.

Inside, Raven was already talking to a smallish bearded man seated behind a counter cluttered with junk. The man himself, in fact, was also cluttered with junk, wearing bits of steel tubing, springs, and metal boxes on leather pads. He was tugging at the chin strap of an old pilot's helmet, regarding Raven with suspicion. "Moscow, eh? That'll cost ya a pretty penny."

The thief glanced back at the other three, eyeing Gwen in particular. "And we're willin' to pay, yeah?"

"For what? How does . . . er . . ." Gwen raised an eyebrow at the cluttered man.

He held up a gloved hand, plated with brass. "Ned."

"How does *Ned* intend to get us to Moscow?"

"Hyperloop, deary," Ned replied. "Fastest mode of transportation outside of rocketry. Without all the fire and fuss, mind you."

Sadie, holding Jack's coat sleeve, pointed to a tin model of a cylindrical pod enclosed within a section of tube. "You mean that?"

"That's right, love. The pod runs through a tube with all the air sucked out of it—feels like flying through space, 'cept it's underground. Real shame, though. The inventor quit the guild. Youngest master we ever had. Ran off to America to build cars and spacecraft."

A light ding sounded from the tinker's helmet, and a sectioned arm with a pair of scissors emerged. The scissors gave his beard a single snip, dropping the trimmings into a brass box on his chest, which snapped closed. There was a muffled pop, and black smoke rose from a tiny chimney.

Jack scrunched up his nose at the acrid smell. "Why would you even—?" The rest of his question came out as an *Oof!* as Gwen elbowed him in the ribs.

Ned didn't seem to notice. He flicked his wrist, and a calculator appeared. He punched in a few numbers, nodded, and showed the final figure to Gwen. "Like I said. A pretty penny." The calculator flipped back out of sight. "How will we be paying, then? Cash? Credit?"

"Cash." Raven produced the pouch from the Phantom's slick.

"Credit." Gwen swiped the pouch out of her hand. "I told you. We're not using this." She stuffed the pouch into her own pocket and handed Uncle Percy's card to the tinker. "Credit," she said again. "Please."

A bar full of lenses swung out from Ned's helmet, and three of them swung down in front of his eye. "Crumb credit, eh?" he asked, inspecting the card. He bit it, grunted with relative satisfaction, and then dropped it onto a silver tray atop a model train, which drove about a foot before dumping the card into a toaster. The coils inside turned orange.

"Uh . . . ," said Jack, but the toaster let out a *ding* and shot the card up into the waiting pincer of an articulating arm. The arm retracted, and the pincer dropped the card onto a second model train, which carried the card all the way around the office, through tunnels and behind cluttered shelves, until it bumped into a register, sending the card through an open slot. The register rang. Four green tickets popped up, and the card slid out into a tray in front of Gwen.

Ned handed the tickets to Jack, whose eyes narrowed. They were completely blank. "What do I do with these?"

"You give them to me," said the tinker, taking them back. "Naturally."

Jack let out a dry chuckle. "Naturally."

Moments later, the four children were buckling themselves into the mismatched seats of a copper pod, hovering in a steel tube. Jack's chair, up front, appeared to have come from a barber shop.

The tinker rested a gloved hand on the dashboard in front of him. "Should anything go wrong," he said, pointing to a lever that looked suspiciously like a brake handle from a turn-of-the-century locomotive, "yank that back as hard as you can."

"Go wrong?" asked Jack, cinching his seat belt tight. "Like what?"

"You know. Cabin leak, maglev failure, or perhaps a

catastrophic—" An alarm interrupted Ned's reply. He rushed back to the control panel. "Another pod's comin' in. You have to go."

"A catastrophic what?" Jack shouted, but the pod door had already slid into place. The tube hatch descended next, cutting off all light from outside. There was a rush of air, and Jack's head was pinned back against the seat.

Chapter Twenty-Nine

THE FORCE OF THE ACCELERATION flattened Jack's cheeks. "Red light," he grunted, staring out through the slanted windshield.

Raven jostled his backrest. "What're you on about?"

"Blinking red light. Coming on fast." Jack scanned the dashboard, repurposed from an old Tube carriage, and found a yellow button labeled HEADLAMPS. With effort, he reached forward and pressed it. A blaze of white lit the tunnel ahead, illuminating a wall of steel.

Jack went for the brake.

Raven caught his elbow. "That's a pressure gate, innit? It'll open. Trust me."

He didn't. Not really. Jack cringed, and at the last

second, the steel wall twisted apart, letting them through.

"See?" The pod settled into cruise speed, and Raven leaned forward out of her seat. "It's safe, yeah?"

Jack rolled his head over and found she was looking at him, so that their noses were inches apart. He had thought her eyes were deep brown before, but they were auburn—right on the edge of purple. "Yeah. Sure."

"*If* you two are quite finished."

Jack glanced back to see Gwen glowering at the two of them. Behind her, Sadie—whose seat was something akin to a La-Z-Boy recliner—had drifted off to sleep.

Gwen pulled her knees up into her own chair, which had *British Airways* stenciled across the headrest, and opened the professor's book. "Assuming you two are still interested, I thought you'd like to know that the giant balas ruby in the Russian crown is a sort of twin to the giant balas ruby in the British crown."

"An' how's that?" asked Raven, sitting back in her chair and giving Jack a little wink.

Gwen shot an extra scowl at the thief. "According to this, the Russian ruby isn't Russian at all. It first appeared on the stage of history in China, where it imbued the emperors with supernatural knowledge." She glanced down at the book, reading on. "It was also said to have driven them mad."

A green marquee on the wall beside them flashed BRUS-SELS, and Jack glanced out the windshield in time to see another red light and another terrifying pressure gate approaching. He ducked as the pod went flying through. "So how did the ruby end up in Russia?"

Gwen flipped the page and turned the book around, showing him an illustration of a man in a simple blue robe, surrounded by books and scrolls. "After generations of absolutely barmy rulers and bloody power struggles, the Kangxi Emperor wised up and unloaded the ruby on the Romanovs." She laid the book on her knees again. "The tsars then suffered a similar pattern of madness, right up to the Bolshevik revolution, when the royal family was murdered, and the crown and ruby were locked away in the Kremlin."

"Where the Phantom plans to steal it tomorrow night," said Jack, finishing for her. He shrugged. "But I don't see how any of that makes it related to the Black Prince's Ruby."

"How about this, then?" countered Gwen. "A mineral study of each stone shows that they come from the same mine. Not in China, or Europe, but somewhere in Tajikistan. These rubies are twins, Jack—giant, cursed twins." Gwen snapped the book closed. "The Phantom is obviously targeting the crowns that hold them, and Tanner was studying them just before he disappeared. That's a pretty hefty coincidence if you ask me."

Jack turned around and sank into his barber chair. "The professor can explain it. I know he can. We just have to find him."

They passed more cities—Hanover, Berlin, Warsaw—until, less than an hour later, a buzzer sounded. Jack dug his fingers into his thighs, having no armrests on his barber chair, as the pod came screaming to a stop in front of a final pressure gate. The marquee on the wall flashed ARRIVAL . . . MOSCOW.

Raven patted his arm. "Faster than the friendly skies, yeah?"

Jack swallowed and nodded, turning to look back at his sister. Sadie had slept through the whole thing.

A short stair and an iron door brought the four up to a walkway beside a frozen canal recessed below the city streets. Raven gathered up a snowball and hurled it at the opposite wall, where it stuck like a splat of white paint. "Welcome to Moscow, yeah?" She tromped off toward a stairwell leading up to a bridge. "Hope you brought your long johns."

Raven led them on a freezing two-kilometer march to

a Thieves' Guild safe house north of the city center. And on the way, they passed through the giant plaza known as Red Square. The high brick wall of the Kremlin ran the full length of the western edge, dark, red, and imposing. And to the east stood a whimsical cathedral, with bulbous multi-colored spires lit by a dozen spotlights.

"Saint Basil's," said Gwen, taking on her Encyclopedia Kincaidia face as they passed the cathedral. "They say Ivan the Terrible had the architect's eyes gouged out after he finished it, so he couldn't make another one. But there's no real proof behind the tale." She went on, talking about the Byzantines and the Soviets, but an image of block lettering stole Jack's focus. It flashed here and there among the noise in his head—a phrase he had seen in the professor's book.

IMPERIAL CROWN.

Jack stomped on a passing flyer. There were hundreds of them blowing around the square. He picked it up and angled it to catch the glow from the cathedral spotlights while the others gathered around.

"What's that, then?" asked Raven.

"Something to do with the heist. I thought. But the writing is all Russian. Maybe I saw something else."

"*Cyrillic*, Jack." Gwen took the flyer away from him. "The

script is Cyrillic. The *language* is Russian." She flipped it over and gave it back. There was an English translation on the other side.

Jack read the ad aloud. "'See the Imperial Crown and the Romanov regalia, on display for the first time in more than a century. Join us on twelve December at Vladimir Hall and view Russia's glittering past. Admission free. One day only.'" He lowered the flyer. "The Russians are pulling the crown out of the Kremlin Armory vault on the eleventh so they can show it on the twelfth. That's why the heist has to go down tomorrow night."

"You mean *tonight*." Raven pulled up her sleeve, exposing an arm laden with watches. She pointed to the fourth one up. "We crossed a couple o' time zones in the loop. It's two in the mornin' here, innit?"

"She's right," said Gwen, sounding more than a little disappointed at having to admit it. "It's already the eleventh of December here. And the heist goes down at midnight. We have less than twenty-two hours to catch the Phantom."

—————· Chapter Thirty ·—————

AFTER SEVERAL MORE BLOCKS of trudging through snow and slush, Raven finally stopped at a decrepit building with a CONDEMNED sign wedged into the crook of a broken window. "This is it," she said, pushing through a rusted door that hung loose from its hinges.

The interior was no better. Flecks of snow floated down through a huge hole in the ceiling, and the walls were stained with streaks of brown. Jack could practically feel the black mold crawling up his nostrils.

"You call this a *safe* house?" asked Gwen, gesturing up at the hole. "The whole place could come crashing down on us at any second."

"You have somethin' better?" Raven struck a match, tossing

it into a rusty fifty-five-gallon drum. Flames leaped up inside. "We need rest, yeah? An' food." She pulled a can from a sagging shelf. "Borscht. Nothin' posh like you crumbs are used to, but I es'pect it'll do."

"But the Phantom—" Gwen argued.

"Will come to us, yeah? We know where he's gonna be and when he'll be there. Meanwhile, we wait." She picked up a ratty bedroll and held it out for Gwen to take. "Don't worry. It's too cold for fleas in here, innit?"

Gwen looked to Jack for support, but he couldn't offer any. He was tired and wet, and his stomach was grumbling. Sadie was already snuggled up beside the fire barrel, wrapped in a moth-eaten blanket. He shrugged. "I'm with Raven."

"Of course you are." Gwen ripped the bedroll out of Raven's hand and stormed off to the other side of the room.

Maybe cold and hunger had altered Jack's standards, but Raven's borscht might have been the best meal he'd ever eaten. Every spoonful of hot beets and cabbage became a rich, orange steam rising through his senses. With his stomach filled and the fire blazing, Jack had no trouble falling asleep. Of course, his sleep was anything but peaceful.

The flame, Jack. Please.

He bolted upright, gasping for breath and reaching for his

sister. But Sadie was still snuggled up, washed in the cold light seeping in through the hole in the ceiling. He must have slept for hours. The dragon had been nothing but a nightmare. Or had it?

Jack felt a press of heat from above. He raised his eyes, half expecting to find the creature salivating there. Instead, he saw tongues of fire hovering over his head, stretching out over the lip of the barrel. There was no breeze in the room, no wind coming down through the hole in the ceiling to bend the flames. Yet there they were, dancing above him, beautiful.

Without thinking, he raised a hand and felt every molecule of the burning vapor like sparking on a gem. He turned a finger in slow circles, and the fire followed, twisting itself into a vortex. He laughed out loud.

"That's a drago trick, yeah? I thought you was a tracker."

Jack jerked his hand away, like a kid caught reaching for the cookie jar. "I was . . . um."

But Raven had already rolled over, tugging her blanket up to her shoulders. Her breathing settled into the steady rhythm of sleep. By the time Jack's gaze returned to the barrel, the flames had retreated. The room was colder, and the light from above was a little brighter. Had it all been a half-waking remnant of the dragon nightmare? Tentatively, he lifted his hand and then pulled it back, snorting at his own foolishness. "Yeah. Like I could really . . . ," he said, but no one was listening. The other three were sleeping.

Jack lay down again, hoping to do the same—hoping the dragon would leave him alone this time.

— · Chapter Thirty-One · —

WHEN JACK NEXT AWOKE, the fire had burned down to coals, and for a few moments, he lay on his back, watching the clouds drift past the makeshift skylight. The daylight had gone out of them, and the significance of that observation took some time to work its way into his brain. "The heist!" he said, sitting up.

"Relax." A red light shined in his face, and he raised an arm to shield his eyes. Through the glint of the beam, he saw Raven, sitting on her bedroll with the blueprints unrolled on the floor. "The Phantom won' hit the Kremlin for hours yet. Too many people wanderin' about." She shifted the light to a pot suspended over the fire barrel. "Have some borscht, yeah?"

"Yeah," he said through a yawn. As he got up to get his

bowl, he felt Raven's gaze still tracking him. "What?"

"Nuthin'." She looked down at her plans. "Strange places make for strange dreams. That's all."

Once all four were up and fed, they gathered around the blueprints—all except Gwen, who paced the floor beside them. Using her red light, Raven pointed out a triangle with two dots inside, then a second, and a third, drawn in the Phantom's invisible ink. "Those'd be guard stations. Two dots is two guards, an' them four slashes by the first two stations means dogs."

"Dogs?" asked Gwen, stopping right above Jack.

The thief ignored her, running her beam along the Kremlin wall. "These Xs is cameras, yeah? An' that blob at the northeast corner is a blind spot." She circled the light around an arrow running through the blob. "That'd be his entry point."

"Why should the Phantom worry about entry points?" asked Gwen. "He can zap himself about—go anywhere he pleases. Why not pop in, grab the loot, and be done with it?"

It was a good question. All four looked at one another, and then Sadie shrugged. "Maybe he can't jump through walls."

"That's it," said Jack, snapping his fingers. "*That's* why he didn't zap himself out of the Ministry of Secrets until we opened the door."

"An' that's why he had to wait for the Russians to move them jewels out o' the vaults, yeah? Tonight's heist is a once-in-a-lifetime shot." Raven shifted her beam to the roof of Vladimir Hall, where the Phantom had drawn a second arrow next to a small blue hexagon. "The crown jewels of the Romanovs—in a room with a skylight."

"Dogs, armed guards, and who knows what else," said Gwen. "We *can't* go in there." She knelt beside Jack and tapped the first entry symbol, the one at the cameras' blind spot. "We have to catch the Phantom here, *before* he goes over the wall. And that means we need to get going. It's a long walk to Red Square."

"Walk?" Raven shook her head and laughed. She stood up, strolled over to a block of floor-to-ceiling cabinets, and swung the whole thing away from the wall, exposing a miniature garage with a pair of rather hefty black scooters. "Who says we have to walk?"

It only took a few minutes to get to Red Square, with Gwen and Sadie on one scooter and Jack hanging onto Raven on the other, feeling Gwen's glare boring through his back the whole time. They parked in the shadow of the State Historical Museum, fifty yards from the Phantom's entry point, which turned out to be a clump of trees beside the Kremlin wall.

While Jack and Gwen settled in to watch for their quarry, leaning against the red bricks of the museum, Raven lifted a backpack from the rear compartment of one of the bikes. "This is the fun part, innit?" she asked, slinging the bag over her shoulder.

Jack and Sadie gave her tenuous smiles.

Gwen gave her no such thing. "What's in the bag?"

"Tools o' the trade, yeah? Little bit of everythin' a cat burglar might need."

"Put it back. I told you, we're not going in. Jack and I will take care of the Phantom *before* he goes over the wall." Gwen patted Jack's leather satchel, with its dart gun and electrospheres. "We have what we need to neutralize his device. And then we'll hand him over to the authorities. End of story."

"*After* he tells us what he's done with the professor," added Jack.

"Yes. That too. All I'm saying is—"

Sadie touched her brother's hand. "*I* know where the professor is," she said, pointing out at the square. "He's right over there."

A hundred yards away, a man in a hoodie and a dark overcoat strolled along the Kremlin wall, pushing a wheelchair. The chair's occupant was shrouded beneath a heavy coat, head slumped over like he was unconscious, but Jack recognized the blanket across his lap. "She's right. It's the professor."

"And the Phantom." Gwen reached into Jack's satchel and drew out an electrosphere. "He's heading for the blind spot. I'll go left. Jack, you go right. Raven, you stay here and—"

"Not likely." Raven slung the backpack over her shoulder and rushed out across the square.

"No," said Gwen, reaching for her, swiping nothing but air. "You're going to blow it."

Gwen was right. Years of neglect and tank parades had made Red Square into a rolling sea of uneven pavers. Twenty yards in, with Jack and Gwen hurrying to catch up—and trying to look nonchalant at the same time—a dislodged stone caught Raven's toe. She toppled indignantly to the stones, letting out a cry of pain and surprise. The backpack fell at her side with a loud *clunk*. The Phantom looked right at her.

Jack sailed past Raven, racing to get close enough to use his dart gun without the risk of hitting the professor. There wasn't time. The Phantom grinned beneath his hood and placed a hand on the professor's shoulder.

Zzzap.

Jack reeled to a stop. He whipped his head around in time to see the thief, the professor, and the wheelchair all hovering in midair over the Kremlin battlements, right in the blind spot by the trees. Gravity took hold. The Phantom's overcoat began to spread, and *zzzap.* All three were gone.

"They're inside," said Jack, rushing back to help Raven to her feet.

Gwen was not so kind. *"You,"* she growled, shoving Raven the moment she was up. "You're all subtlety and grace and the crownless queen of cat burglars. And now, all of a sudden, you're tripping over your own two feet?"

"We're not doing this. Not now." Jack took both girls by the arms and dragged them toward the wall, while Sadie scurried across the stones to meet them. "The professor needs us," he said. "So I guess it's a good thing Raven brought those tools after all."

They used the same spot where the Phantom had gone over, except the teens could not zap themselves to the top of a thirty-foot wall. They huddled at its base, concealed from the locals and the late-night tourists by the trees, and

Raven drew a grappling hook gun from her pack. It made little more than a pop, sending its hook over the battlements while coils of black rope unraveled from the bag.

"You first, yeah?" The thief thrust her chin at Gwen. "Unless you need a *klutz* like me to show you how it's done."

Gwen jerked the rope from Raven's hand and started up without a word, one foot after the other.

"Me next, please," said Sadie, bouncing up and down on the balls of her feet.

"Um. No." Jack took his sister by the shoulders and crouched down in front of her. "I . . . need you to stay here and . . . watch the scooters. Yes. The scooters. Super important job. Whole plan depends on it. Can you do that for me?"

Sadie crossed her arms and cocked a hip, scrunching her face into her I'm-not-eight-anymore-so-I'm-not-gonna-fall-for-that look.

"Please, Sadie. Mom would *kill* me if she knew I let you climb a thirty-foot wall and drop into a compound full of attack dogs and armed guards."

Sadie dropped her arms. "Fine. But you'd better come back out."

"We will. And if we *don't* come out in thirty minutes, find a policeman and tell him your brother climbed over the wall. The rest will take care of itself."

Raven was already at the top. "You comin' or what, Jack?"

Jack gave her a hang-on-a-minute wave and watched his sister skip away toward the scooters, all alone in the great big square, green skirt flouncing back and forth above her sparkly lavender shoes. He shook his head and then turned and took hold of the rope.

Chapter Thirty-Two

JACK SWITCHED THE LINE to the inside of the wall, and the three dropped down into a dark corner. There were several old buildings within the compound, separated by brick roads and courtyards. Spotlights cast overlapping gray circles everywhere. "Which one is Vladimir Hall?" he asked, crouching down between the other two.

Raven nodded toward a green roof that rose above the others. "There. The square piece on the east side of the Great Palace."

"Then that's where we'll find the Phantom." Gwen took a step into the wash of the spotlights. "Let's get moving."

Raven jerked her back again. "Easy does it, yeah? You

wanna get us nicked?" She raised a finger, checking one of her watches. "Wait for it . . ." Then she pointed at the nearest guard shack, a hundred yards away. "Now."

Two men stepped out of the shack, both carrying machine guns, one holding the leash of an attack dog. They walked away from the teens, toward a long yellow structure, leaving the path to the first brick alley wide open.

Gwen eyed the thief. "How did you—?"

"The blueprints." Raven pushed them both out into the open. "The Phantom's chicken scratch said the shift change'll take two minutes. Don't waste it gawkin', yeah?"

They hurried across the compound, scooting from alleys to bushes to parked cars. Raven always seemed to know when the guards would leave their posts or disappear around a corner on a roving beat.

"I didn't see any of this in the Phantom's plans," said Gwen as the thief pulled them down behind a parked sedan.

Raven snorted. "As if you know how to read 'em, yeah?" She took off again.

Their zigzag path brought them to a drainpipe not unlike the one Jack had used during the Hunt, right before it had all gone horribly wrong. He shuddered at the memory.

Raven saw the change in his expression. "You up for this?"

she asked, glancing from Jack to the rooftop four stories up.

He nodded. If it would help him save the professor and prove his own innocence, then he was up for anything. "Absolutely."

Jack's muscles apparently disagreed. Every one of them was burning by the time he reached the top. He rolled, panting, over the gutter and onto the green copper roof, right next to Gwen.

She was breathing as hard as he was. "Please say we're done with all the climbing."

Raven leaned over them, streaked black hair hanging down. "Sorry. There's still the little matter of a fifty-foot drop to the jewels, yeah?"

It occurred to Jack that fifty feet was a little specific, considering he had not seen any measurements on the blue-prints. But then he couldn't read all the Phantom's symbols either.

Raven didn't give him the chance to ask. By the time he got to his feet, she was at the skylight.

If the Phantom had, in fact, used the skylight, he had left no sign. Each of its six triangular panes was still intact, and none would have been large enough for even Jack to squeeze through. "Perhaps he can zap through windows," offered Gwen. "It's possible that all he needs is to see where he's going."

"Or maybe he realized we might call the cops and chickened out," said Jack, pressing his face to a pane with his hands cupped around his eyes. A chandelier hung down from the center support into a sixteen-sided chamber with a balcony around the upper periphery. The jewels of the Russian Imperial Collection sparkled in the darkness far below. Among them, Jack caught a hint of movement. His eyes adjusted, and a dark silhouette formed. "Nope. He's down there."

Gwen frowned at the other two. "And how are *we* supposed to follow? Even if we could cut through the glass, these sections are too small."

"But *three* sections is just right, yeah?" Raven removed a bundle of rails from her pack and unfolded them into a trapezoid to match the outline of three successive panes. "I told you. Tools of the trade. Copper framing melts as easy as glass." She fixed the whole thing to the window with a suction cup and flipped a toggle. The lower half of the rails glowed orange. Acrid white smoke rose into the night. She held out a hand to Gwen. "I'll need your coat, yeah?"

"You most certainly will not."

Raven rolled her eyes. "To set the glass on." She snapped her fingers. "Come on. We don' have all night."

Gwen relented, sliding the coat from her shoulders and grumbling about whose fault it was they were up there in the first place, while Jack kept an eye on the Phantom, making sure he didn't look up from his work. The trapezoid came away from the skylight with nothing more than a light *crick*.

"Now," whispered Raven, setting the pane down on Gwen's coat, "first rule of magic and thievin': never trust your own eyes, yeah?" She lifted a set of brass goggles from her pack and held them to her eyes. After a moment, she nodded to herself and handed them to Jack, bypassing Gwen and getting a dirty look for it.

Jack took a look through the blue lenses. Sparkling lines appeared below. They crisscrossed the room right above the display level. "Laser tripwire," he said, pulling the strap of the goggles over his head. "But I think we can get through, as long as we can see it."

"Look who's a regular criminal now, yeah?"

Jack gave Raven an embarrassed smile.

"*Can* we get on with it?" Gwen was shivering, clutching her shoulders.

He coughed. "Right. Sure."

Jack's goggles amplified light, showing him the entire room below. Cases packed with jewelry lined the floor. There were silver suits of armor, gem-encrusted weapons, and a small fleet of gilded carriages right off the pages of a fairy tale. The centerpiece was a broad pedestal with three crowns, and that's where the Phantom was, pulling the biggest one through a hole he had cut in the display case. He was grumbling, talking to another person. The professor was down there with him, but why would the Phantom talk to him if he was unconscious?

Jack put the implications out of his mind and shifted his focus to the upper level, adjacent to the chandelier. "The nearest balcony is maybe twenty feet away," he said, glancing at Raven. "Can you get us over there?"

"'Course I can." The thief drew a pistol from her bag of tricks, took aim, and fired a dart into the chamber. It was followed by the whistling of monofilament wire. She clipped a D-ring to the chandelier's upper anchor and unfolded a set of handles from the sides of the gun. "Zip line," she whispered, holding it steady for Jack. "After you, yeah?"

As Jack squeezed his legs through the hole in the skylight, Raven waved a hand in front of his goggles. "Wait. Your satchel."

"What about it?"

"Hole's too small. You'll get hung up. Take it off, an' once you're on the balcony, I'll toss it over, along with mine. It'll be safer for the both of us, yeah?"

Jack looked to Gwen, but she only shivered, wearing an expression that said *I'm too cold to care anymore.*

"Jack." Raven made an urgent motion for him to hand over the bag. "We're gonna lose him."

"Yeah. Okay." He passed it over and slid the rest of the way down, holding the thief's hand for support while he reached for the zip line. He cringed as he grabbed the handles and let what was basically fishing line take his full weight. Gravity did the rest.

Jack flew down the line to the balcony and caught the rail with a toe, glancing down over his shoulder. The Phantom still did not look up. He was busying himself with a dental pick, working small diamonds free from the crown and laying them on a black velvet cloth. Jack let out a breath, steadied himself atop the rail, and let go of the device. It whizzed back up to Raven.

Once he had hopped down to the carpet, he took a longer look at the chamber floor, a good thirty feet below him. He could see the professor now. Tanner was indeed awake, watching the Phantom work. He did not look drugged, nor did he look much like a captive. He spoke in low whispers, giving commands like he was in charge. And when the Phantom finally popped the giant egg-shaped ruby from the top of the crown, the professor did something Jack could not rationalize, no matter how hard he tried.

Tanner stood up from his chair.

Chapter Thirty-Three

JACK RIPPED OFF the goggles. "Professor?"

He hadn't meant to say it out loud. Both men looked up, and Tanner smirked—actually *smirked*—at him.

The twang of a cut zip line drew Jack's eyes to the skylight. Raven was gone. Gwen, red-faced, gripped the edges of the trapezoidal hole and shouted down at him. "It's a trap. Get out of there!"

The Phantom swept up the velvet cloth full of gems and shoved them into the inside pocket of his coat. When he drew his hand out again, he was holding the stopwatch device. He looked straight up at the skylight.

"Not this time," muttered Jack, backing across the carpeted balcony to gain some runway. "Gwen, cover the glass!"

Three things happened in quick succession. Jack launched himself from the balcony rail, flying headlong into open space. Gwen threw her coat across the skylight like a tarp, covering the entire thing. And the Phantom vanished.

Zzzap.

The thief reappeared a few feet below the covered window, a mix of surprise and terror filling his eyes, frantically reaching for the chandelier's chain. Jack's gamble had paid off. The Phantom couldn't teleport any farther than he could see. An instant later, Jack slammed into him, wrapping him in a bear hug and sending them both into a violent midair twist.

Adrenaline pumped into his brain. His muddled tracker senses kicked into crystal-clear overdrive, and his topsy-turvy world slowed to a crawl. The Phantom was still grasping but not for the chandelier. The stopwatch floated just beyond his outstretched fingers.

It was Jack's first solid look at the device. Instead of hands and numbers, spirals of silvery script were carved into the dark alloy on both sides—ancient runes, or maybe complex equations—leading to a bright blue gem at the center. With almost academic curiosity, he pushed himself away from his foe and plucked it from the air. He fixated on the only soft thing he could find, a purple cushion just visible through the sunroof of a fantasy carriage, willed himself to land there, and pressed the button.

Zzzap.

Pain.

Atoms turning inside out.

Jack thumped down on the seat with a surprised *Oof* as a glassy blast wave rushed out of him in all directions, cracking the carriage walls. He would have felt guilty about the damage, but the Phantom came crashing down through the sunroof right behind him, showering him with splintered wood and gold leaf.

Alarm bells rang.

The thief had fallen through the laser tripwires. As the Phantom lay groaning on the carriage floor, something else dropped through the ruined sunroof, and Jack reached out and caught it—the Russian ruby. Jack must have knocked the jewel from the thief's grasp when he smacked into him in midair. The Phantom's face contorted into the start of a growl, but then he vanished, along with the ruined carriage, the alarm bells, and everything else.

Jack dropped through a white-out blizzard, with shapes and figures spiraling past him in the vortex—crossbows, muskets, war machines, and chemical formulas—all broken down like three-dimensional blueprints. It was a spark, he knew, but he had never felt one like this before.

He landed with a crunch in a snow-covered courtyard, and the blizzard thinned. An army of men in gray over-coats, collars raised against the cold, stood in rows before him. A few wore the funny hats his mind had forever linked with Napoleon, but they were not speaking French. Their accents were Russian, and they were chanting a name—Constantine—over and over.

A line of mounted men in similar uniforms stretched out to Jack's right, horses stamping the pavement. Several held their weapons at the ready, but no one fired. The snow whirled and tumbled between the two factions, as if it were the only thing keeping them from tearing each other apart.

Jack had to get out of there. Back in reality, alarm bells were ringing, Russian guards were converging on the hall, and the Phantom was about to tear his head off. But he couldn't look away from the standoff.

A horse snorted, sending a puff of hot breath into the frigid air. Jack was resting against its flank. Rather, the Russian ruby was resting against its flank. Jack was watching the spark from the pinnacle of the same crown the Phantom had just picked clean of its jewels. A mounted soldier with a curling mustache and the most epic sideburns Jack had ever seen was holding the crown at his knee. He remained bareheaded, the only bareheaded soldier in that whole disturbing winter wonderland.

"Nicholas." A soldier with gold epaulets and a plumed cap eased his horse closer. He said something in Russian—urgent, pleading.

We must end this, before it comes to blood.

The translation came unbidden to Jack's mind. But how? Sparks showed images and sounds from the past. They did not come with captions. But he had already seen that this was no ordinary spark. What had Gwen told him about the Russian ruby? *It imbued the emperors with supernatural knowledge.* She had followed that with a caution, though. *It was also said to have driven them mad.* Jack mentally cringed. He really had to get out of there.

In answer to the soldier's urging, Nicholas waved a hand high in the air. Instantly, a group of horsemen broke from the line, charging the opposing troops. Yet still they did not fire.

"Constantine! Constantine!" The troops held their ground, chanting the name all the louder. The horsemen faltered and pulled up short. Their mounts slipped and skidded on the icy stone, and two of them went down. One fired a shot and a single chanting man dropped like a marionette with its strings cut. Blood seeped into the snow.

The crowd went silent.

Nicholas let out a string of angry commands, and the rest of the horsemen returned to the line. After that, the only sound was the whistling of the wind and the brush of the snow like grit against patches of empty stone. Then Jack was rising. Nicholas was lifting the crown, not to place it on his head, but to stare at it, as if searching for the answer to his crisis.

Frost tinted his eyebrows, and beneath them, his steel-blue eyes were sad, even confused. But as Nicholas gazed into the ruby, his expression changed. Sadness and confusion twisted into malice.

Jack felt the same mixture of anger and glee rising in his own mind. Ghostly cannons materialized in his vision—men loading grapeshot, white flashes exploding from bronze barrels. The Russian ruby—this source of supernatural knowledge—had shown him how to finish the standoff.

It had shown Nicholas as well.

The would-be tsar set the crown on the pommel of his saddle, letting it hang at an ignoble tilt, and pointed at his cavalrymen. They parted, making way for three cannons.

The troops across the square began to murmur. The men of the front line took a step back into their comrades. But Nicholas gave them no chance for retreat. He pumped his fist. The cannons fired.

Men fell by the dozens, blood spraying across the snow. The rest tried to run. They pushed and scrambled out onto an ice-covered river that bordered the square. Meanwhile, the cannon teams reloaded and fired into their backs. The ice broke beneath them. They sank into pink, frothing water, dragged down by their winter coats.

The whole scene was horrifying. And electrifying.

A part of Jack exulted in the sight of all that death— knowledge of warfare perfectly executed. The rest of him recoiled. Before Jack had the chance to process what was happening to him, Young Professor Tanner materialized out of the smoke and the swirling snow. He strolled up to the horse and reached out, his thin fingers going straight for Jack's face. "I'll take that."

Jack tried to flinch but he couldn't. He'd almost forgotten he was sparking. Tanner wasn't reaching for Jack's face. He was reaching for the jewel. And if the professor was there in the spark with Jack, he must already have a hand on the ruby back in the real world.

Chapter Thirty-Four

YOUNG TANNER'S SMIRK held steady, but the rest of him morphed into Old Tanner. At the same time, the snow-dusted, bloody square behind him became a darkened hall, and the screams of dying men became the alarm bells the Phantom had set off. Tanner's arm was stretched through the carriage window, fingers caressing the ruby. He plucked it from Jack's hand.

"Why?" asked Jack, recovering his voice. "Why are you doing this?"

But Tanner gave no answer. He kicked away the chock beneath the carriage wheel—the one holding it in place on the platform—and then shot straight up through the hall. A pair of quantum thrusters, like those the spooks had used in the Archive, blazed at his ankles.

"Didn't see that coming," said Jack as he and the Phantom watched Tanner nimbly alight on the upper balcony and run away into the shadows.

Slowly, the two tore their eyes from the empty balcony. They stared at each other for half a heartbeat, and then the Phantom snarled and made a grab for the stopwatch device. But the shift of his weight set the coach into motion, sending him sprawling back against the seat instead.

The coach creaked and bounced down a ramp toward a pair of tall double doors, and Jack dug the fingers of his free hand into the velvet cushion as it smashed through. The carriage collapsed to the bricks, skidding to a stop in a sagging heap of gilded firewood, wheels rolling off in separate directions. Jack fought back his shock, pushed his way out through the debris, and took off across the courtyard.

Dogs barked.

Men with guns converged, shouting in Russian.

"Jack!" Gwen waved to him from the corner of a building, next to the alley that led back toward the wall. They would never make it that far.

It seemed the Russian guards weren't too keen on shooting at a couple of kids. They did, however, release the dogs. A pair of German shepherds bolted out in front of their masters, covering the distance at twice the speed. Jack glanced down at the device in his hand and a solution came to him. He held it up so Gwen could see. "This way! Run to me!"

She nodded and sprinted out to meet him.

A dog leaped, teeth bared, just as their fingers touched.

Zzzap.

Pain.

Trees.

An iron grip on his shoulder.

Jack glanced back and saw the angry glare of the Phantom. The thief had chased him from the wreckage, grabbing him at the last moment, and Jack had teleported all three across the compound to the top of the Kremlin wall. As momentum carried them over the battlements toward a grove of tall pines, the Phantom ripped the stopwatch from Jack's hand, growling in his ear. "Turnabout's fair play, innit?"

Zzzap.

He was gone. And Jack and Gwen crashed into the pines.

They tumbled down through bows and branches, letting out a series of grunts and cries until they slammed into the snowbank below. Gwen was the first to crawl out. She pulled a pinecone from her curls and tossed it away. "You all right?"

Jack moaned, sitting up and rubbing his head. "I think so." He let her help him to his feet and together they stumbled out of the foliage. Alarms still rang in the compound. In moments the whole square would be crawling with guards and policemen. The two of them ran for the scooters.

"Raven ditched me as soon as you went in," puffed Gwen.

"Yeah. I know." The Phantom's last taunt was still ringing in Jack's ear. *Turnabout's fair play, innit?* He had heard that before, at the Thieves' Guild. "She's with the Phantom," he said between breaths. "Had us pegged the moment we floated into the guild. I'll bet she wanted us to see her going into the guild master's boat, just so we'd believe she was working for him."

Guards began pouring out from the main gate of the Kremlin, and the few policemen in the square ran to meet them—all except for one, who stood between the two teens and the scooters, scratching his head as he spoke to a little girl in a flouncy green skirt.

Jack swept up his sister as he and Gwen ran past, shouting, "What an imagination, huh?" But he doubted the cop heard him over Sadie's "Wheeeeee!"

—— · Chapter Thirty-Five · ——

ZZZAP.

The Phantom and Raven materialized directly between the scooters and the fleeing kids, knocking the nearest bike over with the blast wave of their arrival. The Phantom revved up the remaining scooter while Raven hopped on behind, and the two spun around in a cloud of smoke and sped away.

"We have to stop him," grunted Jack, righting the fallen scooter. The three piled on, with Gwen shoving helmets down on everyone's heads. But Jack's launch was not nearly so dramatic as the Phantom's. It was more of a slow toe-walk through a 180-degree turn and a lurching, wobbly acceleration out of the square.

"Car!" shouted Gwen as soon as they hit the street. "Lamppost!"

Jack jerked the handlebars to avoid the streetlamp and fishtailed back into the center of the road. "Thanks, but I've got this."

"Really? How many times have you driven a scooter before?"

He didn't answer.

Police vehicles flew down the other side, lights flashing and sirens blaring, all heading for the Kremlin. They didn't seem to care about a couple of scooters racing through the city. The Phantom leaned left and right, dodging the traffic and widening the gap. "They're not even wearing helmets," Gwen complained, apparently adding that nugget to the thieves' growing list of offenses.

Jack would have turned to give her a sarcastic look, but taking his eyes off the road meant certain death. "Why are they bothering to drive at all? Can't they just jump away?"

As if he had heard the question, the Phantom looked back and gave him a three-fingered Boy Scout salute, his other two gripping the stopwatch.

Zzzap.

Zzzap. Zzzap. Zzzap.

The thieves leaped forward through the traffic, blowing out car windows and streetlamps with the blast waves of their jumps, until Jack couldn't see them anymore. He stared after them.

"Car!"

A horn blared. Jack steered back into his own lane, heart pounding. Once he recovered his balance and his composure, he let the scooter coast to the curb. "They did that for our benefit."

"They were toying with us," added Gwen.

"Yeah," agreed Sadie in a muffled voice. "But if we're done chasing them, can you guys stop squishing me?"

Jack lowered the kickstand and stepped off. "Sorry. These things weren't really built for three." He narrowed his eyes at his sister, who looked like a fairy mushroom in her oversize helmet and brightly colored skirt. "Why on earth were you talking to that policeman?"

"You said to find one if you didn't come out."

"In thirty minutes. We were in there like fifteen . . . twenty at the most."

Sadie held up a bare wrist, twisting it back and forth. "If

you want *that* kind of accuracy, leave me a watch next time."

"Hey. Focus." Gwen unbuckled her chinstrap. "What about Tanner? Where did he go?"

"I think he had his own escape plan," said Jack. "He was wearing ankle thrusters."

"What do you mean 'ankle thrusters'?" Gwen dropped the helmet to her hip. "Tanner can't even walk."

"Yes he can. Tanner's legs work fine."

"Get. Out." She punched him in the arm.

"You were right, okay? Tanner's behind the whole thing. He set me up." Jack shoved his hands into his pockets. "Twice. All for a few shiny jewels."

"The jewels." Gwen punched him again. "The Phantom wasn't carrying the jewels."

Jack stepped back out of her reach, rubbing his arm and frowning. "Yes he was. Tanner took the big ruby, but the Phantom stuffed a bunch of diamonds into his coat."

"Not those jewels. Britain's jewels. The Phantom stole a sword, a scepter, and a crown, Jack. A bag big enough to carry that lot would be obvious."

Gwen was onto something. Jack could see it. She paced beside the scooter. "He wouldn't carry a bag that big into the Kremlin. That would be an unnecessary risk. And he wouldn't leave the Crown Jewels at the Thieves' Guild. No way. He'd want to keep them close."

"You mean he hid them somewhere in Moscow," offered Sadie.

"Exactly. They weren't *just* toying with us. That chase had another purpose." She raised her eyebrows, giving him her *now-you-fill-in-the-rest-because-it's-all-so-obvious* look.

Jack had no clue. He spread his hands. "Just spill it, will you?"

"With all that famous loot, our thieves only have one sure means of getting out of Russia—the hyperloop." She pointed back toward Red Square. "And it's that way. They were leading us away from it so—"

Jack finally understood. "So they'd have plenty of time to recover the stashed jewels before we figured it out."

"But we *have* figured it out," said Sadie, looking from one to the other.

Gwen nodded. "Yes we have." She threw on her helmet, heading for the scooter. "And that means we can head them off at the pass."

—— · Chapter Thirty-Six · ——

JACK SPED ALONGSIDE the canal, within sight of the bridge and the hyperloop station. He had gone out of his way to bypass the police in Red Square, and it had cost him. The Phantom and Raven zapped into view in a blast of snow at the water's edge, right next to the station door. Raven immediately hopped off to unstrap a long, hardened case from the scooter's rack.

"The jewels," said Gwen.

"I see 'em." Jack turned at the bridge, back tire slipping out behind him. He skidded to a stop at the apex and jumped off. "Raven! Stop!" He went for the dart gun in his satchel, but his fingers found nothing but cold air and denim. He looked down in confusion.

Jack had no satchel.

The memory of handing it over to Raven on the roof of Vladimir Hall flashed in his mind. He kicked the base of the bridge's stone railing.

"Lookin' for this?" Raven pointed Jack's own dart gun at him. "You didn't think I'd let ya keep it, didja? Not after you shot at me."

"Oh, well done," muttered Gwen.

Jack pushed her behind him, and Sadie behind her. "Don't go with him, Raven. You may be a thief, but you're not like the Phantom."

At the mention of his title, the Phantom tossed back his hood. "The Phantom? Is that what you been callin' me? I told you. It's the Ghost."

"An' I told you, ghosts are pathetic." Raven lowered the dart gun and faced the other thief, puffing herself up. "Ghosts are sad, lingerin' creatures. Leftovers. Phantoms are dynamic and terrifyin'." She threw her hands in the air. "Oh my days, *Arthur*, one's painted right over your bed, innit?"

"Yes it is, *Imogene*. An' I ain't got a wink o' sleep since you painted it there, have I?"

"Arthur?" asked Gwen, peeking out from behind Jack.

"Imogene?" asked Sadie, peeking out from behind Gwen on the other side.

The-Phantom-slash-Ghost-slash-Arthur abandoned his argument with Raven-slash-Imogene and offered a short bow. "At your service, yeah? Spector an' Spector, soon to be the most famous thieves in all the world."

"Yes, but Arthur and Imogene?" asked Gwen, pushing Sadie out of sight again.

Raven shrugged. "Our dad was as British as they come."

"Hey!" Jack slapped both hands down on the rail of the bridge, sharply enough to make Raven raise the dart gun again. He took a deep breath and forced some of the tension in his voice down a notch. "I get it. You're a brother-sister cat burglar team. Cute. Whatever. How does the professor fit in?"

"Tanner?" Arthur snorted—in exactly the way his sister always snorted, Jack noted with annoyance. "Whole thing was his idea, yeah? We use the device he gave us to get in an' out o' Spookville an' the Kremlin." He lifted the long case, holding it up for Jack to see. "An' we get to keep everythin' but them two big rubies."

"The rubies." Gwen stomped her foot. "I knew it. I *knew* this was about those rubies."

Jack glanced back to shoot her a frown.

"Sorry," she whispered, but as soon as he turned back around, she added, "But I did."

Jack rolled his eyes and leaned against the rail. "Is he down there now? Is Tanner down in the hyperloop, waiting for you?"

"Not likely." Arthur tilted his head in the direction of Red Square. "Before we hit the Kremlin, your professor made me pop in an' unlock a door in that cupcake cathedral. I think he planned to have a look inside after we was done fetchin' the jewels. You might still find him there"—he grinned—"assumin' the cops don't nab ya first."

To emphasize Arthur's point, a siren wailed in the distance. Raven pulled her brother toward the hyperloop stairwell and opened the door. "I'm afraid it's time we leave you, Jack. I'd say holdin' the bag, 'cept we're takin' it with us, ain't we?"

While the thief gloated, Jack felt a cold metal ball pressed into his hand, out of sight below the stone rail.

"She didn't get everything," whispered Gwen.

He remembered. Gwen had pulled an electrosphere from his satchel right before Raven took off to have her fake fall and give away their position to her brother. Jack raised his other hand and shouted, "Wait, Imogene!"

The thief extended the dart gun. "Raven. It's *Raven*, yeah?"

"Yeah. Sure. Raven. Um . . . we had some fun, right? You and me?"

She snorted. "I guess."

"I mean we had a sort of connection, you know?"

Arthur's face went flat. "You what?"

Gwen elbowed him hard. "Whatcha doing, Jack?" she whispered through her teeth. "You were supposed to shock her, not hit on her."

"I'll only get one shot at this," he whispered back. "Gimme a minute."

"Awright." Raven shifted her feet, looking off to the side, cheeks turning a little redder than the cold had already made them. "Maybe we did, yeah? So what. If you think I'm gonna hand over the jewels because I gave you a wink and a smile, you got another'un comin'."

"Um . . . no. Nothing like that. But I thought you might want to take something to remember me by. Besides the jewels, of course. And the gun." Jack winced. "And all my candy." He couldn't believe the baloney coming out of his mouth. He doubted Raven would either.

Then again, she was a thief. And thieves are greedy.

"Fine. Sure. What ya got?"

Without risking another word, Jack tossed the electrosphere, letting the chain zip from its housing. He watched the copper ball sail across the canal, almost in slow motion. Raven caught it with one hand and went totally rigid.

"Imogene?" Arthur dropped the case into the snow at his feet, catching his sister as she collapsed. He went rigid as well, and the two stunned thieves toppled backward down the stairs into the black.

"It worked," said Jack, starting to run. He raced across the bridge with Gwen and Sadie at his heels, raising his voice in triumph. "It actually wor—"

A flash lit the doorway, registering as a light crackle in the odd merger of Jack's senses. That was all the cue he needed. He whipped his body around, tackling Gwen and Sadie to the ground as the blast wave hit the bridge. Flames poured over the rail. For a full second there was nothing but heat and the black roar of the fire. Then the cold returned, and with it, utter silence.

Chapter Thirty-Seven

JACK JUMPED TO HIS FEET and ran for the stairs. "Raven!" Black smoke poured from a gaping hole where the hyperloop door used to be. Charred, paper-wrapped toffees littered the snow. "I killed her." He skidded in the snow as he rounded the corner at the top of the steps. "I killed them both."

"Jack, don't." Gwen was right behind him. "It's too dangerous. The pressure gates could—"

A long, whining *screech* drowned out the rest of her warning, ending in a soul-sucking *pop*.

A roar filled Jack's ears. The air was sucked from his lungs, and the snow around him rushed away, mixing with the smoke to form a whirlwind that tried to suck him into the hole left by the explosion. His feet slipped out from under him. He started sliding toward the vortex.

"Oh no you don't." Gwen had him by the collar, leaning back into the steps, boots wedged into the stones on either side.

A string of alarms went off as cars parked along the canal tilted in sequence, asphalt caving beneath them. In the distance, a four-story apartment building dropped about a foot into its foundation, sending up a cloud of snow and dust. The whole section of the hyperloop had collapsed.

A lingering buzz filled Jack's ears. "What have I done?" he mumbled, starting down the stairs again, slower this time.

Gwen followed him down, leaning on the iron rail beside the steps to steady herself. "You couldn't have caused that explosion, Jack. Not with an electrosphere. The hyperloop uses pressure and electricity. There's no fuel down there—nothing that could have made a fireball like that."

Jack touched the stones at the edge of the hole in the canal wall, rubbing the soot between his thumb and forefinger. "You're saying . . ."

"Tanner rigged it with a bomb. He murdered Raven and her brother."

"But why? Why would he do that?" The buzzing wouldn't go away. Maybe it was the shock of seeing Raven and her brother killed, rather than a lingering echo of the explosion. Yes. They were thieves. But they hadn't deserved to die. Just like those soldiers who hadn't fired a shot even when one of their own was killed hadn't deserved to get mowed down by cannon fire.

"He didn't need them anymore," offered Gwen. "He got what he wanted."

Jack turned away from the empty black of the hole to look her in the eye. "The rubies."

She nodded. "And without Raven and the Phantom, we have no proof that he took them. Tanner never set foot in the Ministry of Secrets. And there are no witnesses or video that can place him at the Kremlin, thanks to the Phantom's device." She let out a rueful chuckle. "We can't even turn in the remaining jewels. They're buried under ten feet of rubble and crumpled steel."

"I don't think so." Sadie had come down the steps behind them and was crouched down beside the misshapen remains of the hyperloop door. She pointed to the shadows underneath.

Both Jack and Gwen tilted their heads to look. There, trapped under the door, was the hardened case full of jewels.

It took a good bit of grunting and heaving to move the

door, but they soon slid it off into the icy water. Gwen popped the catches, and all three sucked in their breath as she lifted the lid. The largest of the gems each had their own custom pockets cut into the gray foam liner—two big sapphires and two huge diamonds. Next to these were several square compartments filled to the brim with smaller jewels of all shapes and colors. There must have been thousands of them, sparkling in the white light of Moscow's winter sun.

Sadie lifted a gold ingot, one of several. "But what are these?"

"All that's left of Britain's Imperial State Crown and the Sovereign's Scepter," Gwen replied, recovering the ingot from the little girl. She sighed as she set it back in its place. "The thief must have melted them down. Wouldn't be the first time. The Cromwellians did the same in 1649. The good news is that crowns can be remade. The jewels are the main thing."

The only item of the regalia that had survived intact was the gold-and-silver Sword of State, lying in its own cutout below the ingots. Arthur had probably meant to keep the famous weapon for himself.

Lights flashed in the distance. Gwen slapped the case closed and secured the catches. "We need to move," she said, hoisting it up and shaking it at Jack. "We've got enough here to clear our names at home, but I don't think the Russians will be so forgiving. We have to get out of Moscow if we don't want to end up in a gulag. And I think I know a way."

They took the scooter they had left on the bridge, with Jack driving and Gwen directing him toward some mysterious mode of transportation that she swore would get them safely out of Russia. He slowed to a stop as Saint Basil's came into view.

"Keep going," said Gwen. "I'll tell you where to turn."

"We can't leave yet."

"Jack, whatever Tanner's up to, the ministry can handle it. They'll call in a twelve to hunt him down."

"And how long will that take?" he asked, turning in his seat. "The twelves are dispersed all over the world, and Tanner's already got a head start. Gwen, we may be the only ones who can stop him."

Zzzap.

Jack's eyes jerked from Gwen to the canal, now a good distance behind them. He couldn't have heard what he thought he heard. Both Spector siblings had been immobilized by the electrosphere, unable to use the stopwatch device to escape. And no one could have survived that blast.

Maybe the sound was just a pang from his guilty conscience. Maybe he'd be hearing it for years to come. Still, he had to ask. "Did you two hear that?"

"No." Sadie answered his question quickly, as if she knew exactly what he was referring to.

Gwen squinted at him. "Hear what?"

He turned and cranked the scooter's engine. "Never mind. Let's go."

Chapter Thirty-Eight

ARTHUR HAD CALLED it *that cupcake cathedral.* Jack would have gone with ice-cream swirly church, but whatever.

Saint Basil's stood at the south end of Red Square, lit on every side by spotlights, without so much as a stray dog to darken its cobblestone porches. A few hundred yards away, however, the scene at the Kremlin gate had descended into controlled chaos. Police vans were parked at all angles. A drab rainbow of uniformed men and women milled about in a hodgepodge of activity that all boiled down to one goal—catching Jack and Gwen.

"Are you sure you want to do this?" asked Gwen as Jack pushed the scooter into the bushes beside the church. "Don't you read mysteries? Rule number one for murderers and thieves: 'Never return to the scene of the crime.'"

Jack lowered the kickstand. "That's not a real rule."

"It is if you're a criminal."

"Yeah, well, what about rule number one for agents of the Elder Ministries?"

Gwen pursed her lips. "'Defend the Realm against all enemies' doesn't apply." She gestured all around them. "We're in Russia, Jack, not England. This is not *our* realm."

"Now you're just nitpicking."

As Jack mulled over the risk of leaving the jewel case strapped to the bike, the image of a worn bronze wolf's head flickered in his brain. He grabbed the two girls and dragged them into the bushes beside him.

Gwen jerked her arm away, plucking a dead leaf from her scarf. "What is it?"

He pointed. Not two hundred yards away, talking to a Russian cop and impatiently tapping his wolf's-head cane on the cobblestones, stood Ash. A huge companion stood beside him, wearing a heavy tweed coat with a fur-lined hood.

"Ash," said Gwen, easing herself even deeper into the bushes. "And Shaw. Wherever did he find that ridiculous coat?" She let out a frustrated breath. "I'm not surrendering to those two, Jack. Shaw will hand us over to the Russians without a thought—probably ask for a medal. I *told* you we needed to get out of Moscow."

"We check the cathedral first. Tanner wanted inside. There has to be a reason."

"What reason?" Sadie settled in between them, finding the only stump suitable for sitting amid the wet leaves and mud. "He's already got the Russian ruby."

"Why does any tracker go poking around historic buildings?" Gwen drew out the professor's book. "He's searching for something. Perhaps Tanner has another jewel to find." She opened the book to the last chapter and showed Jack. "Look. There's a third stone." Beneath a picture of a wedge-shaped gem—the same translucent red as the others—the title read THE TIMUR RUBY.

The Timur Ruby. The name hit Jack like a punch to the chest. Tanner had told him the Timur Ruby had sunk to the bottom of the Mariana Trench. But if the professor could walk, then the whole tale about what had happened in that island cave might be a lie. Tanner had never tried to save Jack's grandfather. What if the exact opposite was true?

Jack fell back onto his rear among the dead leaves, shaking his head, not caring about the cold seeping through his jeans. "I don't think Tanner's looking for that ruby."

"Why not?"

"He's already got it."

Jack told the girls Tanner's story, allowing Gwen to reach the same conclusion about how Joe Fowler the Eleventh had really died. The two confirmed it with a silent glance to spare Sadie the pain of hearing that someone had murdered her grandfather.

The nine-year-old seemed to sense it anyway.

Gwen squeezed her arm. "I'm sorry."

Sadie sniffled and nodded. "Me too."

After a long moment, Gwen closed the book and tucked it away. "According to Lazarev, that ruby gave Tamerlane the ability to command men."

The ability to command men. Hadn't Tanner used that exact phrase? "Command," said Jack, repeating the word out loud.

"Knowledge," added Sadie, as if she knew what he was going to say next.

"Loyalty." Gwen finished the thought. "Three rubies. Each grants a different aspect of the power to rule. That's what Tanner's after. He wants to be king."

"Emperor's more like it." Jack glanced toward the Kremlin, checking on Ash and Shaw. They had moved farther up the square with their police escort. "There's more. I don't think the professor was always like this—a murderer, I mean. I think the rubies are changing him."

Gwen offered him a hand and pulled him off his rear, up to a crouch. "Clarify."

"I saw the effect the Black Prince's Ruby had on the Duke of Alencon at Agincourt. It made him . . . evil. And I saw something similar when I touched the Russian ruby. I sparked, and a guy named Nicholas went nuts right before my eyes. He killed a bunch of soldiers with cannons."

"The Decembrist Revolt," said Gwen, looking down at the leaves between them. "It was in the book. Tsar Alexander had died, and the army split into factions, each supporting one of his brothers. The majority supported Nicholas, but a few thousand rebels marched to the palace to demand the throne go to his other brother, Constantine." She raised her eyes to meet Jack's. "Nicholas tried for hours to disperse the rebels peacefully. And then, in a sudden fit of rage, he ordered his cannons to fire into the crowd."

"I saw it happen." Jack grimaced at the memory. "It was as if the moment Nicholas decided to claim the crown he became a different person. In a matter of seconds, he went from berating his cavalry over the death of one rebel to gleefully tearing hundreds to shreds. It was definitely the ruby. I felt it."

Gwen pieced it all together. "Atrocities throughout history are linked to each of these jewels, even though they were separated by whole kingdoms. What will Tanner do once he's got all three?" She glanced at the cathedral. "We really need to get in there."

"Oh. So now you're on board with sticking around. What happened to 'Rule number one doesn't apply'?" Jack didn't wait for a reply. He stood up, only to have her yank him back down again. He let out an exasperated sigh. "But you just said—"

"The police are everywhere, Jack." Gwen nodded at the steps, glowing white in the spotlights, easily seen from the Kremlin gates. "Do you really think the professor used the front door?"

—————· Chapter Thirty-Nine ·—————

JACK KEPT ONE EYE on the Kremlin as the three snuck along the periphery of the cathedral, checking the doors. No sign of Ash or Shaw. He wasn't sure if that was good or bad.

"That one," said Gwen, nodding toward an entrance sheltered from the spotlights by a grove of pines. "He would have entered there." They hurried into the shadows beneath the portico, and Jack tugged at an iron door. It squeaked free of its frame. There was a strip of tape over the latch to keep it from catching.

"See?" said Gwen. "The Phantom was here."

"Wait." Jack held her back with a light touch on her arm. "Lazarev."

"Yes. The guy who wrote the book about the rubies."

"Yeah. I know. But . . ." Why had the archeologist's name popped into Jack's head right at that moment? He let out a breath, trying to bring the noise of the distant police chatter under control. His head was still buzzing from the explosion at the hyperloop.

Lazarev. The name had come to him from somewhere—somewhere close.

Jack slipped a hand into his jacket pocket and took hold of the zed. The buzzing dissipated. He saw the voices from the police radios, like smoky trails of purple script that he couldn't read. He saw the flashing lights, red, blue, and white, reflecting on the wet stones all across the square. He gathered all that useless data, acknowledged it, and let it fade into the gray mist of his subconscious, leaving only the small courtyard behind the church.

Trees: pine boughs waving in the breeze. No Russian names there.

A black marble sign bolted to the side of the cathedral: Cyrillic, with no translation.

A trash bin: crumpled paper cups, cigarette butts, and a gleaming rectangular shape poking out—an ID card, with most of the name visible.

Lazarev.

Jack rushed out across the lighted cobblestones, letting go of the zed. All the noise came rushing in again. He stumbled, almost fell, and had to stop at the trash can to steady himself.

"Jack," hissed Gwen. "Get back here. Someone will see you."

"Like I don't know that?"

He felt something cool on his upper lip and instinctively raised a hand to check. It was wet—a nosebleed. Jack turned and wiped it away with his handkerchief. He couldn't let Gwen see.

"That took *way* too long," complained Gwen, taking the card the moment he got back to the portico. But she didn't seem to suspect anything. She squinted at the name. "Dimitri . . . Lazarev. State Historical Museum of Russia ID. With a data chip and everything." Her eyes widened a touch. "This is an access card, Jack. I remember where I know Lazarev's name from."

Jack beat her to it. "The leftover enquiry from yesterday's filings. Lazarev was the guy who lost his wallet in London."

"You mean the guy who got his wallet stolen. Raven or her brother must have picked his pocket and then passed it on to Tanner."

"So Arthur was telling the truth. The professor was definitely here." Jack pulled open the iron door and waved the girls through.

If the cathedral looked like a collection of cupcakes and ice-cream swirls on the outside, then on the inside it looked like a gingerbread house. Jack felt like Hansel, leading two Gretels into the witch's candy cottage. Every spire represented a single chapel, and each chapel was tight and cluttered, and painted with a bright, hypnotic mix of peppermint stripes, gumdrop flowers, and ribbon-candy swirls.

"I don't see how loyalty, knowledge, and command could be curses," mused Sadie as the three of them explored the first chamber. "Aren't those good things?"

"Not if they're corrupted." Gwen tugged on a narrow door, finding only a shallow closet behind. "And that's exactly what these stones seem to do. Loyalty can be misplaced. Knowledge can still lead you down the wrong path. And you can bet that every sovereign who's ever been crowned has abused the privilege of command at some point. It's human nature."

The first chapel was a disappointment. Jack had been hoping for marble, maybe some bronze or copper, but everything was covered in painted plaster or wood. And all the precious metals were tucked behind glass. Even the floors were a disappointment.

"We'll never find Tanner's trail," he said as he ducked through a candy-cane-striped archway behind Gwen. "This place is a maze. And there's nothing here that's good for sparking."

"What about these?" She knelt beside a line of brick trim that ran along the base of the wall. The bricks were unpainted and formed a continuous line that ran from room to room.

Jack could spark off brick. Maybe. He had done it before, when his skills weren't on the blink. But it certainly hadn't been pleasant. He crouched down beside her, already reaching into his pocket for the zed. "They'll have to do."

A voice deep in Jack's subconscious warned him about using the zed again. It was draining him. He felt it a bit more each time he let go of it. Each time the static and the buzzing in his head grew more insistent. But it also worked. The zed was more than a placebo. That much was clear now. He drew it out, turning so that Gwen would not see, and placed his other hand on the brick.

The wood floor disintegrated in wisps of black dust, dropping Jack into a jagged, incongruous blend of shifting shadows and glimmering specks of color. He landed in the same crouched position, but his surroundings bore little resemblance to the hallway he had left behind. Jack hated brick. It was a hodgepodge, to use Gwen's word—a mix of materials that weren't great for sparking to begin with. The specks were new, though. Some kind of metal. Jack wondered if the sixteenth-century Russian masons that built the place had used iron filings in the mix.

He pushed against the vision, pressing it forward through time, and saw a hundred shadows walk past in just a few seconds. One carried a child, surrounded by others, murmuring sweetly. Another was dragged, kicking and screaming in distorted, broken tones. Beautiful things had happened there, ugly things too.

Finally, the hall went quiet again, and Jack saw a black silhouette stroll by, tall and lanky, walking with the same confident gait Young Tanner had used in the winter square. The figure vanished at the next doorway, and Jack was left with a terrifying choice. If he wanted to follow, to have any hope of finding out what the professor was up to, he would have to interact with the spark. He would have to leave the safety of being a mere observer and push his way into that shifting, shadowy world.

—·— Chapter Forty —·—

JACK MADE HIS DECISION and stood, taking his hand from the brick. Instantly, the strange world of the spark threatened to knock him down again. He struggled to maintain his balance amid the chaos. All around him, the ill-fitting pieces took on greater dimension. The glimmering dust from the iron filings hung in the air like the high-definition remnant of an obliterated reality.

He staggered forward, glancing down at his hands, and found that he too had become a shifting silhouette. The previous morning's fear of being trapped in the yellow gems seemed trivial. Surely, being trapped forever in this disjointed realm as a half-formed wraith would be the very image of hell.

A translucent wall of shade barred his path through the archway where Tanner had gone—a barrier where all definition was lost. Perhaps it was the spark's translation of the grout between the bricks. Jack pushed a hand into the darkness and watched his arm disappear. Not much comfort there. Then again, he was already pretty messed up, so he closed his eyes and soldiered on. There was no sign of Tanner on the other side.

Jack had delayed too long.

The next chapel was shaped like a hexagon, with corridors leading off in separate directions from three of the six walls. Tanner could have taken any one of them. Without considering the potential consequence, Jack looked up into the turning, grinding vision of the spire above. Vertigo took him—nauseating vertigo. He stretched out a hand to grab the wall and touched something living instead.

Beneath the arch of the first corridor, stood a fellow shade. Jack could make out the indistinct shapes of a bowler hat and an ankle-length coat. Why did he keep appearing?

"Dad?"

Jack's voice came out as garbled as the rest of him, somewhere between speaking under water and shouting into a fan.

Instead of answering, the wraith took hold of his arm and

yanked, stepping back and turning at the same time. The figure vaporized into the wall, sending the high-definition dust spiraling away in all directions.

Jack stumbled into the corridor. "Wait, Dad, I—" He cut himself off. At the other end of the hall, he saw Tanner. The young, wraithy version of the professor was gazing intently at a blank wall.

After a time, Ghost Tanner drew what might have been a pad from his coat and scratched at it with something that might have been a pen. Then he turned and entered another corridor. Jack raced down the hall, turned the corner to follow, and felt the ground drop beneath his feet.

"Aaaaah!"

"Hush, Jack. The police are outside, remember?" Gwen stood over him, with the tulips and gumdrops of the candy-painted ceiling standing out in sharp clarity behind her.

Sadie was there too. "Are you okay?"

He was back. With the fright of falling, Jack had thought of escape and fallen right out of the vision. "I'm fine," he said, trying to stand, but he fell back to his knee.

"You're *not* fine," said Gwen, helping him up. Then her eyes widened with concern. "Your nose, Jack."

He turned away and covered the bleeding with his

handkerchief. "It's nothing. We have to keep moving. I've got Tanner's trail." He slipped the handkerchief and the zed into his pocket, trying to push back the static resurging in his brain, and set off into the next chamber.

Jack took a left turn at the archway where he'd seen his dad and followed the short passage to Tanner's blank wall. Except the wall wasn't blank. What had been a jagged, gray emptiness in the spark was actually a huge tapestry, protected by glass and hanging above a wooden table filled with votive candles. The artist had woven the image of a battle, immortalizing an army in spiked turbans attacking a city protected by little more than a wooden wall. A line of angels hovered above the frightened villagers, each holding out a hand to stop the invaders.

"I followed Tanner to this spot," said Jack, striking a long match and lighting the candles. "He fixated on the right side of the picture for a few seconds and wrote something down."

"There's a plaque beneath the frame." Gwen held her scarf to keep it out of the flames as she leaned in to read. "'The angels of heaven turn back Tamerlane's army at the siege of Volga. Circa 1396.'" She straightened, glancing over at Jack. "Makes sense. Saint Basil's was built to commemorate Russia's freedom from khans like Tamerlane. Although it was named for a poor shoemaker that stood up to the tsar."

"A shoemaker. As in . . . a cobbler?"

Gwen raised an eyebrow. "I know, right?"

"Look. Rubies." Sadie had zeroed in on a small unit of riders near the back of Tamerlane's forces, on the right side of the tapestry.

The area was patchy, but Jack could see what remained of four multicolored banners flying in the wind. He shook his head. "Those are flags, Sadie, not jewels."

"No. She's right." Gwen fished a magnifying glass from her pocket and held it close to the tapestry. "Check out the main banner, above the lead horseman."

The foremost of the riders held his flag higher than the others. With the help of Gwen's magnifying glass, Jack could make out three red circles on a field of black, forming a triangle. He frowned. "Three circles. Three stolen rubies. That can't be a coincidence." And there was something else. He could swear there was a tiny discoloration at the center of the triangle. But the tapestry was old. There were discolorations everywhere.

"This battle took place in 1396." Gwen lowered the magnifying glass, scrunching up her brow. "The Black Prince's Ruby was in England by then. And the Russian ruby was wreaking havoc on the Chinese emperors. Even if the three rubies did start out in a mine near Tamerlane's capital, he would only have had the one piece. Why would he put all three on the flag?"

"And why does Tanner care?" asked Jack. "There's another piece to this puzzle that we're missing." He picked up a candle and turned to his right, expecting to find the corridor where he had lost the professor. The wall was covered with a heavy curtain of dusty purple velvet. He reeled back. "I . . . I could swear there was a passage here."

"There is. Look here, on the edge of the curtain—finger marks in the dust." Gwen hauled the fabric off to the side. Behind it was a staircase. "After you two."

Chapter Forty-One

AT THE BOTTOM of the staircase, Jack found a blue door marked DIMITRI A. LAZAREV, PHD.

"Our walletless archeologist," said Gwen, drawing the ID card from her pocket. She slid it into a reader on the wall.

A green light. A beep. The lock clicked.

"Basement office. Windowless door." Gwen pushed it open. "The Phantom couldn't see inside to jump. That's why Tanner needed the card."

"But why would he come here in the first place?" asked Sadie. "He has all three rubies. Why not take over the world already?"

Jack nudged her into the room after Gwen. "Let's find out."

The three of them squeezed into a tight space—so tight

that Jack had to tuck his elbows to keep from bumping his sister as he opened a filing cabinet drawer. "An archeologist who works in a broom closet in the basement of a church," he said as he picked through the papers. "That's a little odd, isn't it? Doesn't that ID say he works in a museum?"

Sadie lifted a shard of pottery from the desk, and Gwen quickly took the piece away, carefully setting it down again. "This *is* a museum, Jack. The Soviets confiscated Saint Basil's from the church decades ago and gave it to the State Historical Museum. The new Russian government never gave it back." She motioned for Jack to join her. "Over here. Have a look."

In order to comply, he had to pirouette around his sister in a little scooting dance. Artifacts of all kinds covered the desk—old books, fragments of pottery and parchment, an aquarium chemical bath filled with ancient coins. Underneath it all lay a map of the world, heavily marked and dotted with Post-its. Gwen traced a line of arrows from Samarkand to India, then out into the Pacific. "Lazarev was tracking the Timur Ruby through history."

"He tracked all three rubies," said Jack. He pushed a notebook aside and exposed another line of arrows that ran from

Turkey through Spain, up to England. "'An eastern usurper to the Moorish throne,'" he said, remembering what the archeologist's book had said about Abu Sa'id and the Black Prince's Ruby. "That's how the British crown ruby found its way to Europe." On a hunch, he eased the aquarium back and discovered yet another set of arrows originating in China, tracking west to Moscow. "And this is the path of the Russian ruby."

At the starting point of each line, Lazarev had pasted a picture. Jack tapped the one at the start of the western line, an illustration of a man dressed in furs and seated on a wooden throne. Above the throne was a long blue flag that bore a familiar device. "Check out this guy's banner."

"A triangle of red dots," said Sadie, squeezing in between them. "Just like Tamerlane's flag on the tapestry."

"And over here, too." He pointed out the picture at the origin of the Russian ruby's line, thousands of miles away in China. The man in the second illustration was sitting on a golden throne with sparrows flitting about the peak. His banner was white, yet there was a triangle of red dots at its center exactly like the others.

Gwen drew her magnifying glass and studied the captions.

She shook her head. "This can't be right. The guy in Turkey with all the fur is Batu Khan, leader of the Golden Horde. And the man on the golden throne is Kublai Khan, ruler of China. How could both kingdoms, along with Tamerlane's, share the same three-ruby emblem?"

As Jack took the glass to have a look, his sister lifted an ancient coin from the map. It left an oily blotch behind. "Ew," she said, rubbing the piece between her fingers. "It's all greasy."

"Because it came from that chemical bath in the aquarium," he said, reaching to snatch the coin away. "Sadie, that stuff might—" The moment the metal touched Jack's skin, Tanner's sinister face flashed in his mind.

The professor had held that coin.

Tanner's smirk quickly faded, replaced by yet another circle-triangle symbol. This time it formed a three-dimensional structure. Jack could see a fractured impression deep within the metal, though time had wiped all visible markings from the surface. He saw all three circles, plus a fourth, much smaller than the rest and set at the very center. With the new addition, the triangle symbol looked exactly like the drawing he had seen in Tanner's office two days before.

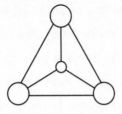

He dropped the coin back into the aquarium and watched the tiny waves it made in the chemical bath. A name wavered beneath the yellow ripples—a label taped to the bottom so that the writing could be seen through the glass.

Meanwhile, Gwen had her fingertips pressed against her temples, rocking side to side, deep in thought. Jack could see that the lack of space in the office was killing her. She preferred to pace when she was working things out.

"Three paths. Three kingdoms. Three flags," she was saying. "All using the same three-ruby symbol. Why?" Then her eyes popped open. "Because it wasn't *their* emblem. It belonged to a common ancestor who *founded* all three kingdoms. Jack, I know how the three rubies were separated. They were divided among the heirs of—"

Jack said the name with her. "Genghis Khan."

Sadie giggled.

Gwen dropped her hands, looking disappointed. "How did you know that?"

"Those are coins from his empire," said Jack, nodding at the aquarium. "And they're stamped with a symbol that I saw in Tanner's office." He found a pen and paper on the desk and started drawing. "There were four rubies, not three, with the smallest one at the center. I'm betting the small dot faded from paintings and tapestries. Over time, it was lost entirely, like a piece of a message lost in the telephone game." He held the paper up, pointing to the central dot. "*This* is why the professor came here. He's still tracking the final ruby."

Gwen took the pad from Jack's hands, tracing her finger along the lines between the circles, listing off an attribute as she touched each one. "Loyalty, command, knowledge. Genghis Khan didn't just divide up the jewels among his sons, he divided up the sources of his power. And the fourth ruby must link them all together."

"Forty million people," Jack said under his breath.

Gwen looked up from the pad. "Say again?"

"Forty million. I remember the number from our history courses. That's how many people Genghis Khan slaughtered. He made towers out of their skulls."

"Gruesome." Gwen scrunched up her face. "Do you think Tanner would be capable of such things? You know, if he managed to claim the power in all four jewels?"

Jack shook his head, remembering Nicholas and the Duke of Alencon. "The question you should be asking is will the power of the jewels claim him."

She stared at him for a long moment, then ripped the page from the notepad and stuffed it into her pocket. "We have to beat him to that fourth ruby."

"But how?" interjected Sadie. "We don't even know where to start."

"Oh yes we do." Gwen pushed Jack into another pirouette, scooting around him, and headed for the door.

Chapter Forty-Two

THE THREE HAD LEFT the urban streets of Moscow behind, heading out into the suburbs. Gwen had insisted on driving, and Jack had let her because, as usual, she wouldn't tell him where they were going. He was regretting it.

"You're squishing me again," complained Sadie, wiggling her shoulders against him.

The scooter *really* wasn't designed for three people. Jack inched backward for the umpteenth time so that his rear end hung in the cold wind. He would get frostbite on both cheeks if they didn't reach their destination soon. "Gwen!" he shouted over the wind whipping past his helmet. *"Where are we going?"*

"A library of sorts!" Gwen shouted back. "British. Centuries old."

Jack tried to scoot forward again, but Sadie reached back a hand to stop him. She hadn't even looked. Then she tapped Gwen on the shoulder. "Why is there an old British library here in Moscow?"

Gwen turned onto a long stretch of asphalt, running between swaths of snow-covered trees. "The Moscow of the eighteenth and nineteenth centuries was all kinds of British, Sadie. The tsarina was Queen Victoria's granddaughter. The Muscovy Company—a division of the Ministry of Guilds— had the biggest trading post in the city. I could go on and on."

"Well I can't!" shouted Jack. "How much farther?"

She acted as if she hadn't heard him. "There was this Scotsman, you see. Jacob Bruce. Astronomer and scientist extraordinaire. Favorite of Peter the Great and all that. The tsar made him a count and everything."

"Gwen . . ."

"He granted Count Bruce an estate. And according to legend, all sorts of wonderment occurred there, genera- tion after generation." She finally slowed and turned down a gravel road, heading for a huge yellow house with lots of white pillars. "Wooden girls walked in the garden. Flying machines rose from the back lawn. The last Bruce was said to shoot lightning from his cane."

They coasted to a stop in the circular drive, and Jack hopped off, poking his buns to check them for feeling. Gwen lowered the kickstand and removed her helmet. She gave him a freckle-bounce smile, taking on her *now-you-fill-in-the-rest* look.

"Flying machines?" asked Jack, helping his sister off the bike.

Gwen nodded.

"And lightning bolts from a cane."

"Yep."

He took off his helmet, frowning at her. "The Bruces were quartermasters. They were part of the Ministry of Trackers."

Gwen waved her hand in a grandiose arc. "Welcome to Monino, Jack. Outpost of the ministry from the mid-eighteenth century until 1917, when the Bolshevik Revolution forced them to abandon it." She shrugged. "Currently it's a summer health spa."

"You still haven't told me how this will help us catch Tanner."

"I was just getting to that." Gwen lifted the jewel case from the bike and took a path toward the back of the house. "Of course, if you'd read the histories of the ministry I gave you," she said over her shoulder, "I wouldn't have to explain."

The rear garden was quite large—pretty, in an unkempt sort of way, except for a rusty metal rail that ran down the middle. Jack stepped over it, following the girls up the porch steps.

Gwen set the jewel case down and examined a set of ornamental columns recessed into nooks along the back wall of the house. There were three, with arched doorways between them. She focused her attention on the center column. "The Bruces were station managers, Jack, and quartermasters to the Fowlers. Joe Fowler the Ninth set up shop here while hunting artifacts in the east. I suspect that's where he met his wife Saraa—your great-great-grandmother and the world's leading expert on Temujin."

"Hold on," said Jack. "Our great-grandmother?"

"Temu-who?" asked Sadie.

"Great-*great*-grandmother," said Gwen, correcting Jack. And then she gave Sadie a little wink. "Temujin was the real name of the man the world remembers as Genghis Khan. Genghis Khan was just his title—universal king or some such rubbish."

Jack looked out at the expansive garden, overgrown and abandoned for the winter. "If this place is still used as a summer health spa, then won't all of Saraa's—I mean my great-great-grandmother's—research be long gone?"

"It's copper."

"What? Her research?"

"No, you wally." Gwen had knelt beside the column. "This base. I thought it was stone like the rest of the column, but it's oxidized copper. And to answer your question, the outpost isn't inside the estate. It's underneath. I'm trying to figure out how to get down there."

Jack crouched beside her. Sure enough, the gray-green base, which had looked like the stone of the column in the dull light of the moon, was really copper. He pressed his fingers against one of three decorative bands, feeling the cold metal. It gave to his touch, turning in place. He tried the next one down. It turned as well. Each was etched with squiggly symbols. "This looks like a combination lock."

"And if I had to hazard a guess," said Gwen, "I'd say those are Mongolian letters. It's written vertically. Perhaps we need to line them up to make the right word."

Jack glanced over at her. "How many Mongolian words do you know?"

Gwen's freckles went flat. "None."

"So there's that."

She shot him a frown and then pulled Sadie over, showing

her the script. "The Bruces loved codes and clues. They would have left some for us. Look around."

While the girls searched, Jack listened to the night. There was a lot less noise this far from the city center—only the constant buzz still hovering in his mind and the white haze of the cold. But a dark, bumpy rumble had been forming beneath it all, still faint but getting louder. "I hear an engine," he said. "A car on the outer road."

"It's a motorway, Jack." Gwen lifted a dead potted plant and checked the underside. "People drive on it. Relax." She set the pot down again, looking disappointed.

"Found one." Sadie sat down in a rocking chair, rubbing one of its arms with her coat sleeve. "It's covered in mold, but I think it's one of those squiggles—a sideways *U* with two dots."

Jack saw the same symbol on the top ring. He turned it until the *U* clicked into place at the front.

Sadie squealed.

Not in a good way.

Chapter Forty-Three

JACK JUMPED TO HIS FEET. The rocking chair was empty. It was also free of mold and grime—an exact copy of the chair his sister had been sitting in but definitely not the same one. He looked to Gwen.

She shrugged. "I was watching you turn the ring."

"Jack?"

The call formed in his mind before he registered it as sound—a muted pink vapor rising out of the porch. That particular shade belonged to only one voice. "Sadie?"

"It's really dark down here."

"She's below us. We have to get down there."

"Then we'd better finish the combination." Gwen looked from the chair to the house. "Sadie found the *U* symbol opposite the first column. That can't be a coincidence." She hurried past Jack to the last column and then paced outward, crouching down when she reached the porch rail. The balusters were shaped like saints and angels. "Eureka. There's a fancy capital *E* on this angel's right wing. Third column, third ring, right?"

The approaching car had reached the intersection of the gravel road. Jack willed it to pass on by as he turned the bottom ring. The *E* symbol clicked into place.

Nothing happened.

"Perhaps you need to set the middle ring first. There's another symbol around here somewhere."

"And it's been right at my feet the whole time." Jack rubbed away the dirt from the plank between his sneakers. Within the grooves of the white-painted wood, he saw a squiggle that resembled a squished horned animal. The same symbol appeared among the script on the rings. He turned the middle band until the squished-horned beast clicked into place.

Again, nothing—at least, not from the porch.

A string of crackles and pops sounded from the other side of the house, the distinct sound of tires on gravel. Headlights washed through the trees.

"Gwen—"

"I see it."

"That'll be Ash and Shaw, and a car full of Russian police."

She wrinkled her nose at him. "Stating the obvious isn't making my brain work any faster, thank you. We lined up the symbols, top to bottom. It should have worked."

"Top to bottom," mumbled Jack. "You said Mongolian is written vertically, exactly the way the symbols line up on the rings."

"Yes. So?"

"Still dark down here." Sadie's pink, disembodied voice floated up through the planks.

Jack gave them a stomp. "I'm working on it." He pointed at each column in sequence. "We've been trying to read them left to right, like English. But what if . . ."

He closed his eyes, visualizing the items on the porch—the arm of the rocking chair, the angel wing, the squished-horned beast carved into the plank. The symbols from each one flew to the center of his vision, remaining at their respective heights. If he read them top to bottom instead of left to right, the last two symbols were reversed.

"I'm trying a different order," said Jack, and turned the middle ring so that the funny *E* from the angel wing came to the center. "Watch out for a trapdoor."

It worked. The baluster rotated, turning the angel's face to the inside. There was a light *click*. "Ha! Missed me," said Gwen, hopping backward. A trapdoor opened right where she landed, and she fell through the porch with a squeal just like Sadie's.

The driver of the car on the other side of the house shut off the engine. The headlights went out, reclaiming the shadows from the pines. Time was short. Jack picked up the jewel case and turned the final ring, clicking the squished-horned beast into place. He heard a ratcheting of gears, and a section of the floorboards at his feet started down like an elevator. But it quickly ground to a halt, leaving him shin-deep in the porch.

A car door slammed.

Gwen's face appeared at his feet, two eyes and a freckled nose. "Are you coming?"

Jack jumped up and down, pounding the planks with both heels. "Why . . . is it . . . always . . . something?"

On his fifth jump, the platform gave. The chains zipped through their pulleys, dropping him into the dark, and he stumbled off the elevator into Gwen's arms. It whooshed back up into place. A gas light, warm and yellow, sputtered to life above him.

Jack didn't move, arms still wrapped around Gwen. Even after all the adventures of the last two days—after dragon fire and borscht and the cold wind—her hair still smelled like strawberries.

"Um . . . Jack?"

"Shh. Someone's coming."

He listened for the inevitable sound of footsteps on the porch—the telltale creaking of wooden planks.

Nothing.

Maybe Ash had found the porch and garden empty and given up.

After a few more heartbeats, Jack backed away, and Gwen cleared her throat, giving him a nervous freckle bounce. "Not much of an improvement, is it?"

It wasn't. They had fallen into a rectangular room no bigger than the porch, steeped in shadow. The gas lamp cast its yellow circle down over a pedestal at the center of one wall, but gave no other light to the place. Jack caught the silhouette of a clothes rack in the corner, complete with a pair of shoes and the brown, musty scent of mothballs.

Sadie stood beneath the outline of an inverted rocking chair, arms folded. "Took you long enough."

Beneath the light, on the pedestal, stood a wooden dove

with a field of stars painted on the wall behind it. Jack recognized the scene from the necklace Sadie always wore, the heirloom their mother had given her. "That's the symbol of House Fowler," he said, and then something strange happened. As if awoken by the sound of Jack's voice, the dove opened its eyes, fluttered its wings, and cooed.

"Oh, lovely." Sadie rushed up beside her brother and stroked its beak. The dove cooed again. "I think he likes me."

"This isn't right," grumbled Gwen, pacing behind the other two. "This place should be much bigger, with more than a rack of clothes and a toy bird. Where are all the books and gadgets? Where is the—?" She stopped and let out a huff. "What kind of outpost is this?"

Jack was still inspecting the dove. The strange pattern of speckles on its chest stood out in his mind. He glanced down at his sister, who was still petting the bird. "Sadie."

She pulled her hand back. "I wasn't going to hurt him."

"I know." The four stars above the bird on his sister's necklace looked a lot like the speckles on the chest of the wooden dove. "But I think I need to borrow that pendant."

Sadie frowned.

"Just for a minute. Then I'll give it back. I promise."

After a moment's consideration, she reached behind her

neck, unhooked the clasp, and lowered the necklace into her brother's waiting hand.

"Thank you." He turned and held the pendent up beside the bird's chest, while the wooden creature watched his every move. The stars and the speckles were indeed mirror images. Jack lined them up, pressed the pendant against the bird, and a *chink* sounded inside.

The beak snapped shut.

Jack stumbled back as the bird launched itself into the air. It flew around the room, picking up speed, and then tucked its wings and dove at the wall behind the pedestal, forcing the children to duck. Jack thought it would smash itself to bits, but it shot through a hole the size of a tennis ball instead, hidden by a wooden flap.

"Well, that was something," said Gwen as all three straightened again.

"I think there's more." Jack handed the necklace back to Sadie, listening to sounds behind the walls. Huge, unseen gears clacked into motion. The wall split, right down the center of the night-sky painting, and the two halves slid apart.

Chapter Forty-Four

THE SLIDING PANELS disappeared into the walls on either side, and behind them was a staircase leading down into a long chamber filled with bookcases. Jack found a forked switch at the bottom. He threw it, and an electric *sizzle* ran away into the dark. Lanterns similar to those in the drago collection bubbled to life all about the room, the liquid inside them roiling as its yellow glow intensified.

"Books," said Gwen, walking past Jack and placing a hand on the first of many freestanding shelves.

"And gadgets." Sadie gently moved the arm of a wooden girl up and down. The life-size doll stood on an ornate box beside the stairs, half-bent at the waist, her arm outstretched as if she might straighten up to bid them welcome at any moment.

Jack was afraid she might. "Maybe you shouldn't touch that."

Books and gadgets, life-size dolls, and disturbing creatures bottled up in jars, not to mention a wooden dove fluttering around the room. Jack guessed the successive owners had been a mix of librarians, tinkers, and mad scientists—exactly as Gwen had described the generations of Count Bruces. And one of those strange men had been a good friend of his great-great-grandmother.

"This is her, I think." Gwen stood on tiptoes next to Sadie and the wooden girl, admiring a black-and-white photo on the wall. A short man with cheekbones nearly identical to Jack's had his arm wrapped around an Asian woman, whose black hair was tied back in a ponytail. The couple was standing in front of a white circular tent, with barren mountains far in the distance. They looked so happy.

Jack cocked his head. "So Saraa Fowler was—"

"Mongolian," said Gwen, lowering her heels to the ground. "I told you Joe Fowler the Ninth met her in the field. Did you think I meant a corn field?"

"But that would make me—"

"A little bit Mongolian too?" Gwen poked him in the chest. "You catch on quick. Perhaps that's where you got those eyes of yours."

He furrowed his brow. "What *about* my eyes?"

Suddenly, Gwen looked uncomfortable. "Nothing. I mean . . . they're . . . dark." She walked off, lowering her voice to a mumble. "And nice. Oo! Look here, Jack. Another picture."

Gwen's new find hung on the wall not far away, above a cluttered credenza. The painting showed a fierce mounted warrior surrounded by a small menagerie—a monkey, a tiger, and several other beasts. On the warrior's golden breastplate were four rubies, joined into the familiar triangle symbol by silver bars. The small one at the center radiated with power.

Gwen read the plaque at the base of the frame. "'Legend has it that in the travels of his youth, Temujin discovered a deep red stone at the heart of a great ruby, so dark it was almost black, like a clot of blood. It is said that this Heart of the Ruby was the source of his power. He wore it into every battle, encompassed by the shards of the jewel it came from.'"

"'The shards of the jewel it came from,'" said Jack, reading the plaque for himself. "Tanner's three rubies didn't just come from the same mine, they're all pieces of the same rock."

"And the Heart is the pulsing center that fuses their powers." Gwen sifted through the papers on the credenza. "It makes sense. The core of a giant balas ruby would be darker and denser than the rest. It would look like a blood clot."

"But the Russian jewel is a faceted egg," said Jack, setting the jewel case on the carpet beside the credenza. "And the Black Prince's Ruby is smooth. They don't look like puzzle pieces at all."

Gwen lifted a notebook, flipped through the first few pages, and set it down again. "Those shards took separate paths through eight hundred years of history, Jack. They were cut and polished multiple times. Of course they don't fit together anymore . . . although"—she picked up a jade turtle from the little shelf that ran along the back of the credenza—"three-dimensional puzzles *are* a Mongolian tradition as old as the empire itself."

She handed Jack the turtle, and he saw that it was indeed a 3-D puzzle carved from a single stone. While Gwen dug through the papers, Jack took the pieces apart. They separated easily. But when he tried putting them back together, he couldn't.

The dove alighted on the credenza shelf and cocked its head, watching him struggle.

He gave the bird a frown. "It's harder than it looks, okay?" Then he glanced over at Gwen. "If the rubies don't fit anymore, how does Tanner plan to link them?"

"Haven't the foggiest." She gave up on the papers and set off into the library. "What's more important is figuring out what Temujin did with the Heart."

Jack set his sad Humpty Dumpty turtle down on the desk and followed.

There were rows and rows of bookshelves decorated with Asian artwork—hangings showing Temujin and his menagerie, blue-and-white vases, jade bowls and statues. Jack eyed a pair of dragon bookends. Each jade beast held a swirl of silver flame in its talons. He remembered what had happened in the Moscow safe house. Raven's comment, whether real or dreamt had stayed with him. He cleared his throat. "Um . . . what do you know about the dragos?"

Gwen stopped and turned to face him, narrowing her eyes as if she had been waiting for the question for a good long while. "Why do you ask?"

"Just . . . curious, I guess."

Gwen chuckled. "Right." She started walking again, letting her fingers drift along the books. "Rumors, Jack. Myths. The dragos keep their secrets well. Some say they can breathe fire, and that's where their scars come from." She glanced at Jack sidelong. "Others say they can speak the dragon language."

"There's a dragon language?"

Gwen shrugged. "Like I said. Rumors. Myths. My favorite theory is that the few dragos with abilities are the descendants of Arthur and Merlin—bloodlines that have become thin and convoluted over the centuries. Arthurians can manipulate fire with a sort of telekinesis. Merlinians can read minds and perhaps predict the future. Some say most of those split off to become the Ministry of Secrets."

"Arthurians," said Jack, trying to get the feel of the word. He tried the other one. "Merlinians. Have you ever . . . seen any of these people?"

She raised an eyebrow. "We both have. Ignatius Gall is one. Arthurian, Merlinian—I've heard it both ways."

"But Gall is a spook. That would make him a Merlinian."

"He is *now*." They came to a collection of silver busts all labeled *Jacob Bruce,* and Gwen paused to examine their wild hairdos and impish expressions. "Gall switched his allegiance to the Ministry of Secrets years ago. I'm betting he was a spy for them long before that. I told you he was connected, Jack."

A glint of brass flashed in Jack's peripheral vision. He looked back toward the stairs and saw his sister climbing up behind the big wooden doll. Sadie teetered on the edge of the doll's base, holding a giant winding key over her head. Jack broke into a run to try to catch her. "Sadie, get down. You're going to fall."

She didn't. Sadie managed to keep her balance and to slide the key into a slot in the doll's back. She wound it several times before Jack could rush over and stop her. After a final ratcheting *click*, she hopped down.

"Sadie," said Jack, jogging up to his sister, "you have to stop playing with—"

The doll turned to face them. Paper-thin eyelids shot open, revealing black, glassy eyes.

"Oh. Not good," said Jack, pulling his sister away.

Gwen skidded to a stop beside him. "Wooden girls in the garden," she said with excitement. "The stories were true."

The doll jumped down, landed in a half squat, and then slowly straightened, joints squeaking from a century of no use. She regarded Gwen with her empty gaze. "Good evening, Dr. Fowler. How may I assist you?"

Chapter Forty-Five

"AAANND IT SPEAKS." Jack inched his sister back a little more. *"Doctor Fowler? Joe Fowler Nine was a doctor?"*

Gwen slapped his arm. "Not him, you chauvinistic wally. *Her.* Saraa Fowler was the doctor—the professor kind." She glanced at the waiting automaton. "And it seems she thinks I'm her." Gwen thought for a moment and then addressed the wooden girl. "Ah . . . forgive me, but I'm afraid I've forgotten your name."

Something clacked inside the girl's chest, like a Rolodex flipping through wooden cards. She blinked. "I am Marta, the first of two humaniform creations made by the second Count Bruce. My sister Margery manages the garden, while I assist in the library. As a secondary function, we are both designed for security."

Her mouth snapped shut. That seemed to be all Marta had to say on the subject.

"She's like C-3PO," said Sadie, clapping her hands.

"Yeah." Jack leaned forward, squinting at the lifelike face. "A creepy wooden C-3PO."

Gwen slapped his arm again.

"What? Tell me this isn't weird."

"Marta," said Gwen, taking Jack by the shoulders and moving him aside. "Can you direct me to my research on Temujin's blood clot? It may also be filed under the Heart of the Ruby."

The doll's internal Rolodex flipped through its cards. She blinked. "The Heart of the Ruby, a possible heirloom of Genghis Khan." Without warning, she set off, marching toward the bookshelves. "You will want the Tomb Room."

"The Tomb Room. Sweet." Sadie raced after her, catching the doll's hand and mimicking the stiffness of her march. "This I have to see."

The Tomb Room? Jack mouthed the question to Gwen as he retrieved the jewel case.

Gwen slapped her forehead. "*Temujin's* tomb. It was never found, Jack. Any Genghis Khan researcher worth her salt would have a tomb file." She hurried off after the other two. "Come on."

By the time Jack and Gwen caught up, Marta and Sadie were waiting for them on a circular platform beneath a giant glasswork dome. The odd pair—expressionless wooden automaton and bright-eyed little girl—stood behind a semi-circular control panel that wrapped around a huge column, framed in brass and filled with water. An empty ironwood moat surrounded the whole thing, passing beneath a bridge at the entrance. "The Tomb Room," said Marta with a sweep of her hand.

Jack stopped Gwen halfway across the bridge. "Why should we look for the khan's tomb? I thought we needed to find his fourth heir—the one who would have inherited the fourth ruby."

"That's what I thought too," said Gwen. "But Temujin was an animist. Spirits of the earth, circle of life, and all that. If the Heart was the source of his power, he might have thought it was part of his spirit."

"Sooo, that means the Heart had to be buried with him to complete the circle of life?"

Gwen gave him an *I'm-just-that-good* smirk. "Exactly." Then she turned and continued across the bridge. "Marta, how does the Tomb Room work?"

Marta made a stiff gesture at the moat. "Just add water."

Sadie was already on it. She cranked a big brass wheel, and a short wall of water rushed around the moat, sloshing over the bridge right where Jack stood.

His toes squished in his sneakers as he crossed the rest of the way to the control platform. "Thanks."

Sadie shrugged. "You're welcome."

No sooner had the water settled than the moat began to hum. Ultrafine mist rose beneath the dome. Jack heard the distinctive whir of several reel-to-reel cameras, and projections shot out from lenses all around the moat, catching in the mist. Mountainous terrain materialized in three dimensions of black and white.

"It's a holographic projector," said Gwen, turning in a slow circle.

"From the turn of the twentieth century," said Jack.

"Sweet," said Sadie.

——————· Chapter Forty-Six ·——————

THE ROLODEX inside Marta flipped through its cards. "The Photo-nebulizer Projection Room was created by the third Count Bruce in 1913," she said, "to aid Dr. Fowler's research. She renamed it the Tomb Room because, as she put it, the phrase 'Photo-nebulizer Projection Room' gave her a pounding headache."

"Marta." Gwen circled her finger around a series of small red blotches that had formed in the mist. "What are these red markings?"

"Those are your potential tomb sites, Dr. Fowler, in Mongolia's forbidden zone—thought to be the birthplace of Temujin. You and your husband took great pains to mark these sites on aerial photos before feeding them into the projectors."

Jack took a closer look at the nearest dots, immediately noticing a common thread. "And why are all the tomb sites near streams and brooks?"

The Rolodex clacked again. The doll turned to regard him with her black eyes. "There are four features found in multiple legends about Temujin's tomb. One: he wanted to be buried at his birthplace—although the Mongolian term used in most cases is better translated as *origin*. Two: his personal guard diverted a river to conceal the entrance. Three: his three greatest subjects bow before him for all eternity. And four: his favorite hawk keeps watch for tomb raiders. All of Dr. Fowler's sites meet criteria one and two. The other features are more difficult to match."

"There are so many," said Gwen, walking from dot to dot. "Saraa spent her whole life looking, and she never found the right one. How are we supposed to do it?"

As she spoke, the wooden dove flew into the mist beneath the dome, interrupting the conversation. Marta swatted at him. "Silly bird. Shoo. Shoo, I say."

The dove dodged her and sailed around the center column, and something about the circular trail it left in the mist stuck in Jack's brain—a phrase Gwen had spoken earlier. He glanced over at her, raising an eyebrow.

"Genghis Khan was obsessed with the circle of life, right?"

"Your wife has already mentioned that, Mr. Fowler," said Marta, taking another swing at the bird.

Sadie poked him in the arm, snickering. "Your *wife*."

The dove flew out the way it had come in and Marta stood at the edge of the bridge, watching it go, hands on her wooden hips.

Gwen touched Jack's elbow. "What've you got?"

"You said Temujin considered his spirit and the spirit of the Heart to be as one. And Marta said he wanted to be buried at his origin—not his birthplace, his *origin*."

"The origin of his *power*." Gwen locked her eyes with his. "The origin of the ruby that he broke into the four stones."

"Tajikistan," they both said together.

Gwen turned to their wooden assistant. "Marta, can you show us Tajikistan?"

"I am not familiar with that term," said the wooden girl, returning from the bridge.

"Right. Of course not. You think it's 1917." Gwen raised her palms to her temples, as if trying to squeeze the right word out of her brain. "Aaaaahhhummm." She snapped her fingers. "Badakhshan! That's the one. Marta, can you show us the Badakhshan mine region?"

"Badakhshan. Yes. Joseph Fowler Eight and Nine photo-graphed much of Central Asia from the second Count Bruce's flying machine." Marta flicked a toggle and turned a pair of knobs on the control bank. The black-and-white terrain shot up into the mist and vanished, replaced by a flat aerial photograph of more mountains, curving around the chamber. "Here we are."

Gwen scanned the map. *"His three greatest subjects bow before him,"* she muttered. "Three greatest . . ."

"There." Jack pointed to the intersection of three hills, converging in a valley. "The great subjects are hills, bowing at his tomb. The intersection marks the gravesite."

"Good thought," said Gwen, "but there's no river." She paced the edge of the platform, moving westward across the map, deeper into the mountainous terrain. "Marta, can you superimpose a map of known ruby mines?"

The wooden girl flipped another toggle and a faded map of the Badakhshan mines appeared, superimposed over the aerial photo.

"Now we're talking." Gwen waved a hand over the periphery of the mines. "It would be close, sharing the same vein of minerals but lost to the maps of the twentieth century." She pointed at another meeting of three hills, with a glade between them. "Here. And there's a stream as well."

"There are a lot of streams." Jack stepped up beside her. "What makes you like this one?"

Gwen traced a finger along the flow of water, cutting straight downhill from a river that meandered east to west through the higher terrain. "How many natural mountain streams have you seen that run in a straight line?"

"'His personal guard diverted a river to conceal the entrance,'" said Jack, quoting Marta. "They dug a channel from the river."

Gwen nodded to the wooden girl. "Marta, if you would, please? We need to see the three-dimensional view of these coordinates."

"You have chosen thirty-eight degrees, twenty-six minutes north, seventy-three degrees, two minutes east." Using the controls, she turned the map on its edge to form a disk around the platform and then stretched it down into a three-dimensional view.

As Marta zoomed in on the spot, the mountains rushed toward them, giving Jack the feeling of flying up the twisting valley between the northernmost hills. The image came to a halt, and there at the base of the southern hill, hanging over the stream, was a beaklike formation of rock.

"'His favorite hawk keeps watch for tomb raiders.'" Jack turned his back to the map to stare at Gwen and Sadie. "Did we just find Genghis Khan's tomb?"

Someone clapped from the library outside the dome—a slow, deliberate, mocking clap. "I believe you did, my boy. I believe you did."

Gwen's eyes narrowed in anger.

Jack spun and saw Edward Tanner standing on the other side of the moat.

The professor laughed. "And I can't tell you how much I appreciate the effort."

—·Chapter Forty-Seven·—

JACK SQUARED OFF at the edge of the bridge, opposite his mentor. "You have a lot to answer for, Tanner."

The wheelchair was nowhere in sight. The professor stood straight and tall, without that absurd blanket that had always lain across his perfectly good legs. Beneath his open coat, he now wore a shirt of gold chain mail, with a triangle of rubies and silver bars on his chest that matched the device Temujin was wearing in the painting—except Tanner's device was missing the center jewel.

Jack could feel the Black Prince's Ruby calling to him, the same way it had called to him in the Vault. He felt compelled to rescue it from Tanner's evil clutches. It dawned on him that the Duke of Alencon had likely felt the same about Henry at Agincourt, and Don Pedro had probably felt the same about Abu Sa'id when the Moorish delegation came to Castile. The ruby put out a kind of beacon that turned man against man—loyalty perverted. Jack gritted his teeth.

Tanner read his expression. "Are you feeling the loyalty, Jack? That aggressive, mindless allegiance to a shiny object? You would kill me for it if I let you."

Kill? Would Jack ever kill a man over a jewel, as those men at Agincourt had killed one another? He felt the steely cold of a hilt in his palm and glanced down. He was holding Britain's Sword of State. The jewel case lay open at his feet. Jack had no memory of popping the catches or drawing out the weapon. Yet, there it was in his hand.

And why not?

Would it be so wrong to run Tanner through? The man had betrayed and murdered Jack's grandfather. He had murdered Raven and her brother.

Jack raised the king-size weapon, gripping the golden hilt with two hands. "This ends *now*," he said, and started across the bridge.

Gwen followed, towing Sadie behind her. "Careful, Jack. Don't do anything you'll regret."

Regret? He laughed—right out loud. He wasn't going to regret this.

Tanner raised his hands in mock surrender, retreating through the shelves. "That's it, Jack. Show me your darkest thoughts. But don't come too close." He pushed out a palm.

Jack froze. His legs refused to move. His arms and torso were free, but from the waist down his muscles felt as if they had turned to stone.

Sadie and Gwen were stuck as well—one beside the other—with Gwen at Jack's shoulder. Gwen tugged at her own leg, trying to pull her foot off the floor. "Jack, what's happening?"

"'The power to command men,' Miss Kincaid." Tanner waved his other hand across the Timur Ruby. It was the only one of the three stones etched with script—Persian, maybe Hindi. "Many rulers tried to claim that power by carving their names into the stone. Fools. Only a strong mind can control it. A mind like mine."

"You're . . . wrong," grunted Jack, still fighting the strange energy holding his legs in place. "You aren't controlling these gems. They're controlling you. Take them off before they destroy you."

"Nice try, my boy. But I don't think so." Tanner turned

his hand and curled his fingers, bringing Jack a step closer. "You're right in one sense. I do not have full control. At the moment I can only bend a few muscle groups to my will—your legs, for instance, and those of Miss Kincaid and your sister. I cannot take the full power of command without the spirit of Genghis Khan waiting within the fourth ruby, just as I cannot take the full power of knowledge or loyalty from the other two." He grinned. "But that is no longer a problem. Thanks to you, I now have the location of his tomb."

"You're cracked," said Gwen. "You've completely lost the plot."

"Have I, my dear? Or have I been driving it from the very start? You three have followed every step of the path I laid out for you. I know"—he removed a gold-plated cylinder from his coat and pressed a button on its top—"I've been watching."

Gwen let out a scream. The left pocket of her coat began to bulge and squirm. Frantically, she reached in and tossed away a leather pouch. It landed on the carpet several feet away, shifting and wriggling.

Jack could see she wanted to back away from it, but she couldn't. "That's the bag of guild coin from the Phantom's desk," he said. "The one Raven waved in front of us at the tinker's place. She tricked us into taking it."

Gwen gave a disgusted shudder. "You mean she tricked *me*."

One of the shiny cubes rolled out onto the carpet, followed by another, and then another, and more until a small army of gold, silver, and copper guild coin had lined itself up in a semicircle. All at once, they cracked open.

Sadie moaned. "Ugh. Spiders."

The edges of the cubes became legs, eight each, some with tiny jewels at their peaks, and the abdomens were glass vials filled with syrupy green liquid. The heads were mostly gears and lenses—and long, glistening fangs. Jack had seen a similar creature in his mind while waiting to enter the arena. He had written it off as delusion. He should have known better. "Where did you get those?"

"A gift from a benefactor," said Tanner. "An investment, if you will, by one who thinks he can control me. He has no idea how wrong he is."

A benefactor. Jack thought back to his spark at the Ministry of Secrets, when he had seen the man with the clockwork eye hand a case to the Phantom. He clenched his teeth. "Gall."

Tanner neither confirmed nor denied Jack's suspicion. "My spiders kept me informed of your progress," he said, waving the control cylinder, "as I nudged you from one step to the next. I didn't follow you here. Much to the contrary. I was waiting under the porch when you arrived—waiting for Jack to unlock the library and find Temujin's tomb. Well done on all counts, boy, but I think you've finally outlived your usefulness." He pressed another button, and the centermost spider reared back and hissed.

"Wait." Gwen held up a hand. "Just . . . wait a minute." Jack could see Gwen was stalling, but it worked. The spiders backed off. "If you were already under the porch," she said, "then who was it that drove up in the car as we came in?"

A wolf's-head cane swung out from behind a bookshelf, hitting Tanner behind the knees. He slammed down onto his back with a pained *Oomph*.

Ash stepped into the open and stood over him, the butt of his cane at Tanner's neck. "That'd be me."

──· Chapter Forty-Eight ·──

THE MOMENT Tanner hit the ground, Jack regained control of his legs. He rushed the spiders, scattering them in all directions.

Shaw appeared next to Ash. "Mrs. Hudson'll be wantin' this," he said, thick fingers going straight for the Black Prince's Ruby.

"No, Shaw!" shouted Jack. "Restrain him first. He's got—"

He was too late. Tanner zipped away across the carpet, a blue-white glow at each heel. He was still wearing the ankle thrusters. With the grace of a superhero, he righted himself and landed halfway up the steps to the entrance. He raised a hand, and the teens and Sadie all froze.

"I can't move my legs," said Shaw, looking frantically down at his wingtips.

Gwen shot him a frown. "Yes. We know."

The spiders skittered out from under the shelves and desks, surrounding them in a tightening circle of pure creepiness.

Jack's eyes went to Sadie, who was clutching her arms to her chest as if trying to squeeze herself out of existence before the bugs could get to her. "Don't, Professor," he begged. "Please."

But Tanner only grinned—with the same malice as the tsar in the snowy square. Perhaps the Russian ruby had shown him how to deal with young trackers, quartermasters, and wardens the way it had shown Nicholas how to deal with rebellious troops. This fight could get just as ugly.

The clockwork spiders reached Marta first. Two of them spiraled up her body and settled on her shoulders, wasting no time before sinking gold-and-silver fangs into her neck. The green syrup drained from their glass abdomens.

"Oh, Marta," groaned Gwen, reaching for her.

But Marta showed no ill effects. She scowled at the creatures and picked them both up by their back legs. "You are a threat to this station," she said. "You will be terminated." And then she crumpled them in her palms and dropped the remains into a waste bin.

"Oh. Right." Gwen glanced over at Jack and rolled her eyes. "She's made of wood."

Marta wasn't bound by the power of the Timur Ruby, either. She immediately began stomping at the other bugs. "You are a threat to this station. You will be terminated." It seemed the biting spiders had activated her security function.

Jack played a hunch. "Marta, Tanner brought those things in here. *He* is the threat."

Marta's foot stopped an inch above a cowering spider. Her Rolodex clacked. "Edward Tanner. Tracker. Ministry authorization nine four seven six."

Gwen nodded, catching on. "That's right. He's a tracker, Marta. But he's a traitor. Listen to me. Listen to *Saraa Fowler*. Edward Tanner is trying to kill us."

The Rolodex buzzed, going into overdrive, and then stopped. "Edward Tanner . . . traitor." A blue glow ignited behind Marta's eyes. The narrow wood panels that formed her shoes, calves, dress, and arms flipped over, exposing bronze plating. Her knuckles flipped last, capped with spikes. She clenched her fists, finished her stomp, grinding the spider into the carpet, and then marched toward the stairs. "Edward Tanner, you are a threat to this station."

Tanner backed up two steps.

"You will be terminated."

"Uh-oh," said Ash, swatting a spider away with his cane. "I think you're in trouble, Professor."

Undaunted by the threat to its master, a spider leaped at Sadie. She raised an arm and screamed, but the creature never landed. The wooden bird swooped down and caught it midair, wings, talons, and beak flipping to bronze to match Marta. It ripped its captive in two, wheeled around, and dove at Tanner.

Ash grinned. "Yeah. You're definitely in trouble."

Tanner seemed to agree. He ran up the steps.

The remaining spiders abandoned their attacks on the children and scurried after Marta.

"A nuisance," Tanner called over his shoulder, waving his arms to protect himself from the bird. "That's all." He reached the top and clawed at the elevator platform, hauling it down. "I am the successor of the Great Khan. I will stand against whole armies. You cannot stop me with wooden toys."

His threat seemed a little empty, given the scene unfolding.

Marta reached him, spiders hanging from every limb, and cocked her spiked fist for a right cross. But Tanner launched himself through the opening, and the elevator slammed into place behind him. She lowered her fists to her sides. "And stay out!"

"Well done," said Ash, tipping his cap.

With Tanner gone, the spiders dropped from the wooden girl and flooded down the stairs.

Jack sidestepped to protect his sister. "I can move," he said, slashing at a jumping arachnid with his sword. He clipped a leg, diverting its trajectory. It landed on seven legs and immediately renewed its attack.

Gwen stomped it into the carpet. "We all can, now that Tanner's gone. But I wouldn't get too excited. This is far from over."

Three of the creatures assaulted Shaw but could not penetrate his tweed coat. The big warden brushed them down his arm into a pile and crushed them under his heel. Sparks flew out from either side of his shoe. Beside him, Ash was knocking spiders away left and right.

Jack stayed close to Sadie, trying to breathe, trying to see. But he had trouble anticipating the spiders' movements. There was too much static in his head. Each attacking creature got closer to victory until, finally, Jack missed one completely, slicing the air beneath its copper legs as it leaped for his face, fangs at the ready.

Gwen's scarf snapped out. The creature flew across the room and slammed into the wall, glass abdomen shattering. It left an oozing green trail as it slid down onto the credenza.

"Thanks," said Jack, catching his breath.

"Don't mention it." Gwen wrapped her scarf in multiple loops around her neck with one graceful motion. "Was that the last one?"

Ash nodded, leaning on his cane and breathing hard. "Think so."

"You are a threat to this station. You will be terminated."

"Or not," said Jack.

He glanced over his shoulder to see Marta marching toward him, spiked knuckles raised like a boxer. With a sudden, cold rush down his spine, he realized she wasn't coming for him. Spiked feet dug into his leather jacket, prickling his back. A huge golden spider, with emeralds at the apex of each leg, crawled over his shoulder. It was going for the exposed flesh at his neck.

Sadie's hand snapped out before Marta could reach them.

Jack swatted at his sister's arm. "Sadie, no!"

Too late. She plucked the spider from his shoulder by its glass vial and tried to toss it away. The eight legs flipped backward and latched onto her finger. She couldn't shake it loose.

The creature's head rotated in place, golden fangs gleaming in the dull light of the liquid lanterns.

Sadie screamed in pain.

—— · Chapter Forty-Nine · ——

JACK SMASHED THE SPIDER away from his sister's hand with the hilt of his sword, and the creature bounced across the carpet, legs curled against its half-empty abdomen. As soon as it landed, the legs uncurled and reversed, pressing their spiked ends into the carpet.

Gears whirred.

Joints clicked.

It jumped.

Jack took a blind swing, and legs, gears, and glass flew in all directions.

It was over.

He let out a long breath, sliding his sword into his belt. But then he heard Sadie moan behind him. Jack turned and saw his sister sinking to her knees. "Sadie?"

Ash and Gwen ran to her side, easing her down.

"No. No, no, no." Jack took his sister's hand. The bite marks on her finger were swollen and red. A trace of green syrup still lingered between them. He wiped it away and kissed the injury. "Why did you do that?"

Sadie gave him a weak smile. "I told you that you'd need me."

He nodded, tears welling in his eyes. "You found the symbol on the tapestry. You gave me the key that got us into the library. You brought Marta to life so we could find the location of Temujin's tomb. I did need you. I'll always need you. So don't go anywhere." Her eyes were closing. Jack patted her hand until they fluttered open again. "You hear me, Sadie? Don't go."

Shaw stared up at the elevator. "The pr'fessor's gettin' away. If anyone cares."

"Quiet, Shaw," said Gwen, glowering at the warden. "Give us a minute."

"I'm just sayin', is all."

Neither Ash nor Jack paid him any heed. The quarter-master wrapped Sadie's forearm with a silk handkerchief, tying it tight. "This will slow the spread of the poison. But it won't stop it."

Gwen pressed a hand to Sadie's cheek. "She's cold. She needs a hospital. Fast."

Jack's mind was spinning. His face and limbs tingled with a thousand pinpoints. He had to get himself together. He draped his sister's arm over his shoulder. "Help me get her up. I'm getting her out of here."

Ash helped him lift her, but he placed a gentle hand on Jack's arm. "You can't be the one to take her, Jack. The Russians are still looking for you, remember? You won't get anywhere near a hospital."

"A hospital won't do her no good, anyway," added Shaw. "It's poison. In the blood. Nothin'll stop it but an antidote."

Gwen glared at him. "I told you to be quiet, Shaw. You're not help—" She stopped, the frustration in her eyes fading. "No. Wait. You *are* helping. Well *done*, Shaw."

Jack watched her carefully, grasping at the hope in her voice. "What do you mean?"

"Tanner said those spiders came from a 'benefactor.'" Gwen made air quotes with her fingers. "That *has* to be Gall, a spook, and spooks have rules just like trackers. Mo-Mos, book two, chapter eleven: Assassination, Subterfuge, and Sabotage. Rule twenty-six states that any agent carrying poison must *always* carry the antidote, for their own protection."

"The case in Arthur's quarters," said Jack, nodding slowly. "The one he got from Gall. There were pockets in the foam— square cutouts for the spider-cubes and an equal number of circle cutouts for the vials of green poison . . . but there was an extra pocket." He closed his eyes, trying to remember what he had seen Arthur handing to Tanner when he spotted them in the arena—the gold control cylinder for the spiders and . . . "The antidote is a vial of blue syrup. Tanner has it. I know he does."

He started for the steps with Sadie, Ash supporting her on the other side. "Get my sister to a hospital," he said to the quartermaster. "Maybe they can stabilize her—delay the poison while we go after Tanner."

Ash narrowed his eyes. "Shaw can do that. I should go with you."

Jack shot a glance back at the warden, whose thick lips spread into a forced helpful smile. Jack shook his head. "Uh . . . no." He pointed at the dome of the Tomb Room. "The rest of the Crown Jewels are over there. I'll trust Shaw with those but not my sister."

Shaw's smile dropped away. "Too funny." He tromped back to the dome to recover the case. "An' 'ow do you propose to go after the pr'fessor, eh?" he called over his shoulder.

"Airport? Trains? Buses? Wherever you go, the police'll be waitin'. You can't leave the city."

"Yes we can." Gwen followed the others up the steps with Marta beside her. "As I told Jack when the hyperloop exploded, there's another way out of Moscow." They reached the top and she nodded to the wooden girl, whose bronze plating was in the process of flipping out of sight. "Marta, we need to borrow Count Bruce's flying machine."

Chapter Fifty

JACK STEPPED OUT of the way as Marta marched over to the corner beneath the upside-down rocking chair.

"Margery won't be happy," she said, holding up her index finger. The tip folded back, revealing a brass key. "She hates it when the count and I disturb her garden." Marta inserted the key into a keyhole and turned it. The wall split and slid open, exactly as the opposite wall had earlier, and Jack caught his breath.

More liquid lanterns roiled to life, illuminating an underground hangar far deeper than the library. A zeppelin hovered at the center, straining against its lines as if the long dead count had taken it for a spin the night before. A great band of some copper alloy formed the central fuselage, with bundles of flared pipes for thrusters and a long, sleek gondola beneath. The gas envelope, pointed at both ends, was made of ribbed purple fabric and decorated with gold geometric figures.

"The counts were nothing if not flamboyant." Gwen started down a wrought-iron staircase that joined a catwalk several flights below.

"Wait," Jack called after her. "Do you even know how to fly that thing?"

"It's an airship, Jack. How hard can it be?"

Marta turned a crank fixed to gears and chains hanging down from the ceiling, and Jack finally understood the purpose of the rusted rail in the garden above. It was the seam of a retractable roof. Two huge panels folded back like accordions, letting in the moonlight and dropping dirt and shrubs into the bay. "Oh dear," said Marta, locking the crank in place. "Margery has let her garden go."

The wrought-iron staircase Gwen had taken down to the catwalk also had a flight going up to the garden. Shaw was already on his way up. Ash, one arm supporting Sadie, offered Jack a hand. "I'm sorry I doubted you."

"I gave you every reason to." Jack clasped his forearm, gripping his shoulder with the other hand. He gave Ash the coordinates of the tomb and made him promise to bring Sadie to him if and when the Russian doctors got her stabilized.

"Are you sure you won't let Shaw do all of that? I should be with you, Jack. Tanner is dangerous, and I guarantee you that tomb is booby-trapped. You'll need a quartermaster."

Jack looked down at Gwen, who was unraveling a mooring line as if she had launched an airship every day of her life.

She glanced up at him and offered a crisp British salute.

He saluted her back. "I've already got one."

A few minutes later, Marta released the final line and waved from the bottom of the hangar. Jack and Gwen waved back from the flight deck, and the airship rose into the night. Once they were well into the air, the garden roof closed beneath them, cutting them off from the warm yellow light of the count's library. And with a burst of blue flame from the pipes, they were off.

Jack walked aft along the cabin's deep bay windows, watching the count's estate pass behind. When they were high enough, he found the main road and Ash's car speeding toward Moscow with his sister. He pressed a hand against the glass.

Once the car was out of sight, he lowered his hand again, and it came to rest on the golden hilt at his belt. "Huh," he said, glancing down absentmindedly. "I forgot to put the sword back in the jewel case."

"Not to worry. You might still have a use for it." Gwen looked back at him as she adjusted the big navigation wheel. "Come up front and help me search for Tanner. He'll be headed southeast—perhaps making for a train station or an airfield. If we can intercept him, we can get Sadie the antidote that much sooner."

Jack nodded and took a few steps toward the flight deck, but the tingling he had first felt when Sadie collapsed was back. A million silvery pinpoints pressing into every square inch of him, as if his whole body was phasing away. His knees buckled and he had to catch the rail that ran along the windows.

"All right. All right." Gwen ran back to catch his elbow and guided him the rest of the way. "Are you sure you weren't nicked by that spider? You look worse than ever."

He looked up at her, scrunching up his face. "Thanks. I appreciate that."

"You know what I mean." She lowered him into the plush captain's chair behind the wheel. "I'm serious, Jack."

"It wasn't the spiders."

"No. You're right. You were like this before we got to

Count Bruce's library. You had that nosebleed at the cathedral. What's going on?" She stared at him hard, waiting for a response.

He didn't give her one.

Beyond the windscreen lay the empty, snow-covered forests of eastern Russia, colored pink by the sun peeking over the horizon. The view would have been breathtaking if Jack didn't have so much riding on his shoulders and so little of himself left to face it. He saw no cars on the few winding roads ahead—no sign of Tanner.

"Jack." Gwen folded her arms, still waiting.

"There's something I've never told you, something about the night we rescued my dad from the Clockmaker." He drew the zed from his pocket, letting its gold lace catch the light coming in through the window. The image of his dad returned to him, slumped over in that wheelchair at the top of Big Ben, face burned and swollen. "He spoke to me."

"You *thought* he spoke to you, Jack. I was there. Your dad was already in his coma."

Jack set the zed down on a flat leather pad that ran along the base of the controls. "Through this," he continued, ignoring her argument, "the zed. It connected us, Gwen. My dad talked to me. He told me to leave him there and go stop the Clockmaker. Since then, it's helped me boost my fading abilities, but every time I use it, I get . . ."

Gwen touched his shoulder. "Weaker."

He nodded.

"Where does it come from, Jack?"

"I . . . I don't know."

"You must know something. You know its name."

"No. I don't. I mean . . . I made it up. There was a funny sort of Z drawn on a folded paper in the spot where I found it."

"A funny Z?" Gwen snapped up a piece of chalk from a small blackboard embedded in the control panel and pressed it into Jack's hand. "Draw it. Now."

He leaned over the wheel and did as she asked.

She shook her head. "No. No. That's not right." Gwen erased the symbol with her sleeve and snatched the chalk away, drawing her own version. It looked the same, except canted sideways. "Like this. Right?"

Jack didn't see much difference. "Um . . . sure."

"That's not a Z, Jack. It's a symbol, one that trackers and quartermasters use *all* the time."

Jack was tired. His sister was on the edge of death. And he and Gwen were drifting toward a confrontation with a maniacal tracker bent on channeling the spirit of the world history record-holder for most millions slaughtered. At that particular moment, he didn't need Gwen's condescending *everyone-knows-this-but-you* attitude. "Fine. You're smarter than me. I get it. So enlighten me. What does this oh-so-common symbol mean?"

Gwen let out a huff at the rebuke, and then she turned and hovered over the blackboard, making an exaggerated tap, tap, tapping with her chalk as she drew another symbol. "Only this."

Jack stared at the board.

She had drawn a skull and crossbones.

────·Chapter Fifty-One ·────

JACK SANK BACK against the cushion. "Poison?"

Gwen flung the chalk at him. "It means danger, you wally—as in dangerous bend, watch out, use caution. Scientists and mathematicians use it in proofs to say, 'Something here is not what it seems.' As you can imagine, the Ministry of Trackers finds uses for it all the time."

"'Not what it seems,'" he repeated, eyeing the zed.

"Exactly. You think that stone boosts your abilities, but what it's really doing is taking them. Jack, that thing is eating you alive."

He grimaced, wondering how close *eating you alive* came to the truth. The winter hills outside had turned from gray to white as the sun climbed higher. The shadows of the trees had shortened, and he felt the passage of time closing in on him like a vise. Jack put the zed away, out of sight. "Let's focus on Tanner. How do you think he plans to get to the tomb?"

"As I said before, a train—a plane, perhaps. The distance is too great for an automobile. Eastern Russia doesn't have too many petrol stations. What we need to do is determine his jumping-off point, so to speak." She bowed her head, drumming her fingertips against her temples. "Tanner claimed he's been guiding our steps, right? He steered us to Count Bruce's estate."

"If that was his game all along, he would have had transportation ready somewhere near . . ." Jack's eyes drifted across the hills. "There." He pointed at a swath cut through the trees, just coming into view. An airfield lay nestled in a shallow valley.

Gwen slapped the arm of his chair. "Private jet. That's how Tanner is getting to the tomb." Even as she spoke, a little black aircraft lifted off, cleared the hilltops, and turned southeast. "That *has* to be him." She punched Jack's arm. "We're right on his tail."

He winced, rubbing the spot. "You *really* have to stop that."

The aircraft pulled away in its climb, leaving the count's

centuries-old zeppelin crawling behind. Jack shook his head. "We're moving at the speed of a flying turtle here. We'll never catch him."

"Is that so?" Gwen reached up and grabbed the lever of a circular control that hung down from the ceiling, with labels like *all stop* and *cruise*. She shifted a big brass arrow all the way to *ahead full*, causing a quaint little *ching*.

The airship continued its slow crawl across the landscape.

Jack opened his mouth to say something snide, but then a *chunk, chunk, chunk* filled the cabin. Air hissed through the spaghetti of pipes in the rafters above them.

Turning in his seat, he could see the zeppelin's fabric envelope expanding. The aft section of the copper fuselage shifted back, lengthening the central section. And from the pocket behind the separating halves, great bat wings folded down. The dark blue fabric on the underside of the left wing was painted with a red griffin. The right wing bore a silver hound. The airship had transformed into a sleek, winged hybrid.

"From the second Count Bruce's coat of arms," said Gwen, nodding at the giant creatures painted on the wings. "On top of the flamboyance, he was a bit of an egomaniac."

Jack stood and leaned into the windscreen to check Tanner's progress. The black jet was barely a speck. "Great," he said. "We look a whole lot cooler now. But we're *still*—"

A light *ding* from the console interrupted his complaint. A green placard flashed READY.

Gwen placed five fingertips on his chest and shoved him back into the captain's chair. She flumped down beside him, scooched him over with her hip, and rested her thumb against a big brass toggle.

She pumped her eyebrows. "I wasn't finished yet."

Chapter Fifty-Two

GWEN FLIPPED THE TOGGLE, unleashing a roar from the pipes and a burst of acceleration that pressed them both back into the cushion.

With his jumbled tracker senses, the roar of the thrusters came to Jack as a hundred ribbons of blue and gold. He strained to look back and saw that the flames streaming behind appeared little different. The bat wings shuddered in the wind. "Can the silk handle this kind of speed?"

"That's not silk." Gwen flopped her scarf at him. "It's Tibetan yak's wool. Finely woven. Tough as Kevlar."

She pulled the throttle back to *high cruise*, narrowing the jets of blue down to fine points. The airship had climbed and gained on the black jet, but the gains didn't last. The modern aircraft could climb higher and take advantage of the upper-level winds. Soon Jack could only find it with the help of some brass and ivory binoculars he had found beneath the control panel. After a while, even those were not enough.

"We're nearly keeping pace," Gwen assured him as he shoved the binoculars back into the compartment. "Tanner will have to land at an airport and hire a helicopter, or find some other means to continue on. But our airship can go straight to the tomb site. We'll catch him, Jack. Trust me." She jerked a thumb aft toward the cabin. "There's a couch back there, and we've a long way to go. You could use some rest. Why don't you lie down for a bit?"

He didn't argue. Jack wandered back into the cabin and collapsed onto the blue quilted cushion, laying the sword on the floor beside him and watching the hills and valleys float past the windows. The buzzing in his head lessened. The tingling faded.

He closed his eyes and let the low drone of the thrusters become a field of blue crystals in his subconscious. They grew and split, replenishing themselves.

Over and over.

Over and over.

After a time, Jack noticed the crystals were no longer a

field. They had become a chamber, broad with tall, arched windows. The crystals above him grew down into the shape of five giant bells hanging from the ceiling. He was at the top of Big Ben—at least, some odd dream-world version of it. At the far end, more blue crystals stacked one upon another until they formed the silhouette of a man in a long overcoat and bowler hat.

Jack found his voice. "Dad?" He crept closer, trying to make out the features on the crystal face. "Dad, is that you?"

In answer, the thing exploded into green flame, forcing him to raise his arms against the heat. When he looked again, he saw a man dressed head to toe in blue-green armor. Jack reeled back in horror. "No. It can't be."

"Hello, Lucky Jack," said the Clockmaker. "How I've missed you." He grinned, the way he had grinned when he had first told Jack how he had wounded and kidnapped his father.

"You're dead. You fell from the top of Big Ben."

"Am I?" The Clockmaker raised an arm and a swarm of clockwork beetles flew in from either side, hovering at his shoulders. "Are you certain of that, *mon ami*? I have so many helpers. And my body was never found."

The spiders came next, copper, silver, and gold—just like

the spiders from the library—gathering at the Clockmaker's feet. Jack looked away.

"Oh, Jack." The Clockmaker clicked his tongue. "What good will it do to hide your face from the truth, eh? You know my handiwork when you see it."

Jack wanted to run, to escape. But he forced himself to hold his ground. "What did you do to my dad?"

"Only what my master asked of me. He wanted access to your father. I obliged him."

"What master?"

The Clockmaker ignored the question. "In exchange for my efforts, he told me how to use you to get the Ember, so that I might create a masterwork of fire." His smile twisted into a scowl and he thrust out his right forearm—a stump capped with bronze. "And you stole it from me."

Jack hated the memory of severing the psychopath's hand, but it had been the only way to stop him. That was when the villain had fallen from the tower. "You left me no choice."

"Heh." The Clockmaker sneered at him. "So you say, greedy child. But you wanted the fire of the Ember for yourself. I saw your eyes light up as you watched it pour from my hand."

"No. I only wanted to stop you. I had to save the city, save my dad and Gwen."

"Denying the truth changes nothing. You are who you are." The Clockmaker pointedly lowered his gaze, and Jack glanced down at his own fists. He opened them. A tongue of green fire sprang up in each palm. He caught his breath and squeezed his hands closed again, snuffing the fire out.

The flame.

Jack's eyes snapped up. The Clockmaker's voice had changed into a deep, horrifying cackle—an echo in Jack's mind. The psychopath grew into a dragon, as big as the white beast from the Archive but formed of gears and gold, with huge blue-green wings.

The flame is in your blood, boy. And one day it will be mine!

The dragon surged forward, shattering crystals and sending up spurts of green fire. Steel jaws opened wide to swallow Jack whole.

The flame, Jack! The flame!

"Jack, wake up!"

"What?"

Jack felt a lurch. He heard a sputter. His eyes popped open and he found he was lying on the couch, forearms shielding his face from a nonexistent mechanical dragon. Gwen was shouting at him from the flight deck. "The engines are flaming out. I need your help!"

"Right." He rolled off the cushion. "Coming."

Gwen had been busy. The carpet of the flight deck was littered with old maps, and she had one of them laid out across the controls. The header read *Badakhshan, 1914.* "Yeah. Like that's gonna help," he said, coming up beside her.

She pushed the map aside. "It may be a tad out-of-date, but the basic geographic features haven't changed. Besides, navigation isn't our problem, Jack. It's thrust. We're out of fuel."

He glanced out the windscreen. The snowy white hills had become stony gray mountains dotted with scrub, and they looked a lot closer. The airship was lower than before. "Gwen, what did you do?"

She chewed her lip. "The tanks ran dry. We were losing speed, so I diverted some hydrogen from the airship's envelope."

"And . . ."

"And I diverted too much. Jack, we're going down."

——— · Chapter Fifty-Three · ———

THE SHADOW of the airship drifted across the scrub, growing larger by the second—and slowing. Jack stared out at a ridgeline rising in the windscreen. They were moving at a good clip, but momentum would only carry them so far. "How close will we come to the tomb?"

"Close enough." Gwen showed him their position on the map. "After this ridge, we should see a lake, here. This hill at the southern end is one of the three 'subjects' from the legends, bowing down before the tomb. And that has to be Temujin's glade just beyond. If we clear the ridgeline, we'll be high enough to clear the hill as well. We can land in the glade."

Jack rested a hand against the windscreen. "That's a big if."

What had looked like scrub before, now proved to be sage-colored trees. And every inch of ground beneath them was covered in jagged rocks.

The ridge continued to rise.

Jack couldn't see all the vectors and angles, but he could see enough. "Pull up," he said, breathing out the words.

"There is no 'pull up,' Jack. It's an airship, not a plane."

"Then give us another burn. Sacrifice more gas."

"We'll lose altitude even faster."

He turned to face her. "Do it, Gwen."

She didn't waste any more time. Gwen spun a valve on the control panel and shoved the throttle to *ahead full*. Streams of fire shot from the pipes, and the airship lurched forward.

After a full second, Gwen started to turn the valve back.

Jack grabbed her hand. "Not yet." He watched the motion outside—ridge coming up, trees and rocks passing below. "Wait for it . . ." He let go. "Now!"

Gwen cut the gas and yanked back on the throttle.

Both of them held their breath as the airship sailed over the rocks, skimming the trees. Bristly leaves brushed the underside of the gondola. And then they were clear.

Gwen collapsed into the captain's chair. "Well, that was exciting."

"It's not over." Jack pointed at the near end of the lake that now stretched out before them. There was an airfield—little more than a couple of hangars and a control tower. A black jet sat parked on the apron. "Tanner's here."

"That's a lot closer than I'd hoped." Gwen handed him the binoculars. "Look for a helicopter or a car. He has to get to the tomb somehow."

Jack raised the glasses.

Airfield: no helicopters, not even an ultralight. A single car sat parked beneath the tower.

A road running south along the lake: no cars or trucks, no traffic of any kind.

A speck hovering above, turning in a circle: too small to be a helicopter—a hawk, maybe. Why was it circling? What was it so interested in?

Jack shifted the binoculars down and saw a white streak on the water. "I've got him." He pulled Gwen up by the arm and pressed the binoculars into her hand. "He's in a boat, and we're gaining, but not for long. We have to stop him."

"How?" she asked, glancing over her shoulder as Jack stormed back into the cabin.

"I don't know. We can drop an empty tank on him or something."

The tank idea was a bust. They were all welded to the rafters, along with the pipes. As Jack was staring up at them, trying to come up with something else, the airship banked. He fell sprawling to the carpet as a brilliant ball of orange flew past the window. "Hey!"

"Tanner's spotted us," called Gwen, righting the craft. "He shot a flare at us."

Jack pushed himself up on one arm, frowning at her. "It's not like it was a Stinger missile. How much damage could it do?"

"Whatever gas is left in that envelope above us is hydrogen, Jack. Extremely flammable. Remember the Hindenburg?"

A photograph from a long-forgotten textbook flashed in Jack's mind. He saw a zeppelin falling from the sky in a huge ball of flame. "Great."

About the time Jack got his feet underneath him again, Gwen banked the other way. Another flare rocketed past. He stumbled into the couch and found a lever on the arm. Small white lettering was stenciled beneath it: PULL FOR EMER-GENCY ANCHOR.

What did he have to lose?

He pulled the lever and the couch rolled forward, exposing a ladder down to a steel grate platform. Right in the middle was something that looked very much like a cannon. He glanced up toward the flight deck. "Gwen, I think I've got something."

Jack grabbed the rails and jumped—rather than climbed—down, landing on the toothy metal grate. The water rushed by beneath his sneakers, two hundred feet or more below.

The cannon was mounted on a swivel, with a set of cross-hairs on the nose and a huge serrated arrowhead sticking out the front. A pair of voice tubes with flared ends hung down from the gondola behind it. Jack held on to a wooden hand-rail for dear life. He pressed one of the tubes to his lips and the other to his ear. "Gwen?"

No response. Jack switched the tubes. "Gwen!"

He heard the sound of bumps and jostles—someone scrambling for the mouthpiece. "Jack? Where are you?"

"The outer deck. I found a sort of cannon-anchor thing."

"Which side?"

"Left."

"You mean port." He could practically hear her rolling her eyes through the interphone.

Jack rolled his eyes right back at her, not caring that she couldn't see him. "Whatever. How close are we to Tanner?"

"Close enough that if he shoots another flare, I might not be able to dodge it."

"Can you turn me broadside?"

A long pause.

"Gwen?"

"We'll lose all our speed and make ourselves a bigger target."

"Then I'd better make the shot count. Can you do it?"

The airship banked, throwing him back against the rail. "I'll take that as a yes."

For a few seconds, Jack saw nothing but blue sky and the red griffin roaring at him from the wing. Then the lake rose into view. He saw the boat, and Tanner's evil grin. Jack tried to push himself off the rail.

He went nowhere.

His arms were pinned to his side.

The professor had his left hand outstretched, using the strange power in the Timur Ruby to hold Jack's upper body captive. The grin Jack had planned to wipe from his face grew even wider, and with his other hand, Tanner raised a double-barrel flare gun.

Chapter Fifty-Four

AS THE AIRSHIP SETTLED, Jack staggered up to the cannon. But try as he might, he could not command his arms or hands to take the handles. He could not so much as flex his fingers.

Tanner took his time, refining his aim.

The airship was a sitting duck.

Jack saw the professor's finger shift back to hook the trigger, and he prepared himself for the worst. But then something fluttered down from the hatch above him. The wooden bird from the library tucked its wings and made a power dive at the boat, bronze beak catching the sun.

Tanner shifted his aim and fired, and in the same instant, Jack regained control of his body. He grabbed the handles, swiveled the cannon to put the sight a few feet in front of the boat, and jerked back on the trigger.

There was an earsplitting *bang*. Black smoke, stinking of powder, billowed back into his face. Steel wire whipped and whistled as it uncoiled from the gun.

He rubbed the soot from his eyes in time to see Tanner bailing over the side, with the huge arrow-anchor blowing through the hull right next to him. The wooden dove, unharmed, circled back toward the shore. Jack let out a cheer.

It was a tad premature.

He was watching the sinking boat pass beneath them, searching the waves for Tanner, when the anchor line went taut. The airship dug in, dumping him over the side. With one hand, he caught the metal platform. The sawtooth edge tore into his fingers.

"Gwen!"

Jack doubted she could hear him through the interphone.

"Cut the line, Jack!"

Or maybe she could.

The anchor had tethered the falling airship to the lakebed, bringing it down that much faster.

"Cut it now, Jack! Do you hear me?"

The cannon had a D-ring on the side that looked a lot like

a parachute ripcord. Grunting against the effort and pain, Jack pulled himself high enough to yank it free. The anchor line zipped away. The airship snapped back to level, slinging him up onto the platform. He rolled over and saw the hill coming up to meet them.

There was no time to get inside the ship. Jack hugged the wooden rail, but the strength of his arms was no match for the raw physics of the crash. The gondola slammed down onto the hillside. He went flying off through the cloud of dust.

Trees.

Rocks.

Dirt.

Blinding pain.

Darkness.

Jack awoke to find the tingling sensation had returned, along with a serious headache. It was aggravated by the sound of sandpaper being dragged across more sandpaper— an odd noise for an arid hillside. With effort, he opened his eyes. A blaring white sun washed everything into a blur of tan and brown, but not all of the forms were stationary. The nearest mass of brown swayed back and forth with mesmerizing rhythm. And then it paused . . . and hissed.

Everything came into focus at once.

The pain in Jack's head and limbs was no match for the need to get away from an angry cobra. He scrambled to his feet and stumbled back against a big rock—the same rock, he realized, that had so abruptly stopped his roll after the crash. The moment he touched it, the cobra uncoiled to twice its former height and hissed even louder.

Jack raised his hands. "Right. Your rock. Not my rock." He shifted ten feet or so to the left and started walking in a wide arc. "Seriously, I don't even like that rock. It's all yours." He gave the snake a final wave and then staggered off toward the wreckage. "Gwen!"

The airship had carved a broad swath through the scrub and lay canted to one side. The near wing and its griffin were mangled beyond recognition. The half-deflated envelope sagged at both ends.

"Gwen, are you in there?" Jack crawled up through the cannon hatch, squinting toward the flight deck. She was still in the captain's chair, head slumped to the side. He struggled forward across the dusty carpet and saw that a trickle of blood colored her hair at the temple. Her eyes were closed. He knelt beside her. "Gwen?"

Her eyes popped open. She shot forward, grabbing the wheel. "Trees! Rocks! Debris!"

"Take it easy," said Jack, breathing a sigh of relief. He eased her back into the cushion. "It's okay. We're sort of past that part now."

Consciousness slowly took hold. "How . . . how long have I been out?"

"Don't know. I was out too. But Tanner's still headed for the tomb. You can be sure of it."

Gwen nodded, wincing. "Then we have to get moving."

"*I* have to get moving." Jack eyed the wound above her temple. A decent-size goose egg had started to form. The sword he had left beside the couch lay at his feet, thrown forward to the flight deck during the crash. He picked it up. "You're hurt. I'll go on without you."

Gwen let out a pained laugh, using the navigation wheel to pull herself out of the chair. "Don't be absurd. You couldn't possibly."

Of course, having Gwen along meant she took charge of their route to the tomb. She argued that the fastest way to the glade would be to work west across the hill to the narrow stream valley, rather than up and over. "It'll be a longer hike but quicker progress," she said as Jack tugged her to the side to guide her around the cobra's rock. "And Tanner will have to walk up the same valley to get to the tomb from the lake."

Her instinct paid off. As soon as they reached the trail beside the stream, Jack noticed a pattern of discolorations on the stones. "Footsteps," he said, handing one of the stones to Gwen so she could feel its wetness. "Tanner passed this way already. He's ahead of us."

"Not by much." She tossed the stone behind her. "Wet footprints don't last long in this climate."

"Why wouldn't he use his ankle thrusters? Wouldn't that be faster than walking?"

"He couldn't," said Gwen, continuing on. "You gave him a severe dunking, remember? And quantum thrusters don't play nice with water." After a beat, she added, "I've heard it helps to immerse them in a bucket of rice, but I doubt he had one handy."

Jack shot her a sideways glance.

Gwen gave him a freckle bounce.

The wet footprints led them up the stream valley and disappeared into a flat expanse of sage-colored grass. The glade looked little different than it had in the black-and-white hologram in the count's library, though the stream meandered a bit more.

"Jack, look," said Gwen, nodding toward a monolithic rock formation guarding a waterfall across the glade. A protrusion near the top looked a lot like a beak. "That's the hawk-rock we saw in the photos. If Temujin's personal guard really diverted a river to conceal the tomb, the entrance will be nearby, under the stream."

They stayed close to the water, but they saw no sign of Tanner, and nothing beneath the surface but weeds and pebbles. Even the deeper section before the waterfall was a bust.

"Maybe the entrance *is* the hawk," offered Jack, running his hands along the stone.

But there were no hidden triggers or panels.

After that, they tried pushing the whole rock. That effort was equally futile, and they quickly gave up, backs resting against it, breathing heavy and staring at the hillside waterfall.

"They diverted a stream to conceal the entrance," muttered Gwen.

Jack was still catching his breath. "You already said that."

"Yes. But do we actually know what it means?" She pushed off and waded into the water. "We assumed Temujin's men dug his tomb in the flat ground—so that the stream runs over it. But who's to say they didn't bore straight into the hillside. In that case, the water would have to pour down over the entrance."

She glanced back at him, and they both said it together. "The waterfall."

Chapter Fifty-Five

FRIGID WATER BIT into Jack's shins as he and Gwen waded into the shallow pool. The cold mixed with the constant tingling in his skin to form a strange and altogether unpleasant mix of white-and-silver flashes. "Tanner's in there," he said, glaring at the waterfall and hooking a thumb in the pocket where he had stashed the zed.

Gwen pulled his hand away from it. "Yes. And we're going to face him together." She intertwined her fingers with his, and they waded through the icy curtain.

Ancient steps led out of the water, up into a long, curving tunnel that ended at a perfectly circular chamber. Twelve stone arches had been cut into the black stone wall, marking twelve new tunnels leading off in every direction.

"Twelve choices," said Gwen. "That, I didn't see coming."

Pots of burning oil, presumably lit by the professor, cast flickering light across a single beast carved over each doorway. The shifting shadows made the creatures appear to move and breathe, so that Jack could almost believe they were alive. He turned in a slow circle, surveying their options—monkey, ox, snake, horse. "Which one do we—? Whoa!"

Jack clawed the air near Gwen's sleeve until he finally caught hold of it and spun her around. Resting in alcoves on either side of the entry were skeletons in leather armor. Rusty swords lay at their sides. He found his voice. "Guards, maybe? Left here to stop tomb raiders?"

"Left here to stop traitors, more likely." Gwen crept up to one of the dead men cautiously, as if he might suddenly wake. "This tomb was well hidden. I'm guessing these two were left behind as a deterrent to those who knew of its existence. A great honor. They must have been among Temujin's most trusted men." Seemingly oblivious to the myriad issues with touching a dead body, she reached beneath its leather skirt and snapped off a femur.

"*Ugh*," groaned Jack. "Seriously?"

"What?" Gwen tore a strip of silk from the skeleton's linen undershirt and wrapped it around the end of the bone. "We'll need a torch, right?" She dipped her stolen thighbone into one of the pots of burning oil and walked along the arches, taking a closer look at the animals. Red dust glittered within the black rock. "This really was a ruby mine."

"It's this one." Jack crossed ahead of her to the third arch, pointing at the birdlike carving above it. "A hawk guards against tomb raiders. I'll bet that part of the legend works on multiple levels." Without waiting for a response, he took a step through the doorway.

Gwen yanked him back by the collar as a giant stone pillar came crashing down behind the arch, missing him by inches. Sparkling black dust rolled out into the chamber. They both retreated to the center.

"How . . . did you . . . know?" asked Jack, coughing in the dust.

"I . . . figured out . . . what this is," Gwen coughed back. She patted her coat, sending up more sparkling dust, and waved a hand in front of her face to fend it off. "It's a zodiac. Twelve animals for a twelve-year cycle, same as the Chinese—year of the rabbit, year of the monkey, and all that."

"So we're looking for the animal sign Temujin was born under. Any idea what it was?"

"Not the slightest. But now we know it's not a hawk, don't

we? Besides, I think that one looks more like a chicken." She swung the torch in a wide arc so that the light passed over the other animals. "We're not even sure when Temujin was born. 1161? 1162, perhaps? Even if we did, neither of us knows the corresponding signs." She glanced down, frowning at the smooth black rock beneath their feet. "Perhaps you could spark and see which door Tanner took."

It was worth a try. Jack crouched down, pressing his palm against the stone. Static. He shook his head. "Maybe if I use the zed."

"No. We're not that desperate."

"Aren't we?"

Gwen pursed her lips at him.

"Fine." Jack stood and paced along the carvings, feeling like an art critic in the world's most dangerous museum. "Monkey . . . ox . . . tiger . . . I've seen this group before. This is the menagerie from all those pictures of Genghis Khan in the count's library." He thought he had something, but his excitement waned when he came to the fifth arch. A cobra glared down at him, like the one he had faced on the hillside. He shook his head. "Never mind. I didn't see any snakes in—"

Didn't see. As those words passed Jack's lips, a phrase came back to him—something Ash had told him during the Hunt.

Sometimes the best clue is the one that you don't see.

"That's *it*." He grabbed Gwen by the arm, pulling her to the cobra's arch. "In each picture, the artist drew a complete Mongolian zodiac. But Temujin himself represented his own sign, rather than the animal. Temujin was the cobra."

"Are you sure?" Gwen cautiously extended the torch through the doorway. Despite the firelight, nothing was visible beyond the first few feet. "Your last guess didn't go so well."

"This time it's not a guess," said Jack, and he stepped into the darkness.

Chapter Fifty-Six

NO GIANT STONES came crashing down. No spears or darts shot out of the walls. And not one single tarantula appeared.

There were, however, a lot of bones.

The tunnel widened and Jack and Gwen followed a long, descending curve, as if spiraling down around the outer wall of a cylinder. Their steps took on a wooden echo, and a sweep of the torch showed ancient planks beneath their feet. On either side lay piles of cattle bones, with yokes at their necks and big wooden wheels between each pair.

Jack eyed a horned skull that looked like it belonged in a Hollywood western. "So they left cows behind as extra guards?"

Gwen elbowed him. "Those were *oxen*. And the wheels were for the carts they pulled. Temujin's men left him some transportation for the afterlife."

The afterlife. What sort of afterlife had been waiting for a man who had killed millions?

Jack glanced over at Gwen. "Do you think Tanner could really harness the spirit of Genghis Khan?"

She stopped walking and looked at him for a long moment, then shook her head and continued on. "I don't think you can trap a person's spirit, or harness it for your own use. But you and I both know that gems capture sight and sound." She passed the torch along the black wall. Red dust sparkled within. "Perhaps this mine's particular brand of balas ruby absorbs and projects negative emotion too— evil, if you like. If anything is trapped in the fourth ruby, I think it's a big ball of greed, hatred, and malice. Not some dead general's ghost."

The tunnel made a ninety-degree bend, and they arrived at the entry to a second chamber, as perfectly round as the first but much larger, with a strange gutter around the periphery and a rock ceiling carved in the sloped style of a circus tent. Silks covered the walls, along with golden shields and silver helmets set with jade and opal.

"It's a yurt," said Gwen, halting with her toes hanging over the gutter. "I get it now. They're all yurts."

"A what?"

"A yurt, Jack. A Mongolian tent, like the round tent in that photograph of your great-great-grandparents." She held the torch out into the room. "Look at the slope of the ceiling, the silks on the walls. Tombs mirror the houses of the living, and Genghis Khan would have spent his last years in a collection of tents that looked like this on the inside—a mobile palace."

Jack looked back over his shoulder at the passage behind them. "That's what the oxen and the cart wheels were for, to pull his palace."

"Both in life *and* in death," said Gwen. "In life, the palace yurts would have been arranged in a circle for defense. I think these tomb yurts are arranged vertically, instead."

The black rock floor bounded by the circular gutter was carved with the same zodiac creatures they had seen in the chamber above. The eleven lesser animals played or hunted between the body segments of a giant cobra that spiraled outward to a doorway on the opposite side. "Vertically," Jack repeated, eyeing the door. "So the tomb chamber will be . . ."

"Directly below us. Yes."

"Then that's where we'll find Tanner and the antidote."
Jack set off across the room. He made it halfway to the
center before he heard a resounding *crack*. The floor
groaned beneath him. "What's happening?" He turned and
thought he saw Gwen rising, along with the entryway.
But that wasn't quite right. Gwen wasn't going up. *He* was
going down.

The floor was one giant stone disk, balanced on a point.

Chains ripped free from the silk coverings on the walls,
pulled by the low side of the disk, and rattled down through
holes at the edge of the ceiling. An instant later, water
poured from spouts farther up. Jack ducked and covered
under the onslaught of a freezing shower and then watched
the water work its way ominously through the carvings.
The extra weight gathering in the gutter tilted the disk
farther, so that he could barely keep from sliding down.
Beneath the edge he saw the dull gleam of bronze spikes.

"The other side, Jack!" shouted Gwen, waving the torch.
"Run to the other side."

He raced up the slope of playing beasts, but not fast
enough. The disk reversed, and momentum carried it past

the balance point too quickly for him to make the door. More chains ripped from the walls on the far side. Before they could unleash another frigid torrent, Jack backpedaled to the center. The disk wobbled. The water behind him spread through the gutter, distributing its weight. The room settled, leaving him inside the central curl of the cobra's tail.

"It's a balance table." Gwen pointed at a total of eight spouts in the ceiling. "Tilting it in any direction brings down water, making things worse."

Jack shivered, soaked to the bone with water from the mountain stream above them. "Really? I hadn't noticed. Now what?"

"Now we figure out how to beat it."

Gwen had not left solid ground, and common sense told Jack she ought to stay there. He thrust his chin at the tunnel behind her. "Toss me the torch and head back to the surface to wait for Ash and Sadie."

"Not on your life, Jack Buckles. Just give me a second to think."

He didn't have a second. Most likely, Tanner's ankle thrusters had dried out and he had simply flown across the disk, getting farther ahead. For all Jack knew, he had already recovered the fourth ruby and was preparing to take over the nearest army. China? Russia? Jack needed a quick solution. "It's balanced now. What if I run to the other side?"

"Won't work. I think those chains operating the water gates were a little sticky after eight hundred years. That gave you some extra time when you first walked out. It won't be so easy the second time."

"Easy?" Jack let out a short laugh. Nothing about that had been easy. "How about this? I'll back up as you come out. Like a counterbalance."

To his surprise, she didn't argue. Gwen took a great big step out onto the disk, and Jack took a hurried step backward. The disk groaned and began to rise on his end. Gwen was too far from the balance point and he was too close. Water rained down. She dropped the torch, covering her head and rushing forward. "Not working!"

Jack jogged backward until the disk reversed, trying to salvage their effort, but the water running through the carvings made the balancing act far too complex. The disk overshot, tipping Gwen way up.

They ran to the center, straight for each other, and Jack

tackled Gwen against the steepening slope. He dug his fingers into the carvings to hold them there. Behind him, he could hear the water spilling out over the gutter onto the spikes below. Everything stopped. Neither of them dared to breathe.

Chapter Fifty-Seven

"WELL ... THIS IS COZY," whispered Gwen.

The bone torch went tumbling past them, and the cracks and clanks of its demise echoed up from the spikes below. "Yeah," said Jack. "I was gonna say 'terrifying.' But okay."

They were in trouble. If Jack shifted his weight down, the disk would tilt farther and they would fall. If he clawed his way up, the disk would reverse, and momentum would carry it far enough to send them rolling down the other way, head over heels. He eyed the grooves of the snake carving. Maybe if he could work his way along the cobra, hand over hand, they could turn around. Then it hit him. "The cobra."

"What?"

"The cobra is the solution. This is just another zodiac puzzle, like the chamber above."

Gwen gave a tiny, ultracautious nod. "If you say so."

She didn't sound too confident, but the disk wasn't going to wait for Jack to explain himself. It let out a deep, disturbing *creak*.

"Just hold my hand and run when I tell you." With great effort, he clawed his way up about a foot, hauling her with him. It was enough to start a reversal of the tilt, and as soon as the disk reached a manageable angle, he yanked Gwen to her feet. "Now!"

They raced along the snake, spiraling outward toward the broad hood at the edge of the disk. It worked. By running in a circle, they kept the table in a constant state of reversal, wobbling like a penny. The oscillations stayed a step behind them, and so did the water raining down. The silk walls rose and fell on every side.

"Jump!"

Jack lifted Gwen's hand and they dove through the arch, tumbling down a set of steps and rolling to a stop at the edge of a cliff. Dust and gravel went flying over the edge. He scrambled back, dragging her with him. For the next few seconds, he sat there, trying to determine if the ground was still swaying, or if it was just him.

There was light in the new chamber. After a time, they helped each other up and peered over the cliff, into an ancient mine. Where the black rock walls in the upper chamber had glittered with red dust, here they sparkled with full-blown rubies, some as big as Jack's thumb. More pots of burning oil sat in alcoves—a sure sign that Tanner had already come through—illuminating a steep path of switchbacks and ladders that led down through the strange underworld to whatever waited below.

But Jack saw another option.

He tilted his head toward a big woven basket, hanging from a sloped pulley system. "We could take the fast way down."

"Not on your life." Gwen tugged on the ropes, sending up a small cloud of dust. "If the bottom doesn't fall out of this moldy basket before we leave the cliff, the line will definitely break. And then where will be? That path is our best—" In midsentence, Gwen's face went slack, freckles falling. She was no longer looking at Jack, but through him, toward the previous chamber.

He heard a monstrous groan.

The disk had continued to wobble after their leap, and Jack had tuned out the noise, assuming it was settling. It hadn't dawned on him that the opposite might be true. He turned in time to see the giant disk reach vertical, slide off its balance point, and crash into the pit, breaking into three pieces. The center section, the size of a tanker truck, fell straight toward the exit and their little cliff.

"Go, go, go!" Jack shoved Gwen backward over the lip of the basket and dove in beside her, knocking the whole thing over the ledge. It dipped down as chunks of stone carved with zodiac animals went flying. Half of a stone monkey sailed over the basket. Jack could swear he saw it wave.

The pulleys squealed.

The basket picked up speed.

"Where are the brakes?" cried Gwen.

There were no brakes. With a tooth-jarring *crunch*, the basket reached the end of its line and tipped over. Both children tumbled out. Jack fell into a cart. Gwen crashed down onto the rock behind it. Jack leaned out, straining to reach her, but he was already headed down the path, wheels squeaking.

"Jump," called Gwen, pushing herself up on an elbow. "Get out before it's too late."

As if he hadn't thought of that.

Jack was already trying to get his legs underneath him for a leap to safety. But in the process, he saw a two-story archway below, guarded on either side by statues of cobras. That had to be the entrance to the burial chamber. A great hawk was carved above it, wings spread. *His favorite hawk keeps watch for tomb raiders.* It *did* work on multiple levels. Too bad there wasn't time for an I-told-you-so.

Only one switchback remained between Jack and the chamber. And at the turn ahead, the path curved up against the wall like a quarter pipe at a skate park.

He could make it.

Tanner would have heard all that racket. He would be ready for them, and if Jack was on foot, the professor could use the Timur Ruby to stop him in his tracks. But no ruby, cursed or otherwise, could stop a speeding mine cart.

Jack pulled himself up to a crouch and reached into his pocket, taking out the zed.

"Don't, Jack!" shouted Gwen from the path above. "That thing will kill you!"

He didn't care.

He shifted his weight to guide the cart through the switchback, willing the wooden wheels to hold together. It worked.

The cart straightened out on the final leg of the path. The professor stepped into view between the cobras, stretching out his hand and looking up with a wicked grin.

His jaw dropped.

"That's right," said Jack, drawing his sword. "This is how I roll."

Chapter Fifty-Eight

THE CART SMASHED into the chamber steps, sending Jack flying. He lowered a shoulder and plowed into Tanner, and the two crashed into the platform together. Jack was the first to his feet. He leveled his blade. "Don't move."

He checked Tanner's legs for the ankle thrusters, but it seemed the professor had dumped them at the entrance, along with his jacket, shoes, and socks. Tanner sat there, leaning against Temujin's sarcophagus, wearing only his wool pants and the gold mail shirt with the triangle of rubies. The center spot remained empty.

The attack had carried Jack to the center of the yurt—the final resting place of Genghis Khan. The sarcophagus lay on a raised platform of white marble with a waterfall raining down behind it. The lid, an effigy of the warrior-emperor, was slightly askew. Bronze poles stood at the head and foot, topped with horsehair banners—one dyed black, the other white.

"Black for war. White for peace," said Tanner, inclining his head toward each banner.

"I said don't move." Jack shook the sword at him.

But Tanner showed no sign of fear. "Men like Genghis Khan and Tamerlane understood that you had to make war to make peace, Jack. They understood that the world is a better, safer place when it's ruled by one man with an iron fist."

"Shut. Up." Jack wasn't playing. The prickling in his flesh—the growing numbness—was getting worse by the second. He wasn't sure how much longer he could hold himself together. "Take off that device. Slowly. If you wave so much as a pinkie finger in my direction, this blade is going straight through your neck."

Tanner laughed, his voice merging with the buzzing in Jack's head. "I don't think so. You won't kill me."

"You really want to take that chance?" Jack extended his arm to press the sword's tip right up against the man's jugular.

But his arm did not actually extend. The sword didn't move.

His eyes darted from the rubies to the professor's hands. In the past, Tanner had held up a palm when using the Timur Ruby. This time he hadn't lifted a finger.

"You misunderstand me, boy." Tanner stood, as casually as an elderly gentleman getting up from his favorite chair. "You have enough darkness inside to run me through, I've no doubt about that. But you won't kill me because you don't have the strength to overcome my power." He opened his right fist. The fourth ruby lay in his palm.

All sense of hesitation was gone. Jack strained with all he had to shove the sword through his mentor's gut. His muscles would not accept his commands.

Tanner walked from one side of the sword to the other, fingers hovering over the blade, daring Jack to cut him. "The fourth ruby holds the power of all the rest, boy. It is the beating heart of the stone. By simply holding it, I can command the finest movements of your muscles—with far more efficiency than I could with the Timur Ruby."

As if in response to the professor's claim, Jack's arm twitched. His hand moved against his will, bringing the sword up to his own throat. He tried to raise his other hand to block it, but that arm wouldn't budge. Neither would his legs. Tanner had full control of his body. Then, somewhere in Jack's subconscious, a voice commanded him to slit his own jugular. It told him that sacrificing himself for Tanner was the right thing to do.

Jack almost believed it.

"Can you see the words implanted in your mind? Can you feel the desire to obey? What you saw in the Black Prince's Ruby was a mere echo of that power. So many of Temujin's enemies turned on their own peoples, marching before his armies to become willing fodder for his next battle. Loyalty to the point of death, Jack. That is what I now control."

Sweat beaded at Jack's brow. He grunted, fighting the thoughts invading his mind.

"You can't stop it. You don't know how. Too bad. All the knowledge of the ages is so close to you, right here in my palm—knowledge that drove the emperors who wore the Russian ruby mad, because pieces were missing. But my knowledge is now complete." Tanner narrowed his eyes, and the blade pressed against Jack's skin.

"Jack!" Gwen came racing down the path.

Tanner glanced her way and she skidded to a stop at the

chamber steps, frozen. Her voice fell to a hoarse whisper—
the voice of someone being strangled. "J-Jack."

The sword cut into him. Sharp red pain flashed in his
mind. And the pain provoked a response from his nervous
system. Not a contraction of muscles—Tanner still had
control of those—but a response only a tracker nervous
system could make. Without a conscious thought, Jack
drew power from the zed squeezed within his left fist.

With a sudden rush of coolness, the soothing energy of
the sphere flowed up his arm. It snaked out across his torso
in curling tendrils. He took hold of it and let out a mighty
growl, pushing the blade from his throat.

The arrogance in Tanner's expression faltered, replaced
with confusion and panic. "How are you doing that? Stop!
I command you!"

Jack's vision began to gray. The buzzing grew louder. A
hundred million pinpoints attacked his body, pushing deep
into his core, threatening to dissolve him into nothing
right then and there. But with each second, he gained
more control of his arm. He gave no more warnings to the
psychopath. He turned the sword, pulling it back for a final
thrust at the man's chest.

"No!" screamed Tanner, slamming the stone into the

center of the triangle. His face twisted into a mask of agony and his hand fell away.

In the next instant, Jack's blade struck home. Drawn like a nail to a magnet, it hit the fourth ruby dead center.

The chamber filled with blinding light.

Chapter Fifty-Nine

WHEN THE FLASH FADED, Jack stood alone on a red lacquer floor, his sword still extended. Rows of gold columns surrounded him on every side, running off into a pink mist. An infinite red dome filtered the light from above, and a gold lattice pattern hovered beneath it like a hologram. The buzzing in his head remained, along with the tingling that threatened to phase his body into nothingness. Jack lowered the sword. At least his neck wasn't bleeding anymore.

It occurred to him that if he had sparked, he had jumped past the observation position, right into the middle of the vision, and he had managed to bring the sword and the zed with him. He wasn't sure if that was a good sign or a bad one. "Where am I?" he asked out loud, partly to hear something, anything, in the deathly silence.

"I think you know." A man in a bowler hat and a suede duster materialized out of the mist, carrying a falcon-head cane. A purple arc of electricity danced within a glass chamber below the head.

Jack went to him, hesitant at first, and then running, racing, practically knocking him down with a hug. "Dad!"

"All right. All right. Take it easy." His father held him tight, with arms as strong as Jack remembered. It had been so long since Jack had smelled that suede, felt that strength surround him. He did not want to let go. But something in the back of his mind told him their time together was already running short. He pushed himself away. "How is this possible?"

John Buckles the Twelfth removed his bowler and scratched his hairline, glancing up at the dome. "You took something from my armory, didn't you? Something dangerous."

Jack looked up at the red dome and the gold lattice. "You mean the zed."

"Is that what you call it?" His father let out a rueful chuckle and started walking, side by side with Jack, through the columns and the cool pink mist. "I wasn't nearly so elegant. I called it the *leech*. And no, I don't know what it is. The zed—to use your word for it—arrived by messenger a few days after my father's death in Salzburg. No letter. Only a dangerous curve sign scrawled on the paper the sphere was wrapped in." The older John Buckles looked down at his hand, turning it over and back. "I felt its power the moment I touched it—a clarity spreading through my senses like I had never experienced. But I also felt something go out of me when I set it down."

Jack caught the edge in his father's voice. He stopped. "What kind of something?"

"A sliver of consciousness. A slice of life, maybe." John Buckles gave a half smile and waved a hand up and down his body. It shimmered, threatening to fade away, as if either he or Jack were fighting to keep the connection between them. "*This*, Jack. That's what *this* is—a thin slice, separated from the whole when I first tried to use the zed."

Jack closed his eyes. He had allowed himself to fall into delusion. This aberration next to him was not his dad, not all of him, anyway. His father was there but not there—right next to him and a thousand miles away at the same time. After all Jack had been through, the injustice of it was more than he could bear. He gritted his teeth, searching for a positive. "Okay. So you're only a piece of Dad, trapped in the zed. That's why I've been seeing you in my sparks. But I'm here now. I can get you out. Maybe this piece is the key to waking you up."

His father shook his head. "That's not why you're here, Jack."

"Not why I'm here? *Not why I'm here?*" Jack lost it. He lost control, and he welcomed the feeling. He had held it together for way too long. "Then why, Dad? Why am I doing *any* of this if it isn't to get you back?" The tears finally fell. "You lie there. Every day. Every night. While Mom pretends she's not crying. While Sadie lives in some kind of spooky, little-girl denial. The doctors have tried every-thing. *We've* tried everything!" He pounded a fist against the suede coat—once, twice, a third time. "What did the Clockmaker do to you?"

The older Buckles caught Jack's wrist and held it to his chest. Then he tucked the cane under his arm and clapped his other hand over his son's. "I know, Jack. I'm sorry. And I wish I could tell you what happened, but all I have from my time at Big Ben are flashes—images I gained when you pressed the zed into my hand." He looked away into the mist. "I saw hypodermic needles, strange gems, and rivers of quicksilver. It was alchemy, perhaps an attempt to transfer my consciousness from the physical to the inanimate. A tracker mind would make the perfect candidate."

Jack cleared his throat, reining in his tears. "But . . . it failed."

"Of course it did. That kind of effort is always doomed to fail. We are more than data, son. We are spirit and soul, and nothing can imprison those. Not the Clockmaker's alchemy"—he turned Jack's fist over and opened his fingers, revealing the zed—"and not this."

Jack nodded, looking down at the stone.

His dad got down on one knee and lifted his chin. "But the zed *has* taken its toll on you. *That's* why you're here. Your subconscious forced you into a kind of pit stop before you charge into whatever battle lies ahead, because you won't survive without it." He gestured at the forest of polished gold columns, and Jack saw that each one held a reflection of him. They had been there the whole time, pieces of him, captured in the zed. "You're not here to get *me* back, son. You're here to get yourself back."

As Jack stared at the columns, a gilded doorway carved with cobras and a hawk appeared at the edge of the mist. The older Buckles stood. "You're almost out of time. You've got to pull yourself together."

"But how?"

"By letting go." He cupped Jack's hand, nodding down at the sphere. "This thing you call the zed, maybe we don't know exactly what it is—but for you, it's a holding pattern. And every time you circle back, you lose a little piece of yourself."

"I don't understand." That wasn't true. He did understand, but he didn't want to. He wasn't ready.

"You're waiting, Jack. You've been waiting ever since Big Ben, hoping this fancy rock will fix me and that fixing me will fix everything else. But the fact is, I'm not that important. Your mom, Sadie, Gwen—they need you *right now*, not when or if I get better." John Buckles placed a hand on his son's shoulder. "Jack, you have to stop waiting. You have to live, even though I may not."

There they were, the words that had been lingering in Jack's mind for a year, and this fragment of his father had dared to speak them. He shook his head. "No. I won't lose you."

John Buckles let out a short, sad laugh. "Who said anything about losing me? Whether I'm standing beside you or looking down on you from somewhere else, I'll always be with you, Jack. Here." He placed his hand on his son's heart. "Put your faith in that, not in some magic rock you carry in your pocket."

The mist had thickened. It was closing in around them. And the gilded door had moved menacingly closer.

"Now's the time, son. Let it go."

A deep voice rang down the silver hall beyond the threshold—several voices, speaking several languages at once. The English voice rang loudest. It was Tanner's. "I know you're there, Jack. Come and stand before your new khan."

The multi-voice reverberated through Jack's body, demanding obedience. He could still feel the sting of the cut at his throat. How could he resist the power of the fourth ruby without the zed? He had carried it too long to let it go the very moment the fate of the world rested on his shoulders.

"The zed won't help you," said his father, countering the argument Jack had not spoken. "It's a burden, and you need to set it down before it's too late."

Jack gazed at the little sphere for a long moment—so

small and insignificant. It should have been a simple thing to toss it away. It wasn't. He closed his fingers around it, shaking his head in resignation. "I can't," he said, and the golden doorway rushed out of the mist and swallowed him whole.

·—— Chapter Sixty ·——

THE MANY VERSIONS of Jack followed him through a silver hallway with sloping walls that joined far above. The reflections walked beside him, and within the mirrored floor beneath his sneakers. A few pointed the other way, urgently signaling him to turn back. But it was too late for that. The golden doorway was gone.

A red light rushed toward him, eerily similar to the red lights in the hyperloop tunnel, and then Jack was standing in a yurt that matched Temujin's burial chamber, carved from pure ruby instead of black stone. A silver throne stood on the platform where the sarcophagus should be, with a cascade of white water behind it. Tanner, or something like Tanner, reclined there, leaning on an elbow, still barefoot and wearing his gold mail shirt with all four rubies in place.

"Welcome, Jack," he said in his multi-voice, including languages that Jack guessed were Mongolian, Persian, and Chinese. Ghostly figures matched his posture on the throne, superimposed over his body. Some wore kingly robes. Others wore armor. Tanner sneered, and they all sneered with him. "I am glad—and I dare say proud—that you've made it this far, boy. You are an excellent pupil. It is fitting that you should bear witness to my full victory."

Jack's reflections filed in on either side of the yurt, barely visible in the translucent walls.

Tanner gave no sign that he noticed them. "Behold, the seat of my power." He waved his hand, a ghostly ripple trailing behind, and the circus-tent roof evaporated, revealing a blue sky so pale it was almost white. Three more ruby yurts were perched up there on ornate silver platforms. They were joined to one another by a triangle of silver halls, sculpted with the forms of the zodiac animals and joined to Tanner's yurt by silver stairwells. "The network is now complete, and with it, I will finish the work of Temujin. The entire world will finally bow before a single khan." He pointed at Jack. "Starting with you."

Jack felt the command to kneel. He heard it in his

subconscious. His knees buckled. He squeezed the zed, drawing what resistance he could despite the tingling that threatened to faze him away. His knees found the strength they needed.

So did his sword arm.

"I don't think so," he said, and charged the throne.

Faceted ruby men grew out of the floor, solidifying into flesh-and-blood Mongol warriors. Jack smashed through a slashing scimitar, cutting into the soldier behind. The man crumbled into shimmering red dust. Beyond the cloud, he saw Tanner lean forward in concentration. The professor was driving the creatures like drones.

A hand caught Jack's arm from behind. And then another. Two soldiers held him fast. Their fists became ruby cuffs. Tanner grinned, a grotesque smile of several evil faces at once, and the faceted ruby shells spread up Jack's arms to his shoulders, threatening to encapsulate him completely. What would happen if Tanner succeeded in trapping his consciousness in the stone?

Jack knew from experience that all of this was happening at the speed of neurons. As far as Gwen was concerned, he was standing in the tomb, his sword just making contact with the ruby on Tanner's chest. But if his consciousness were to become trapped in the jewel, that blink of time might become an eternity. The other Jacks paced within the walls, becoming less visible by the moment. They were fading. *He* was fading.

"Leave my kid alone, Ed."

A bronze falcon head burst through the chest of the soldier on Jack's left. The rest of him shattered and fell away, along with the ruby shell. Jack's sword arm was free. Without hesitation, he shoved the blade through the Mongol warrior on his right. It vaporized into dust. He glanced over his shoulder. "Dad?"

"Didn't I tell you I would always be with you?" John Buckles swung his cane without bothering to look, smashing another soldier coming in from his right.

Tanner bolted up from his throne. "What is *he* doing here?" He made a frustrated gesture at the circular wall. Ruby soldiers stepped out, rushing Jack and his dad.

John Buckles smashed through the first to reach him and pointed toward Jack with the backswing of his cane. "On your left, son. And behind you. Look out!"

Jack turned in time to meet a scimitar with his sword. He chopped the attacker in half and spun the sword on the downswing, thrusting it back beneath his arm. Another soldier crumbled.

He destroyed two more attackers, and then, in a moment's respite, he glanced over his shoulder at his dad. A mystified smile spread across Jack's lips. He had never known the warrior side of his father.

Before the events that had put John Buckles into a coma, Jack had thought he was a salesman. Now he watched in awe as his dad separated the cane into a short sword and a club, thrusting and swinging, suede duster swirling around him like a cape through the sparkling dust. The bowler hat never stirred from its rakish tilt upon his brow.

More soldiers rushed in, and Jack had to focus on his own battle. There were too many. He was tiring. Fast. They piled on by the dozens, hemming him in. A scimitar rose above his head for a killing blow.

"Enough!" The multi-voice echoed through the chamber.

The soldiers backed away into a circle, and Jack saw that his dad, too, had been outmanned. A pair of soldiers held John Buckles fast. A third snatched away the two halves of his falcon-head cane and placed them on the platform beside the throne.

Multi-Tanner and his trail of ghostly khans walked down the steps. He parted the soldiers with a wave of his hand and stepped into the circle. "You brought your father with you,

Jack. Impressive. But I believe I know how you pulled it off. Show me what you're hiding there."

A half-dozen languages whispered in Jack's mind, echoing a command that he couldn't resist. He opened his hand, showing Tanner the zed.

"Do you know what you have there, boy?"

Again, Jack resisted, trying to stop the answer that spilled from his lips. "N-no."

Tanner laughed—an awful, multi-voice laugh. "Well, I do. And I can show you how to use it to bring your father back for real."

———— · Chapter Sixty-One · ————

JACK FOUGHT TO RECLAIM command of his tongue. "I don't believe you. You're a murderer. You killed my grandfather."

"*Killed* Joe?" Tanner looked taken aback. "I couldn't have. He was my best friend."

"You and Grandpa Joe were the only ones on that island. You *must* have killed him."

"You're not seeing the whole picture, Jack." Tanner began a slow stroll along his perimeter of soldiers. "There was someone else. Ignatius Gall followed us to that island."

John Buckles struggled against his captors. "Ignore him. He's a liar."

Tanner whipped his head around to shoot him a glare,

ghostly faces following. "Gall was there, I tell you. Joe tried to use the stone's power to stop him, but it had no effect. Gall killed him, and he would have killed me, too—"

"But *you* offered him your allegiance," said Jack, narrowing his eyes.

"He needed a tracker to wield the rubies, someone he thought he could control." Tanner continued his regal stroll along his circle of soldiers. "And I needed to live to fight another day. After Joe, he killed Bill Shepherd to get the Einstein-Rosen Bridge—a device he passed to the Phantom so he could steal the other two rubies. And there was one other item he wanted." His walk brought him full circle, and he stopped in front of Jack, staring down at the zed. "Your other grandfather, John Buckles the Eleventh, dove off a cliff to keep Gall from learning its location."

As much as Jack didn't want to believe it, everything Tanner had said made sense. It matched what he knew of the deaths of the eleventh-generation trackers. And it matched what his father had told him about the zed. He looked up at his former mentor. "But why?"

"What good is power, if death can take it from you? That sphere preserves life, Jack"—Multi-Tanner made a sweeping, multi-arm gesture—"indefinitely. It is the key to immortality.

And with the knowledge embedded in the khan's rubies, I can help you use it. Together, you and I can bring your father back. Together, we can take our revenge."

John Buckles struggled against the soldiers. "No, Jack. This isn't the way."

"You will be my protégé, boy. You'll be a prince. Not of England or of Persia, but *the* prince—the prince of the whole world. Nothing will be beyond your reach."

Jack couldn't think. The buzzing in his head had grown to an unrelenting shriek. A billion prickling, numbing points sank into his bones, eating them away layer by layer. No matter how hard he squeezed the zed, he couldn't stop it. The zed was the source, but he couldn't resist Tanner without its power. Either way, he would be gone in moments, absorbed into the fourth ruby forever.

"Don't listen, Jack." His father strained against his captors, forcing them to take his weight. "This isn't Tanner anymore. It's a thing—an evil thing—and it's bargaining with you. Think, Jack. Why would it need to do that?"

"Quiet. We've heard enough from you." Multi-Tanner snapped his fingers, and the soldiers on either side of Jack's dad drew their scimitars, holding the points at his ribcage. "Last chance, boy. Join me. Or die."

Jack's reflections were all but invisible. Those he could still see nodded, pleading silently for him to take Tanner's offer. But his dad kept fighting. "It had us beaten, Jack. But something changed. Can't you see? The evil in this ruby took Tanner. And now it wants you, too. But it can't have you unless you give yourself willingly."

"I said quiet!" Multi-Tanner threw a dismissive hand in the air.

The soldiers shoved their scimitars home.

Jack took a step toward his dad. "No!"

Nothing could have prepared him for that sight, watching his father drop to his knees, flickering, bleeding. The zed was forgotten. It fell from his hand, dissolving into red-and-gold dust before it ever hit the floor.

Jack felt himself dissolving with it.

The reflections in the walls—his reflections—faded into nothingness.

And that was the moment everything changed.

── · Chapter Sixty-Two · ──

JACK'S REFLECTIONS had not disappeared. They had been released. Swirls of glowing white vapor streamed from the walls, passing through the circle of soldiers and slamming into him, jarring his body.

The buzzing faded. The tingling dissipated. Clarity returned. As the vapor poured into him, Jack saw every significant moment he had experienced since Big Ben, when he had first used the zed.

He saw the dragos in the train station stare at him, burn scars running down their cheeks.

He heard his sister recite his thoughts before he spoke them.

He watched Gwen recount her tale of Arthurians and Merlinians—fire wielders and mind readers.

He felt the fire that had flashed beneath his hand in the collection of dragons.

Jack could finally see all the data at once.

And it all made sense.

With a resounding *thump*, the last of the vapor entered his body. And in the silence that followed, Jack heard two whispered words.

The flame.

A ring of blue fire shot out from his body, obliterating Multi-Tanner's ruby soldiers in an explosion of red. Free of his captors, his father flickered back into full, solid form. John Buckles took his hands away from his ribs, looking down at cauterized wounds, and then lifted his gaze to his son. "Jack?"

A deep, golden feeling of warmth filled Jack's body, like the feeling he got whenever he touched dragonite. For the first time, it occurred to him that *warmth* wasn't the right word. It was more than warmth. It was *fire*.

The flame.

Jack glanced down. In his left hand, in place of the zed, he now held a spinning ball of blue fire. And yellow fire spiraled up the sword from his right fist. He fixed Tanner with an icy glare.

"Impossible," muttered Multi-Tanner. "You're just like *him*."

Rage built within the many faces, and then he let out a roar and charged, drawing a ghostly scimitar from his belt.

Jack threw his fireball, hitting the creature fully in the chest. It slowed him, but it didn't stop him, and the two swords slammed together with a white flash. Multi-Tanner struck again and again, but Jack saw all the vectors. He anticipated every strike.

"I don't care what you've become!" shouted Multi-Tanner. "You are still nothing but a child—a Section Thirteen."

"Jack, look out!"

Jack didn't need his father's warning this time. He heard the soldiers approaching. He could see them in his mind. With a burst of flame, he knocked Multi-Tanner away and slashed two soldiers in half with a single stroke. He heard a subtle finger-snap and looked up in time to see his dad thrust a chin toward the throne.

John Buckles raised his eyebrows.

Jack knew exactly what he wanted.

Jack hit Multi-Tanner with another fireball, turning him, and then charged, pressing him up the platform steps.

"Mistake, boy," said the creature. "You've given me the higher ground." He raised his scimitar and rained down blows that sent sparks flying. Jack took all the abuse he could and finally jumped back, retreating. The Mongol warrior behind Tanner's face grinned.

But not for long.

John Buckles stepped out from behind the throne and shoved the butt of his cane into the creature's back, firing the stun gun within. Purple arcs of electricity wrapped Tanner's body—just Tanner. The ghosts of khans and emperors flashed out in front of him, faces stricken with terror, and Jack thrust his flaming sword through them all. The image of Genghis Khan reached for him, gnashing its rotten teeth. And then it exploded in a burst of black smoke.

Tanner collapsed onto the steps.

John Buckles doubled over, clutching the wounds in his stomach, but he offered Jack a weak smile. "Well, that's something new for House Buckles."

Fire blazed around them. The ruby palace was burning.

Jack pulled his dad toward a silver staircase. "We have to get you out of here."

"I told you. That's not why you came." He nodded toward the mirrored hall leading back to the pink mist of the zed. "That's my road. This time, anyway."

He started toward the archway, but Jack pulled him into a hug. "I *will* save you."

"Live, Jack. Become the man you were meant to be. Everything else will follow."

Tanner moaned and they both looked his way. Fire had surrounded the platform. Jack furrowed his brow. "What about him?"

"It's a spark, Jack. He has to get himself out." John Buckles backed away as he spoke. The fire spread between them. "Remember. I'm always with you," he said, and placed a hand over his heart. "Right here."

The flames stretched higher, blocking Jack's view. He watched them for another heartbeat and then turned and crossed the threshold, clearing his mind of everything but escape. He took one step up the silver stairway, and he was out.

"Gwen?" Jack lowered the sword. Tanner lay at his feet.

She rushed to Jack's side. "What happened? What did you do to him?"

"I think the professor's mind is trapped in the fourth ruby. I'll explain later. Right now we need to get him—and us— out of here." Jack slid the sword into his belt, checking it for fire, and almost laughed at himself for doing so. That had been a feature of the spark. It was all in his mind. Likewise, the zed had not evaporated. But it was changed. Jack opened his hand and was surprised to find that, beneath its gold latticework, the little red sphere had turned snow white.

Gwen gazed down at it with him. "What does that mean?"

"I don't know." He ripped a strip of silk from the wall, wrapped up the stone, and placed it in her hand. "Keep it safe for me, will you? And don't tell a soul about it."

Gwen nodded, and with his other hand, Jack closed her fist around the sphere. Together the two crouched down beside Tanner, pulling the gold mail shirt up over his belt.

Jack breathed a sigh of relief. "The antidote."

It was secured in a leather pouch at the professor's hip—a glass vial of blue serum. They tugged at it, trying to work it free. As they worked, the four rubies lit up like embers. The jewels crackled and sizzled until fames burst out of them. Tanner sat up, eyes wide and bloodshot, and grabbed Jack's arm. His fingers burned the leather jacket, sending wisps of acrid smoke into the air.

Both teens punched him straight in the face.

He fell back again, unconscious, and the rubies on his chest crumbled into black powder.

Gwen let out a shaky laugh. "I told you we'd take him down together."

Chapter Sixty-Three

EVEN AS JACK CHUCKLED at Gwen's joke, a tremendous *crack* shook the tomb. He sensed a telltale groan from above and jerked her back. A giant chunk of rock came crashing down on the platform, crushing the sarcophagus, and Tanner with it.

Jack surveyed the rubble. His stomach turned. "The antidote. I didn't—"

"But I did." Gwen beamed, holding out the vial of blue serum.

He wrapped her in a hug.

"Hey," she said, grunting under the tightness of his embrace. "What are quartermasters for?"

Another *crack*. Sparks exploded from the circular wall.

The rubies embedded in the rock were burning, just like the rubies on Tanner's chest—as if every bit of the strange red mineral was linked. "This place is coming down," said Jack, taking the vial. "We have to get to the surface."

Gwen took his arm and the two ran down the chamber steps together. "We can't get out the way we came in," she said. "It's blocked by the balance table."

A resounding *boom*.

The whole place shuddered, and both teens covered their heads as rocks and water rained down.

Gwen peeked through her arms. "There," she said, pointing up. A gap had opened in the ceiling, growing wider by the second. The stream poured in. "That's our way out."

Jack staggered sideways as the mine shook again. "How? The path is blocked and the walls are too sheer."

In answer, Gwen hurried back up the steps. She returned a moment later with a pair of high-tech devices—Tanner's ankle thrusters. "With these."

It only took a few seconds to strap the thrusters over Jack's jeans. "How do they work?" he asked as Gwen secured the last buckle.

"Flex your ankles. More flex equals more thrust. Shift your weight to steer." She wrapped her arms around him, preparing for liftoff, and kissed him on the cheek.

"What was that for?"

"Luck."

He gave her a sly grin. "I don't need luck, remember? I'm a Section Thirteen."

Gwen slapped him on the back of the head. "And that's for being cheesy."

He flexed his ankles and the two shot up through the mine, slipping and spiraling on the edge of control.

"Rock!" shouted Gwen, tucking her head into his neck. It missed them by inches.

"Okay. Maybe I need a *little* luck."

Jack managed to dodge the worst of the debris, taking only one bruising hit in the shoulder. What he could not dodge was the heavy mist formed by the stream pouring down through the hole. He remembered what Gwen had told him earlier, that quantum electrodynamic thrusters and moisture don't mix.

The left one sputtered.

They lost momentum.

Jack made it to within arm's reach of daylight before the left thruster failed completely and they started to fall. He caught the ledge.

"Hang on!" cried Gwen, reaching for the cliff. Her fingers missed by millimeters, and she grabbed his neck again, jostling him.

Jack's grip began to fail. "I can't. The rock is too wet!"

One finger slipped. And then another. And then a wooden bird swooped down through the hole, fluttering its wings and cooing madly.

"What's . . . the bird . . . doing here?" grunted Jack, trying to recover his grip. He couldn't. The rest of his fingers slipped free.

Gwen screamed.

In the same instant, a pair of strong hands caught both of Jack's wrists. A familiar face beneath a newsboy cap peered down from the ledge. "The bird's with me."

"Ash!"

"Hello, Jack. Miss me?"

The quartermaster heaved them both high enough to scramble out, and the three ran away before the gap could open any wider. The dove flew ahead into the glade, toward an airship much like the one that had brought them there, with deep green fabric and a gondola riveted together from some silvery alloy.

"You managed to crash half our aerial assets in the region," said Ash. "The old lady brought this one down from Saint Petersburg in a hurry."

"The old lady?" asked Gwen.

Rather than wait to hear the answer, Jack sprinted ahead. He drew the sword and slapped it into Shaw's chest on the way. "I forgot to give that to you back at the library."

"Oi!" the warden called after him. "Wot about them rubies?"

From behind, Jack heard the *thud* of a small fist punching tweed, along with Gwen's voice. "Shut up, Shaw."

Ash had delivered on his promise to take care of Sadie. She lay on a gurney in the gondola cabin, eyes closed, IV bags hanging above her. A heart monitor beeped, showing a rate much too fast for a little girl. Beside the gurney, a doctor stood ready with a syringe. Mrs. Hudson was with him, and Jack's mother was holding Sadie's pale hand. Jack's mom gave him a tearful smile. "They let me come out of the Keep for this one."

Jack pushed the vial into the doctor's open palm and then wrapped his arms around his mother. "Dad was there. He fought beside me."

"Of course he was, Jack. Of course he was."

Slowly, methodically—too methodically for Jack's nerves—the doctor drew the serum into his syringe and eased it into a splitter on the IV line. Wisps of blue swirled down through the solution. "All we can do now," he said as he pulled the syringe out again, "is wait and pray."

They waited.

Jack prayed. "Please, God."

An eternity later, the beeping on the heart monitor slowed, and an eternity after that, Sadie opened her eyes. "Jack?"

"Right here."

"There's a spider."

He laughed, wiping tears away with a sleeve that still bore the black marks of Tanner's burning fingers. "I know, Sadie. I got it."

Chapter Sixty-Four

A SCOUT DISC sailed low and silent over the ever-present mists of the arena's bottom level, curving upward toward Jack, who was crouched atop a peaked turret one level up. He had no trouble seeing the vectors this time. His quartermaster had made a perfect throw.

Jack made an equally perfect catch.

He sparked as soon as his fingers touched the scout. With effort, he settled the spinning vision and surveyed the scene caught in the bronze alloy. The final level represented a single street with a few storefronts and the entrance to a Tube station. A warden sat on a wooden bench, hidden from the levels above by a store awning. The big lummox was goaltending. Jack knew it because the mist, though it gathered in heavy orange balls around the streetlamps and in gray mats over the sidewalks, hung back from the store windows—a sure sign that the particular artifact Jack and his quartermaster were looking for was in there. The bronze lettering painted across the awning read LOST PROPERTY OFFICE.

The spark ended. Jack clambered down a drainpipe, dropping onto a replica of Fleet Street. Mrs. Hudson had configured the arena with select streets from London—a tradition when the Hunt went into a tiebreaker round.

Gwen waited beside a pair of giant double doors, leaning on a wolf's-head cane. "What'd you see?" she asked. "Which street did Mrs. Hudson use for the final level?"

Jack opened a little black door set into one of the big ones and inclined his head, indicating Gwen should go through first. "Baker Street. And I'll give you one guess as to where they've hidden the item."

A QED hovered close, camera twitching. Jack gave it a scowl and it backed away. He could sense the location of every drone in the arena, simply by listening to the hum of their engines. He could hear the whispers, too, just as before.

Section Thirteen.

Freak.

Mrs. Hudson had used the long flight back to London to debrief her wayward team, and Jack had told her everything, with the exception of anything related to fireballs and flaming swords. She had not quite understood how he and Gwen had escaped the dragons at the Archive, but she let it pass. She had also refused to accept that the spooks had opened the cages and released the beasts. "Only the Archivist has the key to that collection," she had told him. "And only a drago can compel her to use it."

The surviving jewels, along with a forgery of the Black Prince's Ruby, were back in the Vault where they belonged. The crown and scepter had been reformed. The Russians had been given a forgery as well, and they had stopped hunting for the mysterious thieving children.

Much to Jack's frustration, though, his allegations regarding Ignatius Gall remained merely that—allegations. According to Mrs. Hudson, they were unsubstantiated and unprovable, since no one but Jack had witnessed any direct evidence whatsoever of the high-ranking spook's involvement. The word of a Section Thirteen was not well regarded, and Mrs. Hudson had cautioned Jack to be quite sure of himself before he told anyone else.

Ash had been given a week's rest, delaying the final round of the Hunt. But when the time came, he had stepped aside in favor of Gwen. Mrs. Hudson, despite an extra-stern scowl, had not forbidden it.

The first levels had gone well for the young team—now the youngest pair ever to compete—but the labyrinth was no less difficult than before, and time was running short.

The two descended the staircase to a second-story rooftop. "There's no fire escape," whispered Gwen as they hurried to the edge. She checked her watch. "Three minutes to go, and we've no way down."

Jack stepped up beside her. "We're not going down. The street entrance is guarded." He nodded at the goaltending warden beneath the awning, pretending to read a newspaper.

Gwen scrunched up her face. "Who does he think he's kidding?" She shifted her gaze to the opposite roof, where there was a broad ventilation shaft. "Across, then?"

He nodded.

"Right. And how do you plan to get over there?"

In answer, Jack pulled up his jeans. Tanner's thrusters were strapped to his ankles. He winked. "Don't worry. I immersed them both in a bucket of rice."

His driving had improved. They reached the other side without crashing or otherwise alerting the sentry below, and Jack shed the thrusters while Gwen used a screwdriver to pry open the grate covering the shaft. Seconds later, they dropped into a room filled with umbrellas. There must have been hundreds, lying on tables and stuffed into wooden cubbies and tall brass cans.

"A minute and a half left," said Gwen.

Jack shook his head and shrugged. "Which one?"

"The biggest. Naturally." She lifted an inordinately long and unwieldy umbrella from the central table. "This one."

As soon as Gwen picked the umbrella up, Shaw jumped out from a dark corner, barreling toward Jack and spreading his arms for a tweed bear hug. "Gotcha, Thirteen!"

But Jack had heard the warden's breathing—smelled him too, Old Spice and stale biscuits. He ducked Shaw's arms and caught the scarf that Gwen had already thrown. Stealing a page from Ash's playbook, the two crossed behind the warden, looped the ends to make a knot, and pulled the yak's wool tight over Shaw's eyes.

A tiny bell rang. A pair of doors slid open.

"Lift," said Gwen, and they ran for it. They turned in time

to see the blinded warden trip over an umbrella can and go down hard. He slammed into the floor. "Buckles!"

One frilled end of the scarf fell into the gap between the doors, and Gwen yanked it through. "Thank goodness," she said as light Muzak floated down over them, drowning out the angry shouts falling below. "I was going to have a beastly time getting this back." She handed Jack the argyle monstrosity. "Presenting the Cloudchaser, the most famous umbrella in golf. A beast to carry, but as long as you drag it around with you, it will never rain." She finished adjusting her scarf around her shoulders and checked her watch. "Fifteen seconds."

The elevator doors opened. The two hurried out onto a platform at the center of the arena's top level, and Jack laid the umbrella on a silver stand an instant before a buzzer sounded. Cheers went up all around.

Mrs. Hudson had been waiting there, and as the stand with the umbrella descended into the platform, a QED flew up beside her, clutching a huge bronze cup in its pincers. She took the trophy and handed it to Jack. "Congratulations, John Buckles the Thirteenth. And congratulations Gwen Kincaid, our newest apprentice quartermaster. After ten years, you have reclaimed the Tracker Cup from the wardens."

Jack gave Gwen a handle, and together they held the trophy high.

The whispers of *Section Thirteen* and *freak* faded. All Jack heard were the cheers.

———·Chapter Sixty-Five·———

THAT NIGHT, Jack showed the Tracker Cup to his father. It was hard to see him that way after fighting beside him against Tanner. So pale and thin. All those tubes. He squeezed his dad's hand and kissed him on the forehead. "I *will* get you back."

He set the cup on the nightstand, jostling a shiny object. A dart gun lay next to the candle his mom always kept burning. It wasn't just any dart gun from his father's armory. The wooden pistol grip was charred, and the copper barrels were nicked and gouged.

"What are you doing here?" he asked, picking it up. He wrapped his hand around the scarred barrels and closed his eyes to get the answer.

Jack fell. He often fell into his sparks, but this was different. It was part of the vision—a dark, disorienting free fall. He pulled with his mind, slowing everything to a crawl.

Iron grate stairs passed by his shoulder, rushing backward. Above, he saw a tilted rectangle of gray light. Below, he saw a copper transport pod hovering beside a platform. And then he saw the first flash of the bomb. Jack knew where and when he was—the Moscow hyperloop station, moments before Raven and her brother were killed.

Instinct told him to get out of there.

Jack knew he couldn't be hurt, but this was not a moment he wanted to witness. All the same, he felt a sense of duty to stay and see it through. Perhaps this was penance for a murder he had taken part in, whether intentionally or not.

Raven was holding the dart gun, falling rigid, thanks to the electrosphere still sending its charge through her body. Her brother—the Phantom-slash-Arthur—fell with her, gripping her shoulder and sharing in the shock. His face contorted against it. His eyes shifted. Jack could tell he had seen the flash.

Still in slow motion, the two thieves crashed down on the platform. The impact shook Arthur's hand free of his sister. His muscles came alive. He rolled to his knees, and Jack saw the stopwatch device—the Einstein-Rosen Bridge—in his other hand. There was still time to activate it. Jack *willed* him to activate it before the blast could reach him. But Arthur didn't. He wouldn't. Instead, he threw his body over Raven's. The last thing Jack saw before the vision ended was Arthur Spector, the Phantom, backlit by a raging mass of fire.

Zzzap.

"Jack?"

He was back at his father's bedside. Jack spun on his heels, tucking the weapon behind him as Sadie peeked into the room.

She held out a pillow and a blanket. "I brought you these."

He gave his sister a halting smile. "Thanks, but I'll sleep in my own room from now on. If we're going to be ready to welcome Dad when he wakes up, we need to take care of each other—Mom and Gwen, too. To do that, we need our rest." He nodded toward the hallway. "Go on back to bed. Pick out a book, and maybe I'll come read with you like I used to."

Sadie brightened. "I'd like that," she said, backing out of the room. "I'd like that a lot."

"Sadie?"

She peeked back in. "Yeah?"

"Um . . . close the door for me, will you?"

As soon as she had, Jack trained the dart gun on a shadowed corner across the room. "Okay. You can come out now . . . Raven."

There was a long pause, and then a figure stepped to the edge of the candlelight. Her face remained hidden beneath a hood, but her voice was unmistakable. "I brought you that gun in good faith, yeah? An' now you're gonna shoot me with it?"

Jack hadn't been completely sure he was right. Now that he knew it was her, he had trouble holding his emotions in check. He lowered the weapon. "Raven, I thought you were . . ." He gritted his teeth. "What about your brother?"

Raven stared out from the shadow of her hood for several seconds, then lowered it, exposing the left side of her face to the candlelight. She was blistered and burned from her temple to her chin.

Jack couldn't help but stiffen.

"Yeah. I know. Would o' been worse, but for Arthur." She looked away, toward the window. "He jumped us both to the roof of a building across the canal, but the blast got to him first. He . . . He didn't . . ." She trailed off, going silent.

Jack couldn't imagine the scene at the top of that building, the horror Raven must have been forced to endure—rolling her dead brother off her, seeing what Tanner's bomb had done to him. "I'm sorry."

"You didn't plant them explosives. Tanner did."

The words were quick, rehearsed, followed by another long silence. The heart monitor at his dad's bedside beeped in a slow, steady rhythm.

Jack swallowed. "So why did you come?"

"I figured you'd want that back," she said, nodding at the dart gun. "It's a family heirloom, innit? What with that seal on the base o' the grip an' all."

Jack turned the pistol over. There was indeed a marking—one he had never noticed before. A falcon and a dragon were etched into the copper baseplate, their wings touching to form an oval seal. The script inside was obscured by soot.

"I figured I owed you, yeah?" continued Raven, lowering her hood. "After what you did to Tanner."

Jack looked down at his sneakers, shifting his weight. "I didn't exactly—"

"It's done, innit? Nuff said." Raven wiped her eyes with an oversize sleeve and then straightened, as if building herself up for the next part. "There's somethin' else, Jack. That spook, Gall, the one who hired Arthur in the first place. He's got it in for you somethin' fierce. This whole deal with Tanner and the rubies was only the beginning." She looked to the window. The Einstein-Rosen Bridge was in her hand. "Watch yourself, yeah? That's all I came to say."

"Wait." Jack reached for her. "Stay. Please. Testify against Gall. You have friends here."

"Like Gwen, yeah?" Raven let out a sardonic laugh.

"Like me. And Sadie. Gwen will come around. Besides, that device you're using—the Einstein-Rosen Bridge—Mrs. Hudson says it's damaging your cells."

She snorted, that same flippant snort Jack remembered from Moscow. For a split second it was a return to something a little less horrible. But then her face went dark. "Thing is, Jack, I don't care if it kills me." She raised her hood, stepping back into the shadows. "An' it ain't Raven no more. It's Ghost."

Zzzap.

She was gone.

Jack let out the half breath he had been holding the whole time. He turned the pistol over again and rubbed the soot from the falcon-dragon seal, careful not to spark on the copper. He didn't need to see that vision again. The script inside read *Familia in Aeternum*. The ministry had pelted him with enough Latin for him to know the translation—*Forever Family*.

A dragon and a falcon. Trackers and dragos. Forever Family.

Were the Buckleses related to the dragos somehow? It seemed likely, considering the flaming sword and the fireballs he had conjured during the fight with Tanner. Still, all of that had merely been part of a grand spark.

Jack set the weapon down, and his gaze fell on the candle. The brush of air from his arm made the flame dance. He thought of his dream beside the fire barrel.

Maybe it wasn't a dream after all.

Forever Family. Trackers and dragos.

Tentatively, Jack poked a finger at the candle. The flame didn't move. He tried again, this time waving a hand over it. He got a flicker, but that was just the movement of air like before.

He sighed, glancing toward the bed, as if his dad might have seen all that foolishness. If he had, he would have laughed and rubbed Jack's shoulders, lightening the moment by saying something both wise and sarcastic at the same time. Jack wished he knew what it would be.

But the candle still burned in the corner of his eye. Jack had always been fascinated by fire, long before he had chased the Ember across London. This was something he couldn't let go. He tried again, going for broke, and shoved his hand directly into the flame. It was too much. The fire burned his palm and he jerked back, knocking the candlestick to the floor.

The fall snuffed out the flame, and Jack was grateful, because setting the floor or the bed on fire would have been a lot worse than simply sitting there in the gloom, feeling alone and foolish.

Of course, his hand still hurt.

As his eyes adjusted, Jack saw a faint glow within his closed fist. He caught his breath. It might have been a trick of the sudden dark—a lingering illusion caused by staring at the candle too long. But maybe . . .

Jack turned his fist over—afraid of what he might find, yet still hoping to find it there. One at a time, he uncurled his fingers and laughed out loud at what he saw.

ACKNOWLEDGMENTS

My wife, Cindy, reads every chapter I write the moment it is written, and she steers me back to safety whenever I am headed for disaster. More than that, she is my sounding board—absorbing, reflecting, and generating ideas before my fingers ever hit the keyboard. Without her, this and all my books would not exist.

I am grateful to David Gale for being both editor and advocate, and to Amanda Ramirez, Jen Strada, and all the others at Simon & Schuster Books for Young Readers who have employed their considerable expertise in developing this series. I am also grateful for my agents, Harvey Klinger and Sara Crowe. I could not ask for more wonderful human beings to be the champions of my work.

Finally, there are a number of volunteers to thank. These have shaped this book through critiques, encouragement, and advice. Rather conveniently, they also all come in pairs: John and Nancy, Seth and Gavin, Danika and Dennis, Chris and Melinda, Scott and Ethan, James and Ashton, Rachel and Katie, Steve and Tawnya, Nancy and Dan, Randy and Hulda, and—of course—the Barons.

Thank you all for everything.